"Men simply ♢ P9-APD-621 how to take care of themselves."

Gabrielle sat down beside him and began to unwind the bandage. "I knew I should not have let you out of my sight," she sighed. Her cropped hair had grown out into dark, glossy ringlets; long lashes veiled her eyes; her mouth was soft, serious, the tip of her tongue visible as she concentrated.

Her hand brushed his skin. As if the shock that ran through him touched her also, she raised her eyes to his momentarily and a deeper rose tinged her cheeks.

He was shaken by a fierce desire to hold her in his arms . . .

◆

PRAISE FOR CAROLA DUNN'S PREVIOUS REGENCY NOVELS

ALSO BY CAROLA DUNN

Lord Iverbrook's Heir
The Miser's Sister
Angel
Lavender Lady

Published by
WARNER BOOKS

GABRIELLE'S GAMBLE

Carola Dunn

Previously published as
THE MAN IN THE GREEN COAT

WARNER BOOKS

A Warner Communications Company

All the characters and events portrayed in this story are fictitious.

WARNER BOOKS EDITION

This book was previously published as The Man in the Green Coat.

This Warner Books Edition was published by arrangement with
the Walker Publishing Company, Inc.

Warner Books, Inc.
666 Fifth Avenue
New York, N.Y. 10103

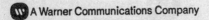 A Warner Communications Company

Printed in the United States of America

First Warner Books Printing: April, 1989

10   9   8   7   6   5   4   3   2   1

GABRIELLE'S GAMBLE

—1—

"WHEW, I'M GLAD that's over!" The tall youth emerged from the candlelit dimness of the small chapel and took a deep breath of fresh, incense-less air. Turning to his companion, he added, "Gaby, we *must* go to England now!"

"Don't call me Gaby!" said Gabrielle automatically, then sighed. "I wish we could have held the service in Notre Dame." She pulled her hood over her dark curls as they stepped out into the chilly April shower. "Marthe did so love it. Even in winter, she always struggled up the hill to Mass." She looked up the cobbled street at the castle of Neuchâtel and the ancient church beside it.

"A bit above the touch of a mere serving woman," snorted her brother.

"How can you say such a thing, Gerard! Marthe looked after us all our lives. She was much more than a mere servant to us, and well you know it."

A black-clad priest hurried out of the church behind them.

"*Mademoiselle, Monsieur Darcy*, permit that I offer my condolences. You will have, perhaps, need of another housekeeper, *n'est-ce pas?*"

Gerard was still gazing up the hill at the castle. Gabrielle knew by the tautness of his arm under her hand how his anger flared at the sight of the flaunting red, white and blue French flag on the battlements.

"*Merci, mon père*, but we have not yet decided what to do next." Gabrielle's French was pure Parisian, without the

1

priest's faint Swiss accent. "Marthe was with us for many years, you understand."

"A good woman who is now in heaven," he said, crossing himself. "I have not seen you before in my humble church. You are Protestants, perhaps?"

"Yes," she said briefly. "Come, Gerard, we must not keep *le bon père* out in the rain."

Obedient to her tug on his arm, her brother followed her down the narrow street, walking carefully on the slippery cobbles.

"Nosy old man," he growled.

"You are in a difficult mood today. He's not nosy, just mildly inquisitive. If it were not for our situation, we should not be so sensitive to such questions. I wish Papa would come home!"

"As do I! Seven months and never a word! I tell you, it is past time we left Switzerland."

"I begin to think you are right. He has never been gone so long before, and with Marthe gone, and the news from Paris . . ."

"A month has passed since that business, and they are still negotiating. It is hard to believe it meant anything serious." Gerard's boyish face was despondent.

"They are playing for time. Bonaparte insults and threatens the British ambassador in public, accuses England of breaking the Treaty of Amiens. It will surely lead to war."

"Gaby—sorry, Gabrielle—we must leave for England at once! If I do not soon join the army, I shall be too old to fight Boney."

"At nineteen? Come now! All the same, if we stay we must find another servant, and no one could be so discreet as Marthe. We will never be able to conceal that we are English, and we cannot afford gossip about that, or about Papa's absence."

"And he has been gone forever. He told us not to wait if he did not return by spring."

Gabrielle shivered. "You call this spring? The roads

through the mountains are barely open. We must go by La Chaux to Nancy, I think, and across northern France. Papa said it is best to avoid Paris."

"We are going then? Huzzah!" Gerard seized his sister's fur-gloved hands and swung her around, then hugged her.

"Silly boy," she said indulgently.

"Watch who you're calling a boy," he retorted, grinning. "You are precisely one year and three days older than me, so don't try to come the high and mighty, miss! I daresay it will take you days to pack up all your things. How soon can we leave?"

"The sooner the better." Gabrielle had already considered all the difficulties before them, and having made her decision she was not one to dither. "We must leave things in order in case Papa returns, and leave him some money, too. We cannot afford to hire a carriage, so we will have to ride—the *diligence* is far too slow—and we can only take what a packhorse can carry. And Gerard, I think it will be safer if I dress as a boy. I could pass as your younger brother, do you not think?"

"Famous! Shall you really? I daresay Madame Aurore will be vastly shocked."

"I shall change back before we reach London. Do you think Papa is right when he says Madame will welcome us to her home?"

"Who knows?" said Gerard blithely. "We shall find out when we get there, shan't we?"

Nearly a week passed before Gabrielle locked the door of the yellow stone townhouse that had been home for ten years, and turned to survey the mounts Gerard had hired from the inn. The sun had not yet risen, and she hoped none of the neighbours was watching her departure, dressed in a hastily altered pair of her brother's breeches and riding astride.

The Seyon gorge was dark and mysterious in the early morning light, the spring-flooded river bellowing invisibly below wraiths of mist. As the path rose, they emerged into pale sunlight. They passed processions of slow amber cows heading for the high meadows, and the sound of cowbells followed them up the steep slopes. At Vue des Alpes they paused to rest, and gazed across the wide green vale at the towering snow-clad mass of Mont Blanc.

"Goodbye, Switzerland," whispered Gabrielle.

"Neuchâtel is part of France now," Gerard pointed out, "and before that it was Prussian, and anyway we are still in it. The old border is beyond La Chaux."

Gabrielle sighed. "I was being sentimental, not political," she explained. "We may never return. I wonder what it will be like to live in England?"

"Let's get moving, or you may never find out!"

By the time they reached La Chaux-de-Fonds, Gabrielle's thighs were sore and tired and she would gladly have never seen a horse again. Her spirits revived over luncheon at a small, cosy inn, especially as no one questioned her appearance in male attire. Her disguise was a success, it seemed.

Slim, of middling height, her curly hair cut short, Gabrielle presented the appearance of a youth of fifteen or sixteen summers. And a good-looking youth at that, with her smooth-skinned oval face, tip-tilted nose and merry brown eyes. The blond-pigtailed maid who served them flirted with Gerard, but had an admiring glance to spare for his little brother.

"*Le petit frère* will break a few hearts when he is grown!" she exclaimed.

Le petit frère groaned when faced with a fresh steed, but declined Gerard's help in mounting. Though the rest had turned her legs to lead and every movement was an effort, to accept assistance would be out of character. Gerard, at her apparent age, had always refused aid indignantly. One of those strange masculine traits that she must attempt to adopt temporarily, she thought, struggling into the saddle.

They crossed the old border and rode north into France.

It began to rain. The road was unfamiliar, and full of potholes hidden by deep grey mud. The charming inn at La Chaux had provided them with a pair of sorry nags, and a packhorse that seemed to be asleep on its feet. As night approached, they were miles short of Belfort, their goal, and just entering a dreary village. Half the cottages were in ruins, mute reminders of fourteen years of revolution and war.

Gabrielle was so weary that she made no protest when Gerard helped her dismount in the yard of a small hostelry, barely more than a tavern. She could summon up no appetite for cold pigeon pie, and so went fasting to bed.

After a night spent between damp sheets, it took all her resolution to descend the stairs in the morning.

"Stiff?" asked Gerard, grinning.

"I *cannot* ride today!"

"There is a *cabriolet* we can hire as far as Belfort. And from there, there is a *diligence* to Nancy that our host swears will take no more than two days. It is the fast *diligence*."

"Two days to Nancy! I had hoped we might be there tomorrow. Oh Gerard, at that rate it will take a month to reach England!"

"Hush! I fancy the people here are not overfond of Napoleon, but it is best that they do not know our destination. If you cannot ride, we have little choice, do we?"

"I shall be better presently. Let us take the gig to Belfort, and find an inn where I can take a hot bath!"

"An excellent idea. I could do with one myself," he said, grimacing.

A hot bath did help the stiffness, but Gabrielle's thighs had been rubbed raw in her unaccustomed breeches.

"I'm so *sore!*" she told Gerard, meeting him for luncheon in the coffee room of the Hôtel du Tricouleur.

"Perhaps you should go back to skirts," he suggested, helping himself to a large serving of a casserole from which rose a mouth-watering aroma. "The more I consider, the more I think Papa would be horrified that I have allowed you to gallivant about in male dress."

"Nonsense! Papa will not care a farthing. And besides, you have not 'allowed' me, I chose for myself. He knows very well that I do not do what you tell me, so he will not hold you to blame. And I shall not wear skirts again until we are safe in England. By the time we reach Nancy, I shall be well able to ride."

"And half dead again a few hours later. No, Gab, we had best stick with the *diligence*. A few more days on the road will make little difference, after all."

"I believe you are still stiff yourself! I own I shudder at the idea of a saddle. Very well, if you promise to remember that it was your notion, and not to sulk, we shall go with the *diligence*."

Grinning, he promised.

The promise was not easy to keep. The coach to Nancy was the only "fast" one they found. All roads, it seemed, led to Paris. As they did not wish to visit that great city, they were reduced at times to carrier's carts, moving at barely a walking pace. Often they did walk, alongside or ahead of their baggage; Gabrielle grew sun-browned, developed a boyish stride, and ceased to worry about curls out of place, dust on her boots or a rip in her jacket. Not one of the French soldiers or officials they met gave them a second glance.

Gerard fretted at their slow pace. Listening to gossip in taprooms, to the chatter of fellow-passengers, he heard that the crowds of English fashionables who had flocked to Paris after the signing of the Treaty of Amiens were in full retreat towards Calais and the Channel ferries. Lord Whitworth, the British ambassador, went with them.

"You must be right," Gerard said, "it will be war, and soon. Everyone says so. The Channel ports will be closed before we get there."

"Then we must head for Dunkerque. Do you not remember the man Papa told us of, the Flemish fisherman?"

"Willem Snieders, was not that the name? Though I doubt I pronounce it correctly. We say that 'Le Hibou' sent us, and he will take us across."

"Yes, that is the one."

"What do you suppose 'Le Hibou' means?" "Gerard asked. Papa was so mysterious about it, told us never to mention 'The Owl' unless in dire need."

"As I recall, we discussed it endlessly and uselessly when first he mentioned it! He never would explain. Best we do not even say the word unnecessarily."

"Yes, ma'am!"

They were descending from the *diligence* at an inn in Tourcoing, still some two score miles from the coast, when they learned that King George had declared war on France. The borders were closed and all British citizens who had not left in time were under arrest.

"We ride for Dunkerque," decided Gabrielle. "Better sore than in one of Boney's gaols. I am grown used to breeches now, so perhaps it will not be quite so bad, but do please try to find me an easy-paced mount! Gerard, I think we must abandon the baggage. We will arouse less suspicion, besides being able to ride faster. Just one saddlebag each, for I must at least keep by me a gown to change into."

"It is almost dark. Will it not draw attention if we leave tonight?" In the street outside the inn yard, a detachment of brass-helmeted dragoons clattered by.

"First thing tomorrow. Have them call us at dawn. I hope William Snieders is at home and ready to sail!"

— 2 —

BEFORE SUNRISE THEY left the town behind them and rode
west across the flat, green countryside of Flanders. Tough-
ened by weeks of travel, Gabrielle found herself enjoying
the ride. For the first time since Marthe's death, she raised
her voice in song, and Gerard's clear tenor joined her until
they heard hoofbeats on the road behind them. Exchanging
a guilty glance, they dropped "Greensleeves" in the middle
of the refrain and took up "Alouette" with scarce a break.

"*Holà, citoyens!*" called a gruff voice. "*Halte là!*"

They drew rein, and found themselves surrounded by
soldiers.

"You come from Tourcoing?" demanded the sergeant.
Wordless, the brother and sister nodded. "You have seen
perhaps *un petit bonhomme* in a brown redingote and leggings?" They shook their heads. "*Sacre bleu! Il nous a
échappé.* If you see him, report at once to the nearest official,
compris?"

Once more they nodded. Gabrielle's heart was beating so
hard she was surprised the Frenchman didn't hear it. The
squad passed them and galloped on, raising a swirl of dust
that made them cough and splutter.

"I must suppose they did not appreciate our singing,"
said Gabrielle wryly, when she could draw breath.

"No more music for me until I am safely ensconced in
Madame Aurore's drawing room!" said Gerard firmly.

Not long past noon, they topped a gentle rise and saw in
the distance the port of Dunkerque, dominated by its

modern fortress, and beyond it the blue sparkle of the English Channel.

"Thank heaven!" Gabrielle exclaimed. "I am not in such agony as I was after that first ride, but I shall be heartily glad to see the last of this beast."

Gerard scanned the road ahead and the fields and farms to either side. A cloud of dust rising from a farm track caught his attention.

"I believe that is our friends down there," he said grimly. "I saw a flash of polished steel. We must go cautiously."

"The soldiers? I do hope they have not caught the little man in the leggings, whatever he has done."

They started down the slope. At the bottom a small stone bridge crossed a stream lined with silver-green willows. Before they reached it, a uniformed figure stepped out of the shade of the trees and barred their way with bayoneted rifle.

"*Qui va là?*" he demanded sharply. "*Ohé, les jeunes citoyens!* You have still not seen the one of whom the sergeant asked? It will be easier to recognise him now, for he is wounded."

"Who is this person?" asked Gerard. "Why are you hunting for him?"

"It is an *espion anglais*. Come to count the troops at Boulogne, *sans doute*. Much good may it do those cursed English to know with how many men we shall invade!" He spat in the dust.

"An English spy!" gasped Gabrielle. "He has been shot?"

"Yes, *mon petit*. Have no fear, we shall soon capture him. And you, *le grand*, how is it that you are not in the army?"

"I was sent home during the peace," Gerard improvised desperately. "Now I go to rejoin my unit, but first I must take my brother to our uncle's house in Dunkerque."

"A fragile youth," said the soldier, looking Gabrielle up and down condescendingly. "But you will fight for *la patrie* when you are older, if we have left any enemies for you!" He sniggered and winked at Gerard. "*En avant, alors, et vive la France!*"

"Vive la France!" they echoed with what enthusiasm they could muster, and rode on.

They were within a couple of miles of the town before they saw more soldiers. Gabrielle straightened wearily in the saddle as Gerard pointed out a group of cavalry approaching the road across a field to their left. Impulsively she turned down a lane to the right, where an avenue of poplars offered a certain amount of cover.

"If they tell me again how they are going to catch the English spy, I shall scream," she said. "If only we could find him and help him hide."

"I think it is time for *you* to hide," suggested Gerard. "It will be far less noticeable for just one of us to enquire for Willem Snieders, and I'll wager you won't even be able to walk straight when you dismount. There's a barn over there, let's investigate."

Gabrielle was too tired to protest. She followed her brother to the ramshackle barn. When she slid off her horse to lead it through the half-open door, she discovered how right he was: she staggered in and collapsed on a bundle of sweet-smelling hay.

"Wait here," Gerard said, "and I will return shortly, whether I find the man or not. If you hear the soldiers coming, burrow into the hay or climb into the loft or something, but I'm sure they must have searched this place already." He leaned down and kissed her cheek. "Don't worry, Gab. We're nearly there."

She watched him lead his mount out of the barn and listened to the receding sound of hooves. He was growing up at last, she thought, taking charge like that instead of waiting for her to make the first move. Doubtless there would be a few good arguments before he accepted that she would not necessarily follow his lead, that she was as independent as he was learning to be.

Papa would be pleased. If they ever saw Papa again. Where had he been all these months, and what was the mysterious business that so often took him from home?

A moan interrupted her musings.

"*Qui est là?*" she demanded sharply. A horrid feeling in the pit of her stomach told her she already knew. "Where are you?"

A hoarse whisper, in English: "Betsy, is that you? Betsy, I'm hurt ever so bad. Come closer, I cain't see you."

Trembling, Gabrielle stood up and peered around in the dim light. Another moan led her behind a heap of old sacks. Huddled in a corner lay a small man in a brown redingote, ominously stained, and leggings.

She knelt beside him. "I'm not Betsy," she said in English. "Is there anything I can do for you? Where are you hurt?"

The man opened his eyes, but they had an unfocussed look and she thought he could not see her.

"Who is it? Who's there? I heered an English voice."

Gabrielle took his cold hand. "I'm English. How can I help?"

"I'm done for, miss. Bain't nowt you can do for me. But if'n you love yer country, go to the King's Head, at Dover. Ask mine host for the man in the green coat." The man paused for breath, shifted a little and moaned again. "Water, Betsy, I'm devilish thirsty. Give us a drink, love."

Gabrielle hurried to the horse and took a water bottle from the saddlebag. She held it to the man's lips and he sipped a little. He coughed, and a froth of pink bubbles ran down his chin.

"Ta, love." He made a vain effort to sit up. "Where was I?"

"Dover. The King's Head. The man in the green coat?" prompted Gabrielle.

"Tell him . . . tell him Le Hibou says, de la Touche is Fouché's man. Can you remember that? I cain't see you."

" 'Le Hibou says de la Touche is Fouché's man.' I have it. Is that all?"

"Ask him to look after Betsy for me. He'll do that. He's a good man, a real gentleman. Always done right by me. Tell Betsy I love her an' I'm right sorry I been such a bad

husban'. Duty first, that's me, but it's hard on a woman."
His voice was fading. Another fit of coughing shook him,
and the dark stains on his coat spread a little wider.

Gabrielle wet her handkerchief and gently wiped his
face. His eyes were closed and he lay still. She sat beside
him, holding his hand, until she heard her brother's return.

"Gerard?" she called softly.

He came to her. "What the deuce?" he demanded.

"Hush! It's the English spy. He's dead, the poor brave
man."

"Poor fellow. We'd best go at once, then. I'd hoped to
hide out here till nightfall, but they'll be on his trail."

"I think he must be Le Hibou, the man Papa mentioned . . ."

"I daresay," Gerard interrupted, "but come on, Gab,
there's a good girl. It is already dusk, so at least they won't
spot us from a distance. I'll tell you what, my horse is tired
and yours is rested, so you had best come up behind me on
yours, and we'll leave mine here. One will be less conspicu-
ous than two, and we've not far to go."

"You found Willem?" Gabrielle asked as he hauled her up
behind him. She put her arms round his waist and held on
tight as he kicked the horse into a trot.

"Yes, easily. It's a smallish town and everyone knows
him."

"But not his unpatriotic activities, I hope."

"If they do, they sympathise. There are a lot of Flemings
here, and they don't care for the French. They directed me
to his house and he was there. He's going fishing tonight,
and he says there will be no difficulty about landing us in
England. All we have to do is get aboard his boat, and we'll
have help for that."

"You know where to find it?"

"Of course!" Gerard's voice was full of scorn. "You need
not think you are the only practical one in the family!"

"I beg your pardon," said Gabrielle meekly, and then in
alarm, "What is that noise?"

Gerard reined their mount to a halt and swung round to

look back. Through the gathering dusk they could see a group of horsemen riding up to the barn, several hundred yards back. Without a word he turned and urged the horse to a canter.

"Should we not cut across country?" asked Gabrielle, raising her voice to be heard above the drumming of hooves.

"No, we'd only get lost or lame the horse, then we'd really be in the suds." He continued down the farm track towards the road.

Peering back, she saw several soldiers run out of the barn, shouting and pointing in their direction.

"I think we are, anyway. Here they come!"

Gerard kicked the horse into a gallop. Unused to having such a pace demanded of it, it snorted indignantly, then settled into a steady gait. It was carrying two, but neither was heavy, and it had rested for several hours while the troopers had been out quartering the countryside. Gradually it pulled away.

They turned onto the road and saw the lights of Dunkerque, seeming near enough to touch. Closer and closer they came, and then shots rang out behind them.

"They cut across!" shouted Gerard. "We were getting away from them. This paltry beast cannot run any faster but we're nearly there."

Gabrielle was wondering just what good it would do them to reach the town, with the cavalry on their tail, when she felt a burning pain in her side and a throbbing ache that spread throughout her body. Dizzy, she slumped against her brother's back and concentrated on holding on with every last scrap of strength.

In a dream, she heard hooves ring on cobbles, felt the horse swing left and strong arms pluck her from the saddle. She could make no sense of the hushed gabble of voices, quickly cut off. There was a sensation of being carried down steps, then Gerard's anguished voice came to her clearly.

"It must be bound before we take her any further!"

"He's right. *La petite* will bleed to death. But first, a drop of *eau de vie* against infection."

The smouldering in her side suddenly burst into flame, and she lost consciousness.

When she came to, the first thing Gabrielle was aware of was a foul stench of ancient fish. It made it hard to breathe, and breathing was painful anyway, so she vaguely considered stopping. At least until she could get out from under the suffocating pile of whatever it was she was under. She moved feebly.

She hurt even more.

One deep breath to shout for help, she decided. She opened her mouth, gagged on the fetid air, and closed it again, fast.

She had remembered why she hurt.

If she was hidden under a heap of fishnets, it must be for a good reason. She lay still and listened.

A light gleamed through the chinks in the net. *"Ohé!* You on board!" someone cried.

Hollow footsteps sounded. Gabrielle realised that the surface beneath her was rocking gently. *"Qu'est-ce que vous voulez?"* came a different voice, surly, slightly accented.

"This is your boat? We are looking for an *espion anglais*. Or rather, two of them now. Have you seen any strangers?"

"No."

"We'd better come aboard and search, or the lieutenant will have our livers. Faugh, don't you fishermen ever clean your nets? What a stink! Who are these in the cabin?"

"My partner, Jan, and my sister's boy. A useless fellow, but what can one do when all the stout young men are in the army? It takes two to haul a net, clean or dirty. And the tide is on the turn, so I'll thank you to move along."

"Leclerc, look in those barrels! If that's where you keep the fish, I hope they are cleaner than your nets! Nothing? *Eh bien, en avant!* Good fishing, *citoyen*."

"To fill your bellies, you parasites!" muttered the second voice, just loud enough for Gabrielle to hear.

The flickering torchlight passed over her hiding place again, bright enough to illuminate the red, white and blue cockades in the soldiers' brass helmets, not bright enough to reveal the trail of dark, sticky spots on the deck, leading straight to the pile of nets.

The motion of the deck became more pronounced, and Gabrielle heard the creaking of ropes, the lapping of water against the hull. How long would it be before they judged it safe to let her out, she wondered? She would never eat fish again for the rest of her life!

At last footsteps approached, and the clear, solid light of a ship's lantern. The nets above her shifted.

"Gerard?"

"Gabrielle! Are you all right? How long have you been conscious?" Gerard's voice sounded very young and scared.

"Long enough to be heartily sick of this nauseating odour! I never knew fishing nets stank so!"

"In general they do not, *mademoiselle*. Naturally, they are washed daily as we cast them into *la mer*. I have hidden a piece of rotten fish underneath, to dissuade the *salauds* from searching too closely."

"This is Willem Snieders, Gabrielle. Oh, there you are." The last of the concealing nets was hauled off. "You look terrible!"

Painfully, Gabrielle sat up. "*Enchanté, monsieur*, and thank you very much for rescuing us."

The stocky fisherman, clad in blue homespun, bowed over her hand.

"You are welcome, *mademoiselle*. We of Flanders have little love of the French. How do you find yourself?"

"Stiff and sore, but most of the smell seems to have departed with your rotten fish, *Dieu merci!* However, a bath would not come amiss. How long will the crossing take?"

"The wind has changed, *mademoiselle*, and we are in for a

16

rough sail. If we miss the tide at Dover, it may be a full day before you can go ashore."

At that moment, the boat left the shelter of the harbour for the open sea. Gabrielle shivered as a stiff breeze from the west filled the sails.

"Will you come into the cabin, *mademoiselle?*" asked Willem anxiously. "It is a little warmer there."

"Thank you, I will. Perhaps you can provide some water to wash with? Even cold seawater would be better than nothing. And I should like to change my clothes. Our saddlebags are within?"

"*Je regrette, mademoiselle*, that the saddlebags were lost in your flight from the soldiers."

"So I shall after all arrive in England in breeches! Well, it can't be helped."

"There is some bread and sausage in the cabin if you are hungry." The fisherman seemed anxious to make amends for the missing saddlebags.

"I am indeed! Gerard, help me up, if you please. Gerard? What is the matter?"

Even by lantern light, Gerard's face was greenish. One hand to stomach, one to mouth, he rushed to the rail and leaned over.

Willem laughed. "*Le mal de mer*! Never fear, *mademoiselle*, no one dies of seasickness, though one may wish to. Permit that I assist you."

He helped her up, and leaning on his strong arm, she stumbled painfully to the cabin.

— 3 —

THE LAST LIGHT of the setting sun shone golden on the whitewashed walls of the King's Head at Dover; after the storm, the sea air was fresh and clean-smelling.

The Honourable Lucius Everett lounged in the doorway of the inn, half-listening to the buzz of conversation in the coffee room behind him. A high-pitched voice rang out complainingly above the hubbub.

" 'Pon rep, my lord, I was forced to leave half my gowns behind in Paris, such was our hurry. All the latest French modes! Do not tell me I shall find anything to equal them in London."

Mr Everett's lip curled. It was not the first time he had heard that lament. England at war again, and all the silly chit cared about was her Parisian fashions! Not that she differed in that from the majority of her class, both male and female, he thought with scorn.

Much milady would have cared for his opinion! A single glance in the passageway had classified Mr Everett as a nobody.

He was a gentleman of some thirty summers, slightly above the average in height and well built, but plainly dressed in a slate-coloured frock coat. Though his thick brown hair was cut short and unpowdered, it was brushed back from his forehead in a far from modish manner. His features were nothing out of the ordinary; certainly no one would have described him as handsome. Yet a perceptive observer might have noticed a clear lucidity to his gaze, an unusual, almost piercing quality, and the stern line of his mouth spoke of determination and purpose.

The innkeeper stepped out for a breath of air, wiping his round, shiny red face with a spotted handkerchief.

"Whew!" he exclaimed. "It's right glad I am the high quality generally patronises the Ship, for we ain't set up to cope with their whims and crotchets and it's no good pretending we are. Still, that's the last of 'em running from Boney. We'll soon be back to business as usual, for they'll be on their way to London soon as I can get enough carriages to take 'em. You've dined, Mr Everett?"

"Not yet, Colby. I'll wait till the crush is gone."

"Right you are, sir. I'll warn the wife to set aside some mutton pasties and a dish of mushrooms, for we don't want our regulars complaining of poor service."

"In that case, send Baxter to bring me a mug of ale!"

"Mr Baxter is a guest here just like you are sir. I'll fetch it myself."

The stout landlord hurried away. His place was taken by three fashionable bucks. Mr Everett moved aside to give them space, and they stood there on the threshold, blocking the doorway, discussing the shocking lack of entertainment to be found in Dover.

They had just decided that a game of hazard in their private parlour offered the best chance of amusement, when a hackney pulled through the archway into the courtyard. As it drew to a halt, a pale-faced youth jumped out, steadied himself against the carriage, and addressed the group at the door.

"Sirs, pray tell me, is there a room available here?"

The dandies turned to stare. One of them raised a quizzing glass to examine the lad's scruffy clothing. None deigned answer; they resumed their conversation.

Mr Everett stepped out of the shadow.

"I fear the inn is full," he said. "Have you tried elsewhere?"

"Yes, everywhere." The boy sounded exhausted and

desperate. "My sister is hurt. She can go no further. What am I to do?"

From the carriage came a low, sweet voice. "Gerard, perhaps there is a corner where I might sit for a while. Let us go in and ask." A wavering figure appeared, dressed in grey breeches, white shirt and blue jacket. "Help me down, I can walk."

"Gabrielle, no!"

"Your *sister*, you said?"

"Yes sir. We thought it safer for her to dress so."

Mr Everett noticed a red stain on the jacket. He sprang forward as the girl crumpled and caught her in his arms. Her brother seemed dazed, and looked to be in not much better case.

"Gabrielle . . . Sir, let me take her . . ."

"Hoy!" interrupted the jarvey. "What about me fare?"

"Do you pay the driver," directed Mr Everett, "and I shall carry her in. You have money?"

"Oh, yes, sir, but Gabrielle . . . I . . . oh, very well. Thank you."

Mr Everett, his face expressing none of the curiosity he felt, shifted his burden into a more comfortable position and turned to find the landlord awaiting him, a mug of ale in one hand, the other planted on his solid hip.

"We haven't got room, Mr Everett, and well you knows it. Partickly not for the likes o' these."

"They may have my chamber, Colby, and I shall answer for them. If I am not mistaken, they are just escaped from France like most of your other guests."

"Oh, in that case, sir, if you say so. You'll want your dinner sent up?"

"We may need a doctor, not dinner. This child is injured and I do not know how badly."

"I am not a child," said Gabrielle, faintly but indignantly. "Pray put me down, sir. I am quite able to walk."

"No, you are not, Gaby. I am scarce able to walk myself and I have no bullet hole in the ribs." Gerard's gait as he approached the group was as unsteady as if the deck still heaved beneath his feet.

"That is because you were so stupidly seasick. And *don't* call me Gaby!"

"A bullet hole, is it? No wonder you are bleeding all over my coat," said Mr Everett grimly, and strode into the inn, the girl in his arms. "You'll do no more walking till it's been seen to, if then. Colby, send for the surgeon at once, and have Baxter come to my room, if you please."

Dimly lit by a single candle, the low-ceilinged chamber to which he carried Gabrielle was nearly filled by a huge, old-fashioned fourposter bed of dark oak. He laid her gently on the patchwork counterpane, and placed a pillow under her shoulder so that she lay half on her uninjured side. Gerard sank into a chair.

"Why do I feel as bad on dry land as I did on the boat?" he groaned.

"It is often so, I believe," said Mr Everett unsympathetically. "I suppose you are too ill to aid your sister. I must cut away her clothing around the wound, for the blood is drying and it will stick. At least you can act as chaperon."

A small, balding man, neatly dressed in black, slipped into the room.

"Sir?"

"Baxter, I need plenty of light and a pair of scissors."

"Sir."

The servant lit a branch of candles on the mantelpiece and another on the dressing-table crammed into a corner between bed and tiny window. The light revealed his lugubrious face, jowled like a bloodhound. He opened a leather box on the dressing-table and offered it to his master.

"Scissors, sir."

"Thank you. That is not enough light. Is there no lamp in here?"

Baxter bent down and pulled an oil lamp from beneath Gerard's chair. He lit the wick at a candle flame and moved to hold it over the bed. As he looked down at Gabrielle, his face grew gloomier.

Gerard stood up and leaned against the nearest bedpost. Mr Everett had pulled back Gabrielle's jacket and was cutting away the shirt, revealing a huge purple bruise. He looked up at her brother, saw his sweat-beaded forehead and white lips.

"Sit down, lad," he said. "It will not help Miss Gabrielle if you pass out on us. Baxter, I need warm water and a clean cloth."

"Sir." The servant departed as silently as he had come.

Mr Everett sat on the edge of the bed and studied Gabrielle's face. Beneath the unladylike tan it was pallid, and a tiny frown of pain contracted her eyebrows. Her hacked-off curls were draggled and stiff from the salt sea air. He leaned forward to loosen her none-too-clean neckcloth, and she opened her eyes and smiled at him.

"Thank you," she whispered. "Thank you for everything. You are very kind to come to the rescue of perfect strangers."

For a moment he gazed at her unsmiling, then his stern mouth softened, giving his expression a curious vulnerability.

"Allow me to introduce myself," he said. "I am Luke Everett. I must assure you that I do not make a practice of removing the clothing from young ladies to whom I have not been presented in form."

Her eyes danced. "Nor I of being carried into unfamiliar bedchambers by gentlemen with whom I am unacquainted. I am Gabrielle Darcy, sir, and this poor suffering soul is my brother Gerard."

Gerard looked up, gave a sickly grin, and returned to the contemplation of his own misery.

"If I might make a suggestion, Miss Darcy, I should not be too free with your name. It might prove embarrassing at some future moment, considering the—ah—circumstances of your arrival."

"You refer to my dress, I take it. I expect you are right. We are but now come from France, Mr Everett, and have had such adventures on the way!"

"The evidence of that is plain before me, ma'am. Ah, Baxter, bring the bowl here, if you please. You see the fabric is stuck and I must soak it off. Miss Darcy, I fear this may be painful."

"Merely breathing is painful, sir. Pray don't mind me."

He took her hand and squeezed it, then wet the cloth and laid it on her side. After several applications, he began to ease off the patch of her shirt he had cut loose. Gabrielle squeaked.

He stopped at once. Her eyes were screwed shut, her fists clenched, but she murmured, "Go on. Finish it."

The rest came off more easily. Mr Everett looked at the wound and shook his head.

"It appears to be considerably swollen. I fear the bullet may still be there. Where the devil is that doctor? Baxter, go and make sure Colby sent for him."

Before the servant could go about his errand, there was a knock at the door and it was flung open. Framed in the doorway stood a huge woman, mop cap askew, wheezily trying to catch her breath. Her triple chin shook with the effort. Behind her, a tall, thin man tried in vain to push around her.

"You should stay in the kitchen, Mrs Colby, you should stay in the kitchen," he admonished. "Climbing stairs is excessively bad for you. Let me pass, I say, let me pass."

The innkeeper's wife recovered enough to gaze around the room.

"What's all this carryin' on then, Mr Everett?" she demanded breathlessly. "I runs a respectable house, I does."

"Get on with you, woman, you have known me for years. Do you still harbour doubts about my respectability?"

"Nay, sir, but I hear there be a young woman in here

without an abigail, and I cannot spare a chambermaid to sit with her, the house being so full and all."

"The young lady's brother is here; you need not fear for her reputation. But for her life, perhaps, if your husband has not sent for a doctor."

"Which he has done. Let be, doctor! Push, push, push till I don't know if I'm on my head or my heels. I'm moving quick as I can."

Apparently deciding the chamber was already too full, Mrs Colby lumbered backwards into the passage and the tall, thin man darted in.

"Dr Hargreaves, sir, Dr Hargreaves. What seems to be the problem now? Aha, the young lady has been shot, has she? She's been shot?" He put down his green cloth bag on the foot of the bed and peered at Gabrielle's side. "Nasty," he decided, "nasty. Bullet's still in there, don't you know, still in there. Have to get it out or it won't heal properly, get infected, *finis*, as you might say."

Gabrielle's eyes flew to Mr Everett's face. He took her hand and held it in a comforting grasp as the doctor fumbled in his bag. Gerard staggered to his feet.

"What are you going to do?" he asked belligerently.

"Have to cut it out, have to cut it out. Looks to be close to the lung, very dangerous, oh very dangerous. The lady must keep very still while I work. There's two ways to do it, don't you know. We can hit her on the head or we can give her half a pint of brandy and hold her. I'll need help, I say, I'll need help."

Gabrielle clutched Mr Everett's hand convulsively. "Please, no!" she gasped.

He sat down on the bed and looked into her eyes with his compelling gaze.

"He's right. But if you are unused to spirits, as I hope is the case, a glass of warm wine should be enough to deaden the pain somewhat. I take it you had rather that than be hit on the head, as the good doctor so uncouthly put it?" He raised his eyebrows questioningly.

25

She managed to smile. "Yes, of course. Please, you will stay?"

He smoothed her hair back from her brow. "Indeed I shall. You do not think I should permit anyone else to help you keep still? Except your brother, if he is up to it."

"I can manage perfectly well," said Gerard with dignity. "The floor is not moving near as much as it was."

"Need both of you, gentlemen, both of you. One at the head and one at the feet." Dr Hargreaves was removing from his bag a series of evil-looking instruments. At least they were clean and unrusted.

"Baxter, go and fetch a mug of mulled wine for Miss Darcy. And hurry, man. Anticipation is half the agony."

"Not in this case," muttered the doctor forebodingly. "Not in this case. I shall need plenty of hot water, too, and ask Mrs Colby for a couple of old sheets. Old sheets, I say."

When Gabrielle woke in the morning, Gerard was stretched out beside her, fully dressed and snoring slightly. The multicoloured counterpane had been folded back over her as a coverlet. On her other side, Mr Everett slumped in a hardbacked chair, his head leaning back against the wall, eyes closed.

She regarded him with interest. His face relaxed, he seemed considerably younger than she had thought. There was a hint of melancholy about his mouth, a sadness of lost hopes, perhaps. Otherwise he looked like a plain country gentleman, very ordinary in his crumpled, slept-in clothes.

Last night he had been a much more romantic figure. Coming unexpectedly to the rescue, he had immediately won her trust with his gentle, comforting assistance. She had not hesitated to accept his assurance that the dreadful operation was necessary.

Her memory of it was mercifully blurred. He had made her drink a huge mug of wine, then lifted her so that the sheets could be spread beneath her. By the time he laid her down again, her head was full of cottonwool. She had been

vaguely aware of Gerard's hands on her ankles and Mr
Everett's firm grasp on her wrists, until a piercing pain,
worse than the original bulletshot, had driven her into
oblivion.

She moved, cautiously. The dull ache in her side flared
into life, but it was not much worse than a scraped knee or
banged elbow, she decided. Her chief sensation was of
hunger, and she thought with longing of the garlic sausage
and heavy, dark bread that she and Willem and Jan had
shared on the boat.

There was a soft knocking on the door and Mr Everett's
manservant opened it just enough to stick his head round.

"Come in!" hissed Gabrielle. "Can you get me something
to eat?"

Baxter shook his head, then jerked it at his sleeping
employer. "Ask the master," he whispered in a hoarse
voice. "Said not to."

"Why?" asked Gabrielle indignantly.

She tried to sit up, groaned and lay down again. Mr
Everett's eyes opened instantly.

"Miss Darcy, are you in pain?"

"Not in the least," she lied.

He woke up enough to realize that she was regarding him
with disfavour.

"Perhaps you do not recall who I am?"

"Certainly I do, and I should know what makes you
think you can dictate whether I eat or not!"

He glanced at Baxter, who shrugged expressively.

"Pray hold me excused, ma'am. I have no wish to appear
dictatorial, but Doctor Hargreaves advised that you should
take nothing until he has examined you. He will come as
early as may be, I assure you."

"But I am hungry!"

Before Mr Everett had to think up a response, Gerard
stirred and stretched.

"Where the devil am I?" he mumbled. He sat up. "Oh, I
remember! How are you this morning, Gab? I could eat a

horse, I vow!" Swinging his legs over the side of the bed, he stretched again and yawned.

"So could I, but Mr Everett will not let me."

"Oh, good morning, sir! I must warn you that it is not the least use telling Gabrielle what to do. Even my father gave up trying some years back."

"Papa did not 'give up trying,' but recognised that I am an adult and quite able to decide for myself. It would have been very inconvenient for him to have a daughter who could only act upon instruction, since he was so rarely there!"

"Enough, Miss Darcy! I shall not attempt to rule you, but I am sure it would be unwise to ignore the doctor's suggestion."

"Oh, if the doctor said so!" Gerard was obviously relieved not to find himself on a field of battle. "Surely you will not argue with that?"

Gabrielle sighed. "I suppose not. I daresay the two of you will repair directly to the coffee room and break your fast?"

Her brother looked guilty. "You cannot expect *us* to starve because *you* cannot eat. Besides, I have not so much as tasted a morsel since . . . since noon on the day before yesterday. Lord, no wonder I am sharp-set! I'll tell you what, if the sawbones has not come by the time we are through, I shall go and fetch him myself."

"At least you will not leave me lying here. Help me to sit up, Gerard."

He stood up and moved to assist her, but Mr. Everett forestalled him, raising her shoulders and pulling pillows behind her back.

"Thank you," she said faintly, leaning back against his arm.

He looked down at her critically. "You are dizzy," he said. "I do not believe you are well enough to sit up."

"Yes, I am," she insisted, raising her chin. "If I cannot eat, I should like more than anything in the world to wash myself. Do you suppose a maid could be spared to help me?"

"Baxter, see to it," ordered Mr Everett, cautiously removing his arm. He stroked his chin, and added wryly, "You are not the only one in need of making a toilet. I shall have to see if Colby can find us a private corner. I am sure at least a few of the other guests will have left already for London. Like you, most of them had just escaped from France, though with whole skins. Come, Gerard, we will leave your sister in peace, and we will not again mention breakfast in her presence."

"Wretch!" Gabrielle flung after him.

The reminder of their escape brought to mind the events leading up to the last frantic dash to safety. Gabrielle thought, for the first time since leaving his cold body in the barn, of the English spy who had given his life for his country. His message and directions were clear in her memory and she was determined to carry them out. When a short while later a chambermaid arrived with hot water, soap, sponges and towels, the first thing she said was, "What is the name of this inn, pray?"

"The King's Head, miss. Cor, miss, there been't much left o' your clothes!" She helped Gabrielle take off the ruined jacket and shirt.

"Good, that's just where I wish to be. There isn't, is there? 'Tis past time I changed to skirts again, at all events."

"The mistress sent up a nightgown, miss. It's ever so pretty. A grand lady left it ahind when she went off to London."

"That's very good of her. I shall pay her, of course. Would she let you go out and purchase some clothes for me, think you?"

The maid was more than willing to be of assistance, though she could not answer for Mrs Colby. "She's a good heart, though, miss, for all she do shout fit to wake the dead when summat goes wrong."

"What is her husband like?"

"Oh, the master's easy enough. Lives beneath the cat's-paw, like, and he don't raise his voice often, but when he do, even *she* jumps."

"I must speak to him. Will you tell him so?"

"O' course, miss. Now if you'll put your arms out, miss, let's see if we can get this nightgown on wi'out hurting your poor side."

The nightgown was an insubstantial creation of frothy lace and pale pink ribbons. Gabrielle felt better just for having it on. The maid brushed her hair, and then held up a mirror.

"You look right pretty, miss," she declared with satisfaction. "No one wouldn't take you for a boy now, even wi' your hair cut short like that. It'll soon grow out, I make no doubt. If there's nowt more I can do for you now, I'll fetch up Mr Colby to see you."

=4=

GABRIELLE AWAITED THE landlord's arrival with eager curiosity. Who was the Man in the Green Coat? Still more interesting, who was Le Hibou, whose name they had used to persuade Willem Snieders to help them? Were the little spy in the Flanders barn and The Owl one and the same person? And if so, how had Papa known of him? What with soldiers, seasickness, and surgery, she'd had no chance to tell Gerard about the spy's message. Now she decided that it was not her secret to tell.

Mr Colby knocked and entered.

"You sent for me, miss?" he enquired, breathing heavily and wiping his forehead.

"You are the innkeeper? Yes, I did. Please close the door." When the man had done so, Gabrielle went on in a low voice. "Someone I met in France told me to go to you. He said to ask for the man in the green coat."

"The man in the green coat, miss?" Colby asked cautiously. "That's an odd one. I don't believe as we has any guests what wears a green coat."

"Then you must know where I can find him. I have a message for him that someone died trying to deliver."

Mr Colby looked startled. "Died, did he, the poor cove? And how did he happen to give you the missige, eh, miss?"

"I don't believe I ought to tell you any more," said Gabrielle consideringly. "It is clear that you know what I am talking about, so will you please stop shilly-shallying and tell this person that I must speak with him."

"And who's to say as you been't sent to trap him, miss, if you'll pardon my plainness? Partickly seeing as how . . . Nay, I can but give him the word and let him decide. Right you are, miss. If'n he comes, he'll come right soon. And if'n your tale be true and you've brung the missige at cost of a bullet, I'll take leave to tell you that you're a right brave young lady, and I be proud to have you staying at the King's Head."

Gabrielle blushed. "Thank you," she said. "It is true, I do assure you, and I hope you will persuade this man of mystery to listen to me."

"Ah, that's as may be." The innkeeper turned to leave, and stepped back with a gasp of surprise as the door opened and Mr Everett came in, followed by Gerard. "Sir, he stuttered, "a word with you outside."

"What is it, Colby? Is your wife questioning my respectability again? Baxter told me you were up here; I hope you have not been upsetting the young lady with questions."

"Oh no, Mr Everett, it's not my place to . . . Please, sir, just a word." He tugged on the gentleman's sleeve. Mr Everett glanced at Gabrielle, noted that she looked not only well but positively glowing, and allowed the agitated landlord to lead him out.

"Whatever are you wearing?" demanded Gerard. "It is downright indecent."

"Oh, do not say so. I believe it must be Parisian. It was left here by one of the guests and Mrs. Colby sent it up for me. Is it not pretty?"

"Yes, but cut much too low. You must wear a shawl."

"How can I, when the saddlebags were lost? Not that I brought a shawl anyway. However, the chambermaid is going to buy some proper clothes for me. Gerard, how much money do you have left? I hope it was you who took off my money belt when I was shot, and not the fishermen."

"Yes, I have it, or the contents anyway. There are

twenty-five *écus d'or* and some silver. And the draft on Hoare's bank, but I daresay that is useless until we reach London."

"Oh dear, that is less than I had supposed. You must have clothes too, before we go to Madame Aurore's, and there is the shot here to be paid, and the doctor, and the fare on the stage. We shall have to be very careful."

"I daresay Mr Everett would loan us something. He is a great gun for all his grim looks."

"Grim? I do not know what you mean, I'm sure. He is not in the least grim. All the same, I should not dream of borrowing from him. It would not be at all the thing."

"And nor is your nightdress. Do cover it up before he comes back."

"With what, pray? Really, Gerard, it is perfectly unexceptionable. And besides, I believe I hear Dr. Hargreaves outside. There is no time to find something."

The lanky doctor bustled in, Mr Everett a step behind him. The latter had a curious expression on his face, which Gabrielle read as disapproval of her dress. At once she felt both self-conscious and defiant.

"I do not think Mr Everett should be present," she said primly.

He looked surprised. "I beg your pardon," he apologised stiffly. "You are right, I have no business here. I had not considered." He left without more ado, but Gabrielle, listening hard, thought he did not walk down the hallway. He must be waiting outside.

"How are we feeling today?" asked the doctor. "I say, how are we feeling today?"

"Ravenous," complained Gabrielle.

He laughed heartily. "Appetite excellent, a very good sign, a very good sign." He felt her forehead. "And no fever. We have here a young woman in prime form, yes, in prime form. Would that all my patients were so healthy. Allow me, ma'am, to examine the wound."

With Gerard's help, he unwrapped yards of bandages from about her middle. Gabrielle held her breath while he studied it, probing with unexpected gentleness.

"Still sore, of course it is still sore. But no swelling, no infection and already beginning to heal, I say, already beginning to heal. An amazing constitution, ma'am, allow me to congratulate you. I shall not come again unless I am sent for. You will send for me if you see any untoward signs. We will put on a fresh bandage, which must be changed daily. It must be changed daily. You will remain in your bed today; tomorrow you may rise but do not overtire yourself. I say, stay abed today but you may rise tomorrow."

"May I eat?" asked Gabrielle.

"Eat? Eat? But of course you must eat. And drink as much liquid as you can, for the blood you lost must be replaced. You must drink plenty of liquids. There, is that quite comfortable? A pleasure to be of service, ma'am, a veritable pleasure. Good day to ye."

"I think," said Gerard as Hargreaves hurried out, "that he must have a lot of patients who do not listen to his instructions the first time he give them."

"Yes, indeed! I hope you were listening when he said that I might eat?"

Her brother grinned. "Never fear, I heard. I'll go see what I can scrounge up for you."

When he opened the door, Mr Everett and the doctor were disclosed in close consultation without. The gentleman looked up and smiled at Gabrielle.

"I hear comfortable tidings," he said. "It seems you are already on the road to recovery. May I come in?"

"Pray do. Gerard is off to find me something to eat," she added firmly, seeing him hovering in the passage. He shook his head dubiously, but left, and she continued, "I must beg your pardon for being so rude as to forbid you your own chamber."

"Not at all, Miss Darcy. It was perfectly proper of you."

"But unfriendly and ungrateful after all your help last night. Indeed, I am truly grateful. I cannot think what we should have done without you."

He flushed slightly, but his searching gaze held hers. "My pleasure, ma'am. I must confess to considerable curiosity as to the adventures that placed you in such a dangerous situation."

"If you will be seated, sir, I shall be delighted to favour you with a recital of our story," said Gabrielle graciously. "It all started in Switzerland, when we decided it was time to go to England. We . . ."

"Stop, stop! Begin at the beginning, if you please. Why were you in Switzerland and why did you decide to leave?"

"You cannot be interested in my life story, sir! The answer to those questions begins before my birth!"

"Then that is where you must begin," he said firmly. "Regard it as payment in some sort for the small assistance I was able to render yesterday."

"Then it will take forever, and you must not mind if I eat in the middle, for I assure you that as soon as Gerard returns I shall devour everything he brings me. Very well, it begins in Louisiana, in 1780 or thereabouts, when Papa met Mama. He was English, she French. My English grandfather despised the French and forbade Papa to return to England as long as he lived—my grandfather lived, that is. So Papa and Mama went to live in France with her family, and Gerard and I were born there."

"So you are citizens of France."

Gabrielle frowned. "Are we? I suppose you could say so. We were brought up to think ourselves English, and generally spoke English at home, for Mama spoke it very well. We had an English governess too, who stayed with us even when we went to Neuchâtel. She did not leave us until I was seventeen. Her sister's husband died, you see, and she went home to live with her."

"When did you go to Neuchâtel?" asked Mr Everett, uninterested in the vagaries of governesses.

"In 1792. Papa decided that in spite of his democratic principles it was too dangerous to stay in Paris. He was right too, of course. Poor Madame Aurore's husband went to the guillotine, and she would have, too, had Papa not rescued her. When Mama died on the way to Switzerland, Madame was the greatest comfort to him, and to us too, for I was but nine years old, and Gerard eight."

"So this Madame Aurore lived with you thereafter?"

"Not for long. She thought Neuchâtel vastly stuffy and bourgeois! She went to London, to join the other French aristocrats, but we have always kept in touch and she sent us all the latest English novels and gossip. So even though we passed for French, we still felt English. Papa always spoke of returning to his native land once his father was gone."

"Who was his father? I take it Darcy is your real name?"

"Yes, of course! But that is all I know, for Papa always refused to talk about his family. He said we should learn all in due time if it became necessary. Darcy is not an uncommon name, I think?"

"No, there are any number of families of that name. You are not seeking shelter with your family, then. Where shall you go when you leave here?"

"To Madame Aurore, in London. She has always pressed Gerard and me to visit her, even if Papa could not go. And when Papa left, he told us to go to her if we felt it necessary to leave without waiting for him."

"Your father left?"

"Yes, and he was gone longer than we expected," said Gabrielle hurriedly, obviously glossing over that part of her tale. "And then we heard of Bonaparte's quarrel with Lord Whitworth, and I was sure there would be war again. And then Marthe died. She was our nurse when we were little, and then our housekeeper. I thought if we found a new servant, we might be exposed as English, and of course Neuchâtel had been part of France for years by then. So we left. And that is where I should have started my story if you had not asked for all that ancient history!"

"I apologise, Miss Darcy. Perhaps we had best delay the rest of the telling, for you look a little pale. Would you like to lie down?"

"I shall be perfectly all right as soon as I have eaten. Oh, there you are at last, Gerard! I had almost given up."

Gerard held open the door, and Baxter carried in a tray loaded with covered dishes.

"Thank you," said Gabrielle with satisfaction. "You may take away all the covers, for I shall certainly eat everything. It appears that Mrs Colby has a proper appreciation of a deprived appetite!"

"One has only to look at her to expect it," Gerard pointed out. "I am hungry again, Gab. Can you not spare me a roll?"

"Just one, then, if you will butter mine for me." She took a large forkful of steaming omelette. "Mmm, delicious. Will you have anything, sir?"

"No, I thank you," said Mr Everett, laughing. "Unlike the two of you I am not suffering from starvation, and I had an excellent breakfast not two hours since. I shall leave you to eat in peace while I step out for a breath of fresh air, but I shall return presently, if I may, for I greatly desire to hear about your travels. Baxter shall stay to serve you."

Her mouth full of fried ham, Gabrielle nodded. Nor did she reply when Gerard commented disconsolately that he supposed they were stuck here for several days while she convalesced.

"I believe I shall go for a walk," he said at last. "I cannot sit here watching you make a pig of yourself."

"Yes, do go, for seeing your long face is almost enough to make me lose my appetite. Go and buy yourself some decent clothing."

Gerard brightened. "That is a good idea. I feel like a tramp in these after wearing them for three days."

"You look like one. Now go away and let me eat, there's a dear. Baxter, be so good as to fetch me some more chocolate. My brother has drunk the half of it."

The two departed, and Gabrielle set to in earnest to

provide Mrs Colby with proof that her cooking was appreciated. When Baxter returned with a pewter pot of hot chocolate, she was leaning back against her pillows feeling somewhat overfull but much stronger.

"Thank you," she said as he poured her a cup. "Have you been with Mr Everett very long?"

"Aye, miss."

"Where does he live?"

"Mostly London, miss."

"Has he family there?"

"Aye, miss."

"Children?"

"No, miss."

Gabrielle decided that she could not ask outright whether Mr Everett was a married man.

"Will he stay long in Dover?"

"Can't say, miss."

"I expect he has business here?"

" 'Spect so, miss."

She looked at the gloomy, close-mouthed little man with irritation. How could she find out anything about her rescuer if he would not cooperate? She was not sure if he was merely taciturn or if he was being deliberately secretive.

"Where does Mr Everett live when he is not in town?" she tried.

"In the country, miss."

Gabrielle gave up, finished her chocolate, and requested the removal of her tray.

Alone at last, she managed to pull a couple of pillows from behind her and lie down. The sun shone through the tiny but sparkling clean window and she could hear the mewing of seagulls and a distant dog barking. Drowsy, she closed her eyes; the sounds faded, and she slept.

A light tapping on the door roused her.

"Come in," she called sleepily.

"Did I wake you?" asked Mr Everett, coming in. "I'm

sorry. I came up earlier and when you did not answer my knock I was worried, so I looked in. Since you did not hear me then, I thought you would not this time if you were still sleeping."

"I must have been ready to wake up. What time is it? Past noon? I'll tell you what I should like above all things: a cup of tea."

"If I send for a pot of tea, will you tell me the rest of your adventures?" he asked, smiling.

"If you don't, I won't!"

Tea was procured, along with a tankard of ale for Mr Everett and a plate of currant cakes ("The mistress says they's to build up the young lady's strength," confided the maid). Gabrielle sat up and, between sips of hot tea, took up her tale.

She explained her decision to dress as a boy, and described the agonising ride which had persuaded them to continue the journey on the *diligence*, however slow.

"You must not laugh," she said severely, seeing his lips twitch. "It was excessively painful, much worse than I feel now. It is not that we had not ridden before, but never for so long, only around the lake usually. And of course, I had always ridden sidesaddle."

"I should not dream of laughing," he assured her. "Go on."

"There is really not much more to tell." Gabrielle had rapidly reviewed the rest of her story and decided that the part about the spy was not hers to tell. She could not think how, but somehow it might endanger other patriotic Englishmen still in France. "We walked a great deal of the way, because the stagecoaches did not go the way we wished to go."

"Since it did not kill you, that is doubtless why you are in such excellent health and recuperating so quickly."

"I daresay. It took forever. In Tourcoing we heard of the declaration of war, so we took horses to ride to Dunkirk. We were nearly there when a group of French soldiers began to follow us, and when we rode on, they fired. Fortunately it was nearly dark, so we managed to get away and sailed here on the next tide. And that is all there was to it."

"Now why do I think you are concealing the best part of the tale?"

She flushed and raised her chin. "You may think what you please," she said tartly. "Do you call me a liar?"

"I should not dare. I expect you would call me out, for you are certainly a redoubtable female. No, not a liar, but certainly a prevaricator. You must believe me when I say I am thankful for your ability to hold your tongue, for I am the Man in the Green Coat."

Gabrielle gaped. "But you can't be," she said inanely. "Your coat is grey!" He grinned. "Oh, I didn't mean that. Of course it is a code name, like Le Hibou. But . . . you? Why did you not tell me before, as soon as Colby told you I was asking for you?"

"You may think me very imperceptive, but I was not sure how far I could trust you. Tell me, what do you know of Le Hibou?"

"Very little." It was her turn for suspicion. "If you are who you say you are, you must know all about him. Why do you ask me?"

"*Touché!* However, I can call on Colby to vouch for me. He has known me for years as the Man in the Green Coat. There is no one to vouch for *you*."

"No, only a bullet in my side! I assure you I did not have it placed there on purpose to deceive you. And Dr Hargreaves can swear that it was real, if you doubt it."

He leaned forward and took her hand. "I know that it was real. Let us not quarrel, Miss Darcy, for I am more and more convinced that we are on the same side. Forget the Owl for the moment, and give me the message."

"It is from the Owl. In truth, I know so little, I will tell you all. Papa told us to ask for passage at Dunkirk in the name of Le Hibou. Gerard went into the town to make arrangements, while I hid in a barn. There were soldiers everywhere searching for a wounded spy, and though not so sore as the first time, I was tired from riding all day. The spy was there in the barn, a little man in a brown coat and leggings, just as they had described him."

"John Waterbury," murmured Mr Everett. "Poor John."

"He heard me and thought I was his Betsy. When I spoke to him in English, he gave me the message. Then he died."

"And the message?"

" 'Le Hibou says, de la Touche is Fouché's man.' "

"*Fouché's* man!" Mr Everett jumped to his feet and began to stride up and down the narrow chamber, a dangerous exercise in view of the low ceiling and the numerous articles of furniture. "Le Hibou is back from Russia then. I must return to London at once."

"What does it mean?" asked Gabrielle. "I know that Fouché was once Minister of Police, but who is de la Touche? And who is Le Hibou? And come to that, who are you?"

"I cannot explain now, ma'am. I must leave immediately. Pray excuse me, and allow Baxter to come in to pack my things." He turned to the door.

"Wait! I had almost forgot: he—the spy—asked that you take care of Betsy."

"You may be sure I shall do so. If you remember anything else, it will have to wait until the end of the week, when I shall return to escort you to your friend's house. This news is urgent, and too important to be entrusted even to Baxter." Without another word, he was gone.

Gabrielle looked after him in exasperation. "If he expects me to remain here awaiting his pleasure," she muttered, "he is in for a surprise!"

—5—

MY LADY HARRISON was in a puzzle. As her abigail delicately brushed the merest *soupçon* of rouge onto her plump cheeks, she squinted sideways at the three invitations lying on her dresser. With the London season drawing to a close, half the ton was trying to squeeze in the entertainments they had postponed earlier, before the Fashionable World dispersed to the country to take up more rural pastimes.

"Devonshire 'Ouse," pondered Lady Harrison. "Of course it is a *grand triomphe* to be invited by the Duke of Devonshire. I shall go to Devonshire 'Ouse. Only it is to be a musical evening, and you know, Marie, that I am *not* musical. It promises to be very tedious."

"*Madame* ought not to have accepted so many invitations," said the maid severely.

"I turned down at least as many others," pointed out her ladyship. "I ought to go to Mrs Levis's card party, for her husband was a very old friend of poor Sir Cosmo's, but I vow I cannot afford to play more than silver loo and the stakes are always high at Mrs Levis's. I shall go to Lady Boniface's drum. She serves an excellent supper."

"If *madame* will stand, we will attempt the fastenings of *madame's* gown."

Lady Harrison sighed. "I know, Marie, I cannot afford Lady Boniface's supper either. Devonshire 'Ouse it is."

A discreet knock at the door of the dressing room called the maid away, postponing the moment of truth. Her ladyship took a few surreptitious deep breaths in preparation for the ordeal. Marie was very clever with her needle, but even she could not let out old gowns beyond a certain point, and where the money was to come from for new ones was more than my lady could tell. What poor Sir Cosmo would have said if he could see how she had to scrimp and save on the generous jointure he had left her! But it was her own fault for taking in as many of her penniless countrymen as the house would hold, as Marie had pointed out to her more than once.

"What is it, Marie?" she asked.

The abigail turned to her with a disapproving face. *"Rien, madame,* it is nothing."

"Now tell me at once. I will not have you concealing things from me. Is that new mantua-maker dunning me already?"

"Certainly not, *madame.* It is a pair of good-for-nothings who have heard tell of your so generous heart and are come to take advantage."

"Who? Who is it?" Lady Harrison jumped to her feet and scuttled to the half-shut door. She pulled it open, to the confusion of the powdered footman standing without, who averted his eyes from the generous figure that matched his mistress's generous heart. "Who is it, Roger?"

"It's a Mr and Miss Darcy, my lady. Just come from France, it seems, and Miss Darcy don't look too well, if you arst me."

"Madame did not ask you," said Marie sourly.

Lady Harrison squealed in delight.

"Gerard and Gabrielle! At last! *Mais c'est formidable!* The papa, he is not with them?"

"No, my lady. Just the two young 'uns, like I said."

"Marie, my wrap! I go to them immediately. Prepare two chambers, Marie. And Roger, have Mrs 'Odge provide refreshments in the drawing room, and cancel the carriage for I shall not go out tonight after all. And . . ."

"Which two chambers did *madame* have in mind?" queried the maid, draping a shawl of Norwich silk about her ladyship's dimpled shoulders. "I remind *madame* that all are occupied at present."

"Oh dear, you are right! Well, Gabrielle must sleep in here for tonight. Make up a bed on the couch. And Gerard will have to share with Alain. I am sure they are much of an age. I very much fear that Monsieur Lecarreau will have to leave tomorrow, so that Gabrielle can have his chamber."

"And a very good thing too! It is four months since *madame* first asked Monsieur Lecarreau to depart. *Madame* is not of sufficient firmness!"

"I know, Marie, for you tell me so often enough. He is a very disagreeable old man, and I am certain he has enough to live on, but it is not easy to turn anyone out, I assure you."

As she bustled out, Lady Harrison thought she heard a mutter from her maid to the effect that, if it caused the departure of *le vieux crapaud*, the arrival of the Darcys might be considered a blessing in disguise. She hoped that meant her maid would treat the newcomers with complaisance, sparing them the acid tongue she usually used on those she described as leeches who were sucking her mistress dry.

Gabrielle and Gerard, waiting wearily on hard chairs in the marbled entrance hall, were startled to see a large, half-dressed lady bearing down upon them, beaming. As they rose, she enveloped them both in a warm, scented embrace, pressed kisses upon their cheeks, then stepped back to look at them, retaining a hand of each.

"*Mes chéris!*" she cried. "You are quite grown up, I do declare. *Que je suis heureuse* to see you again! But where is *le bon papa?*"

"We don't know," said Gerard, pink-faced, extricating his hand with difficulty and making his bow.

Gabrielle curtsied, swaying a little. "It is good to be here, Madame Aurore. Papa told us to come to you."

"And have I not invited you many and many a time? I am Lady 'Arrison now, not Madame Aurore, but we will talk of that later. For now that I look at you, Gabrielle, I see that Roger was quite right and you do not look at all well. Come into the drawing room, my dears, and sit down while Marie prepares a bed for you."

Gabrielle leaning on her brother's arm, they followed her into a room strikingly decorated in pale blue and gold and white. The furniture was simple and elegant, but somewhat worn.

A young man was standing by the window, gazing out into the darkness of Russell Square. He turned as they entered, displaying dark, wavy hair, blue eyes and classical features, adding up to a face whose undoubted handsomeness was marred only by his moody expression.

"Alain!" exclaimed Lady Harrison. "Let me present you to Mr and Miss Darcy. No, wait a bit. Gabrielle, sit down, *chérie*, here on this sofa and put your feet up. You are very pale, *mon enfant*."

"I am a little tired from the journey, my lady."

"That sounds so strange! Perhaps you had better call me Madame Aurore after all, as you used to. Have you dined? Then no wonder you are pale. I ordered refreshments. Alain, *mon ami*, pray go ask Roger what is become of them. No, wait, let me introduce you first. Here are Gabrielle and Gerard Darcy, but now arrived in England. My dears, this is Alain de Vignard. I know you will all be friends, for Alain and Gerard must share a chamber, at least for the present."

The young man was dressed as elegantly as the room was furnished, and with the same hint of shabbiness. Looking at them with eager curiosity, he bowed politely and expressed his willingness to share his accommodation.

"Though indeed I can do no other!" he admitted, with a charming smile that robbed the words of any offence. "If milady had not taken pity on me, I should be living in a garret. If you will excuse me, milady, Miss Darcy, I shall go and clear out my things to leave space for Mr Darcy."

"No hurry," said Gerard. "My possessions are all on my back."

"Then I shall make sure that the admirable Mrs Hodge is

46

indeed preparing refreshments for the travellers." With a slight bow he left.

"Poor Alain!" said Lady Harrison. "His parents died in the Terror and he escaped alone to England when he was scarce sixteen years old. He is some five years older than you, Gabrielle. He had a very difficult time before he came to us, but he has been living here for several years now. Dear Sir Cosmo was so generous in allowing me to help my countrymen! Alain is employed now as a secretary to *le général* Pichegru. But enough of that. Tell me, my dears, are you come direct from Switzerland?"

By the time they had given her a brief explanation of their arrival, Roger had carried in a tray with a silver teapot and a plate of plain biscuits.

"Oh dear, that will never do!" Lady Harrison said in dismay. "Roger, pray go back to Mrs 'Odge and tell her to make some sandwiches, and some of the asparagus soup we had at dinner. It is all Marie's fault," she explained. "She has persuaded the good Mrs 'Odge that I am not to eat between meals. You do not know Marie, of course. She was maid to *la vicomtesse de Brabant* and was turned out when *madame la vicomtesse* arrived penniless in England. She is a treasure, but very strict!" Her ladyship looked round guiltily and took a biscuit.

Following her example, Gerard soon cleaned the plate, while a cup of tea revived Gabrielle. Neither was surprised when Lady Harrison helped them demolish the pile of sandwiches that soon appeared. As there were only two bowls provided, she left the soup for them.

By the time they finished eating, Gabrielle was half asleep and even Gerard owned he was ready to retire.

"In that case," said their hostess buoyantly, "I believe I shall go to Lady Boniface's after all, for I am sure the supper will not tempt me now. I shall see you tomorrow, my dears!"

Gabrielle slept till nearly ten o'clock the next morning and woke feeling very much refreshed. Her side still ached a little when she moved, but she was ready to abandon Dr Hargreaves's voluminous bandage in favour of a small court-plaster over the scar of her wound.

She pushed back the bedcovers and, going to the window, drew the curtains. Russell Square was rain-slicked and deserted, the trees in the central garden collecting grey moisture from the sky and dispensing it in larger drops upon the brilliantly green grass below.

Hearing no movement in the house, she went to the door that had been pointed out to her as that of Lady Harrison's bedchamber, and listened. Silence. She opened it a few inches and peeked in.

The widow of the late Sir Cosmo Harrison, and of his predecessor, Monsieur le Comte de Lavardac et Casteljaloux, lay fast asleep in her fourposter hung with pink silk. On her head, a nightcap of Valenciennes lace was tied with a matching pink ribbon. She looked like an overgrown cherub.

Gabrielle looked again at the clock on the mantel. Ten o'clock it was, and the church bells were beginning to ring out their urgent summons all over the city. Lady Harrison slept on.

A pier-glass caught Gabrielle's attention, and she examined her reflection. Her brother was right, the Parisian nightgown was anything but decent! She blushed to think of the long conversation she had had with Mr Everett while wearing nothing more. Except, of course, for a sheet and a couple of blankets, she reassured herself. And she did look quite pretty in it.

A forget-me-not painted ewer on the marble washstand held a little cold water, so she washed in the matching bowl and put on her only clothes. The maid at the King's Head had bought her a cambric round-gown in a disagreeable shade of yellow, a green spencer which went with it abominably, and a poke bonnet at least a size too large. Perhaps it was just as well she had woken too late for morning church, as she would not dare show herself in fashionable London dressed thus. Nor were her garments in the best of condition after two days on the stage from Dover.

Looking in the mirror again, she decided she looked bilious. Tomorrow Gerard must present their draft at Hoare's Bank, and then she must persuade Madame Aurore to take her shopping.

Madame Aurore needed no persuasion. When Gerard returned from the bank with a pocket full of what he referred to as 'flimsies,' she sent for her carriage and the two ladies set out for Bruton Street. Madame knew all the best modistes, and had for some years been unable to indulge to the full her penchant for the latest fashions. She was delighted to help, and had not lost the elegant taste of the true Parisienne.

Gabrielle, however, had been parted in early youth from the extravagant frivolity of Paris and brought up in the thrifty atmosphere of Switzerland. She was shocked by the prices, and no amount of urging from her ladyship would persuade her to buy on tick.

"But your papa will certainly pay!" exclaimed Lady Harrison.

"I expect he would if he were here," agreed Gabrielle mildly, "but he is not and we have no idea when to expect him. We have limited funds, and Gerard wishes to purchase a commission in the army, which will certainly be expensive, will it not?"

Her ladyship sighed and took her charge to Grafton House.

"Fortunately," she said, "the season is nearly over. One ball gown, a promenade dress and a simple *toilette de soir* will do for now."

"But I have no intention of going to parties!" cried Gabrielle. "I shall just live quietly until Papa comes."

"Nonsense, *chérie*. Believe me, Papa would wish it so. And it will be such a pleasure for me to chaperone a pretty girl instead of going about by myself. Sir Cosmo was a pillar of the Foreign Office and he had friends in the very best society. They are kind to his poor widow, so we shall not want for invitations."

"Tell me about Sir Cosmo, *madame*."

With a mixture of complacency and becoming modesty that made Gabrielle want to laugh, Lady Harrison described how she had found herself a second husband within six months of her arrival in London.

"I had rather have wed your Papa," she admitted with a deep sigh, "but I could not abide Neuchâtel and he refused to come to England, or even to go to Vienna. I was so sorry to leave you two little children, but you had still the admirable Mademoiselle Wilford."

"Whom I must go and see," Gabrielle murmured to herself.

"And now," my lady continued sadly, "your Papa is coming at last, and I have grown so fat since Sir Cosmo died that he will not like even to look at me!"

Unable to deny that Madame Aurore had lost the sylph-like figure she remembered, Gabrielle asked hurriedly, "I suppose my grandfather is dead, or Papa would not be willing to come here now?"

"La, child, has he not told you?"

"No, he never told us anything. He is the most abominably secretive man you can imagine, and we know nothing about his family. So you can begin at the beginning and tell me everything you know."

"Oh dear," said Lady Harrison. "I should like to, of all things. But if Maurice does not wish you to know, I must not. Maurice never does anything without a very good reason. You will have to wait until he arrives."

No amount of pleading would change her mind, though Gabrielle returned several times to the subject as they pored over silks and satins, laces and ribbons. At last, surrounded by packages neatly tied in brown paper and string, they drove back to Russell Square.

The front door of Lady Harrison's house stood open. As they alighted from the carriage, they heard loud voices within. Her ladyship laid a trembling hand on Gabrielle's arm, but trod bravely up the steps.

The footman met them at the door.

"It's the chandler, my lady," he whispered. "Says the bill for candles hain't been paid in six months."

Peering past him, Gabrielle saw Gerard confronting a burly individual with a very red face and bristling mustache.

"Thank you, Roger," said Lady Harrison with dignity. "Please fetch our parcels from the carriage. I shall deal with this person."

"I dunno, my lady. Looks nasty to me. Maybe I better stay."

"My brother and I will be here," reassured Gabrielle. "But hurry!"

Her ladyship sailed into the hallway, looking the very picture of outraged virtue.

"*Qu'est-ce que c'est?*" she demanded. "Gerard, what goes on here?"

Gerard and the stout chandler both spoke at once, but the tradesman's louder voice prevailed.

"It's me bill, my lady. Hain't bin paid in ever so long and I'll thank you to see to it, for I've babes to feed same as the next man."

"It must have been mislaid," declared Lady Harrison. "It shall be paid promptly at the quarter, I promise you, my good man."

"Oh no, I hain't budging till I got the blunt, and that's the truth, my lady."

Gerard pulled a much diminished roll of notes from his pocket. "How much?" he asked briefly. He whistled when he heard the figure, and glanced at his hostess. Her plump cheeks trembling, my lady nodded. Gabrielle helped her into the drawing room as Gerard handed over the money.

Lady Harrison sank onto a sofa and burst into tears. "I

simply do not know where the money goes!" she moaned. "Sir Cosmo left me an excellent income as well as the use of the town house. But, every quarter, Oswald sends back half the bills unpaid and says I have overspent again. And I *will* not call him Sir Oswald, for he has always been most disagreeable to me and I am sure he does not deserve to have inherited poor Sir Cosmo's title!"

"Sir Oswald?" Gerard followed them into the room.

"My stepson. He has a wart on his chin and his eyebrows meet in the middle, and try as I may, I cannot trust a man whose eyebrows meet in the middle."

"Sir Cosmo left your jointure in his charge?" asked Gabrielle.

"Yes. Every quarter he sends me a certain amount for small expenditures, and I send him my bills, and he is supposed to pay them, but there is never enough money. It is all my fault because I cannot refuse shelter to my friends. But I shall pay you back, Gerard, I promise, on the first of July."

Gerard and Gabrielle exchanged glances. "Certainly not," Gabrielle said gently. "If you offer us shelter, you must let us help with expenses, or we cannot accept your hospitality."

"But we cannot have burnt a hundredth of those candles since you arrived! And besides, you are practically family."

Gabrielle patted her hand. "Come, dry your tears, dear Madame Aurore. I have no head for figures, but Gerard has always kept the family accounts. He will go through your expenditures, if you should like it, and find out just why you are in such difficulties."

Gerard pulled a face but nodded.

"I'm sure I never spend a penny on my dress, nor on furnishings," wailed Lady Harrison, wiping her eyes, with disastrous effects on her rouge. "As you may very well see for yourselves, and it is excessively mortifying to appear so shabby when people call."

Gabrielle stood up. "Speaking of dress," she said, "you

promised to show me a picture of a ball dress that will suit me to perfection, so that Marie and I may start sewing."

"Yes, indeed! It is in the latest *Ladies' Magazine*, in my dressing room. The apricot crêpe lisse will be perfect, with a white satin petticoat. Was it not fortunate that we found the matching slippers?" Prattling gaily of fashion and fabric, her ladyship forgot her sorrows as she led the way above stairs.

— 6 —

LADY CECILIA EVERETT's drawing room was crowded with morning callers. Muslin-clad debutantes scarce out of the schoolroom chattered like a flock of sparrows, while matrons in silks and satins exchanged the latest *on dits* in lower tones. Gentlemen leaned on the backs of sofas, joining in, or posed in solitary splendour, displaying either a new waistcoat or a superior degree of lovesickness.

Usually Mr Lucius Everett was highly gratified by this evidence of his half-sister's popularity, but today he desired a word in private with his stepmama, and in consequence wished the crowd to the devil.

He stood leaning against the doorpost, his eyes fixed critically on Dorothea Everett's ethereal beauty. For the first time, he wondered what her many suitors found to admire in that air of fragile docility, which he had always thought highly appropriate in a young lady.

Judging by the sample in the drawing room, Dorothea's friends were all equally well-bred, insipid females, though none compared with her in looks. Her suitors ranged from infatuated youths, who found her gentleness unthreatening, to a wealthy earl in his forties on the lookout for a conformable bride. For leavening, he noted, there were one or two out-and-outers, with rakish reputations. He was not worried. A word in Dorrie's ear and she would unquestioningly drop their acquaintance.

There was something to be said for docility, after all.

At last, the last visitor took his leave. Mr Everett strode across the room, bowed to his stepmother and kissed her hand. She was no more than three or four years older than he, but he made it a point to treat her always with punctilious courtesy when anyone else was present, even her daughter.

"Good morning, ma'am. I trust I did not wake you when I came home last night? Morning, Dorrie. You are a little pale today. Do not wear yourself to a shadow with gadding about!"

"Oh no, Luke!" She looked up at him apprehensively. "I am very well, truly."

"I did not like to see Sir Hubert here, nor Lord Aintree. You must not allow them to dangle after you. I know you will do your best to discourage them."

"Yes, Luke."

Satisfied, he turned back to Lady Cecilia. "I need your help, ma'am," he requested. "You are better acquainted with the ton than I. Do you know of a lady who goes by the name of Madame Aurore?"

"Madame Aurore? A Frenchwoman? I have never heard of such a person, but I am not widely acquainted with the *émigré* community. Dorothea, pray go and fetch my embroidery."

"Yes, mama. Luke, if you have the time, I should like to speak with you before you go out."

"Of course, little sister. I have an appointment with the Foreign Secretary at two, but there is plenty of time before I need leave."

As Dorothea closed the door behind her, he once again turned to his stepmother, with raised eyebrows.

"Luke, are you sure this Madame Aurore is a lady? Such an odd name!"

"I believe it to be a nursery name, such as young children might call a friend of their parents. I most sincerely hope you are not about to tell me of someone by that name who is less than respectable!" Mr Everett's brows were drawn in a forbidding frown.

"Oh no, Luke, I have never heard it in any context, I promise you. Can you tell me no more about her?"

"Only that she is a widow who came to this country some eight or nine years ago."

"A widow!" exclaimed Lady Cecilia with evident relief.

"Cecilia, you thought me entangled with an unknown charmer, confess it!" Luke laughed, and she smiled in reply.

"Of course, there is no reason you should not be 'entangled' with a widow, but you would surely have a little more recent information about any 'charmer.' However, it is past time that you fell in love, Luke!"

His mouth took on its usual stern line, and his searching eyes held hers. "I was in love once," he reminded her.

She dropped her gaze and blushed, but said sharply, "Calf love, and well you know it, Luke Everett. We were children. Do not pretend to me that I blighted your life when I married your father. I believe you have persuaded yourself of it, and used it as an excuse for wearing the willow!"

"No, you are fair and far out there. But I was in love with you when my father wooed and won you, and I have not quite forgiven him."

"Have you forgiven me?" she asked softly.

"Long since, Cecilia. What future was there for you with a boy of sixteen? I could wish that it had not been my father you married, but if you had married someone else, we should not have become such good friends."

"We are friends, are we not? I am glad of it. If only you would recognise your father's good points, for in spite of his faults, he has many."

"We will not discuss him, if you please. Cecilia, keep your ears open for news of my entangling charmer. For all she's an elderly widow, I am anxious for news of her."

"Is it something to do with the Foreign Office?"

"Now, you know I cannot tell you that!"

"Then it is! I shall be very discreet, I promise. Ah, Dorrie, have you found it?"

Dorothea came in carrying a tambour frame and a basket from which dangled lengths of coloured silks.

"Here, mama. It was in your chamber."

"Thank you, child. I believe I shall not do any now, after all. I must see Cook before we go shopping, so I will leave you to talk to your brother. Shall you be home for dinner, Luke?"

Lady Cecilia sailed out, looking dignified and matronly but still reminding him of the girl he had loved so many years ago. He shook himself mentally and turned to his sister.

"What can I do for you, Dorrie?"

"Lord Thirsk wants to marry me!" She sat pale and still, her hands clasped in her lap, but her voice was full of suppressed agitation.

"Do you want to marry him?"

"Mama says I must, because he is very rich. He could provide for my brothers and sisters, and then you need not work any more."

Luke moved to sit beside her and took her cold hands in his. "Dorrie, I may once have resented having to give up a life of pleasure, but I enjoy my work. It is interesting in itself, and of use, I hope, to the nation as well as to my family. If you married Golden Ball himself, I should not give it up."

"Then I do not have to marry him?"

"Of course not, goose. You need not marry anyone you don't want to."

"But if you did not have to pay all the bills, you would have more money for yourself."

"I do not pay the bills, Dorrie. I can see it is time things were explained to you, for otherwise who knows what you will imagine!"

"I know Papa is a terrible gambler and lost lots and lots of money."

"Yes, but fortunately it was not in his power to dispose of our lands. Since he has been devoting himself to them, they pay for necessaries. But there is nothing to spare, because of the old debts that must be paid."

"So you pay for my brothers' schooling and horses, I know that. And for my come-out, and my sisters', and our dowries. You would be better off if I never married!"

"Nonsense! Do you think I want an old maid for a sister?" teased Luke. "Cheer up, Dorrie, and believe me that I have all I want in life, and that being able to provide for you all is a matter of pride and pleasure as well as duty. So now you can consider Lord Thirsk's offer without thinking of anything but whether you wish to marry him or not."

"He frightens me."

"Then you shall on no account marry him. Have you told your mother this?"

"Oh, no. She is not afraid even of Papa in one of his rages. She would not understand at all."

"Then I am very glad that you told me. I will speak to Lord Thirsk and he shall not bother you again."

"Thank you, Luke! You are truly the best of brothers, even though you are sometimes just as frightening as Papa and Lord Thirsk!" She kissed his cheek and skipped out, leaving him wondering whether his fainthearted sister would ever find a suitor who did not make her tremble.

He had always thought Lord Thirsk a thoroughly inoffensive gentleman, and as for himself—only Napoleon's spies had any cause to fear him!

Was Gabrielle Darcy a French spy? Ever since he had returned to Dover two days ago and found her gone, his suspicions had reawakened. Why else should she flee before his promised return?

He had little reason to trust her. The message throwing doubt on de la Touche's royalist credentials might serve

59

Bonaparte's turn whether it were true or not. And the French intelligence service could have picked up hints of the existence of Le Hibou and his own alter ego, the Man in the Green Coat.

But he had seen with his own eyes Dr Hargreaves removing a bullet from her side.

Who the devil was Madame Aurore?

Would he ever see Gabrielle again?

It should not be for want of trying, vowed Mr Everett, and sent for Baxter.

The taciturn manservant had many talents besides those of a gentleman's gentleman. If anyone could run to earth an elderly French widow of uncertain antecedents, then Baxter was the one.

And still more important, the mysterious woman would never know she had been found.

Some hours later, the Honourable Lucius Everett emerged from Lord Hawkesbury's office and made his way to his own.

His elderly secretary, a tall, thin, meek-looking man, took one glance through wire-rimmed spectacles at his grim face and asked, "They didn't believe it, sir?"

"They do not choose to believe it, Davis."

"But the message was from Le Hibou! He has always been the most reliable source we have, since before you joined the service even. His lordship was grateful enough for the information we received from Russia last month."

"The message purported to be from Le Hibou. I am just sufficiently uncertain of its actual provenance to argue convincingly."

"You were convinced last week, sir, when you returned from Dover in such a hurry."

"Something has happened since which I cannot but regard as a cause for suspicion. The person who brought the message out of France . . . Hush! There is someone at the door."

The door was flung open and a large gentleman breezed in. Taller than Mr Everett, he was not precisely stout, but rather bulky in an unhealthy manner; flabby, with the look of muscles gone to waste. His bushy eyebrows, joined in the centre in a straight line, contrasted oddly with his nearly bald head.

"Everett, there you are!" he exclaimed jovially, if unnecessarily. "I hear you've been closeted with the Secretary for hours. And young Monsyer Cadoudal and the French General too. Pichegru, isn't it? Hawkesbury been giving you a hard time, has he?"

"I am not at liberty to discuss the matter, Sir Oswald. You must excuse me, I have a great deal of work to accomplish."

"Piled up while you were gone, did it? Popping in and out like Punch and Judy, off to Dover and back again, they say. Daresay if the truth were known, you were just off on a repairing lease to your country place, eh, you sly dog?"

"Who told you that I went to Dover?"

"Oh, I'm not complaining, mind. 'Pon my soul, a man deserves a break now and then when he sticks as close to his last as you do, Everett. Just like Sir Cosmo. You remember my father, Davis? Always nose to the grindstone. I like to pop in now and then to see how the old man's office is managing without him. Of course, I've all sorts of obligations meself—head of the family, estate to run, and so on. Matter of fact, my place ain't so far from yours, Everett. Near Sevenoaks, isn't it? Surprised we don't see you in Kent more often."

"I spend very little time at Wrotham, Sir Oswald. Now you really must excuse me, if you please."

"Of course, of course," replied the baronet testily. "I hope you will dine with me tonight? Just a small card party, you know, nothing special."

"Thank you, but I have promised to escort my sister tonight. Another time, perhaps. Goodbye, Sir Oswald!"

Mr Everett and his secretary converged on the unwanted

visitor and at last succeeded in forcing him to retreat through the open doorway.

"Nosy," said the secretary disapprovingly, closing the door with a decided click. "You didn't know his father, sir, but it was quite otherwise with him. Many's the time I heard Sir Cosmo described as a pillar of the Foreign Office."

"Hence, no doubt, the son's unjustified belief that he is welcome here. Davis, send someone to find out where my sister goes this evening, and to inform her that I go too!"

Lady Cecilia was pleased to learn that her stepson intended for once to do his duty by his sister. Dorothea, however, regarded him with mingled alarm and delight when he joined them in the drawing room before dinner. She thought he looked magnificent in knee breeches and ruffled shirt, but his expression was not appropriate to an evening of merrymaking.

"We are going to a ball, Luke," she said timidly. "You abominate balls above all things. Indeed, you need not come, for Mr Gardiner is dining here and will escort us."

"Did I tell you that I abominate balls?" Luke said, smiling. "That was a great exaggeration."

"But you do not care to dance, I know. You do not think that I will stand up with Lord Aintree, or Sir Hubert? I promise I shall not, since you dislike it."

"I begin to think you do not want me to go!"

Lady Cecilia intervened. "She means no such thing, Luke! We are both happy to have your escort. It is entirely your own fault if your offer takes us by surprise, for the only ball you have attended this season was our own."

"And a frightful crush it was, ma'am!"

"Yes indeed! Excessively gratifying when your father and I have rusticated for so long and you do not lift a finger to maintain your position in society," she said with acerbity.

To Dorothea's relief, Mr Gardiner was announced. Luke

observed him closely, decided that he was a milksop who was as little likely to attract his sister as to frighten her, and resigned himself to a tedious evening.

Half an hour at the ball did nothing to revise his expectations. Dorothea had correctly diagnosed his dislike for dancing; since discovering, seven years ago, the extent of his father's gambling debts he had taken no pleasure in play; and none of the cronies with whom he enjoyed political discussion had graced the event with their presence. As he dodged, for the third or fourth time, a matchmaking mama with eligible daughter in tow, he wondered if it had been wise to conceal from the world the depth of the family's financial misfortunes. Apparently he was generally regarded as a good catch.

His evasive manoeuvring had brought him close to the entrance, and he considered abandoning Lady Cecilia and Dorothea to Mr Gardiner's care. However, his host and hostess were still standing there, greeting a few late arrivals. There was no way to sneak past without being seen, and it was by far too early to make his departure with propriety.

Frustrated, he watched a group of two ladies and two gentlemen approach the doors from the hall beyond, wishing they were going the other way and he with them. He was turning away when he stopped suddenly with an arrested look and glanced back.

With a shock of recognition, his eyes met Gabrielle's.

=7=

GABRIELLE WENT THROUGH the introductions in a heedless daze. She curtseyed prettily, thanked her hostess for including her in Lady Harrison's invitation, and moved on on Alain de Vignard's arm without the least idea of what she was doing. The brilliance of the scene was lost on her—the gay music, twirling dancers, gems flashing in the light of a dozen chandeliers.

Mr Everett here! And looking as elegant as any gentleman in the room. But had he really, as their eyes met, given the tiniest possible shake of his head, and if so, what did it mean?

Was it possible that he did not recognise her in her finery? The apricot ballgown was certainly a far cry from the men's clothes he had first seen her in, and her hair had been dressed by a fashionable coiffeur who had done wonders with the wreck she had made of it. Yet she was sure he knew her.

She could only suppose he wanted her to pretend she did not know him. That was fair enough: it would be difficult to explain their prior acquaintance without referring to circumstances best left unmentioned. But how she wished she had met him under other circumstances!

She pulled Gerard's sleeve and drew him aside.

"Mr Everett is here," she whispered, "but I beg you will not approach him unless he should indicate a desire to recognise us. We cannot wish to appear encroaching, and it might be best that no one should know of our adventures."

"You are afraid it will get about that you arrived in England in breeches!" said Gerard with a grin. "Mum's the word."

"It would ruin my reputation before I have time to establish one!" she said, laughing.

She wished he knew about the message she had carried to the Man in the Green Coat. Once she had met Mr Everett, she had been sure that she was right not to tell that the fewer people who knew his alias the better. She had always been close to her brother, though, and it was hard to keep a secret from him.

As they made their way through the crowd, Gabrielle spotted Mr Everett talking to a tall, blond lady in a ravishing but matronly gown of lilac silk. They looked towards her, but made no sign of recognition. His wife? she wondered. With a sigh, she followed Lady Harrison to a row of crimson velvet-covered gilt chairs, and the ladies were seated.

"Are you sure you will not dance, Miss Darcy?" enquired Alain de Vignard, bending solicitously over her. His English was accentless, only an occasional turn of phrase betraying his origin.

"What, and betray myself for a country bumpkin, *monsieur?* I do not know any of the dances and should undoubtedly tie myself in knots, along with my partner and all those about me!"

"We must engage a *maître de danse*," declared Lady Harrison.

"Not for me," shuddered Gerard. "Gaby, you don't mind if I walk about, do you? There is so much to see."

"If you will stop calling me Gaby, you may walk about as much as you please for all I care, but it is Madame's leave you must ask."

He looked abashed. "I beg your pardon, Madame Aurore."

"Silly boy! Of course you are accustomed to attending to

66

your sister. Me, I do not take offense. Run along and enjoy yourself."

"Monsieur de Vignard, you must not think yourself tied to my apronstrings. Pray go with my brother. I expect you have a great many acquaintances present."

"A few," he admitted, "and I shall make Gerard known to some of them later on. But first let me procure you a glass of lemonade. It is deuced hot in here."

"Thank you, I should like that." Gabrielle smiled up at him. It was a relief, in a ballroom full of strangers, to have a handsome young man considering her comfort.

In the three days she had been in London she had seen little of Alain, but that little had favourably impressed her. He was kind and charming, properly grateful to Madame Aurore, and Gerard liked him. He seemed thoroughly gentlemanly, and she could only deplore the ill luck that had forced him to make his way in the world without family or fortune to help him. At that, she gathered from Madame Aurore that he was in better case than many of his countrymen, some of whom had been driven to such menial occupations as cobbling shoes for a living.

Pondering his fate, she listened with half an ear to Lady Harrison, who was issuing, in an undertone, condensed biographies of the people around them. She had a certain gift for capturing the essential points of character or career in a few phrases, and Gabrielle was soon absorbed in her words. Some of the names she recognised from the reams of gossip Madame Aurore had penned to them over the years. It was fascinating to see in the flesh the fops and exquisites, Corinthians and court-cards whose exploits she had exclaimed over and giggled about with Gerard.

The dress of the ladies was equally interesting. Lady Harrison had an unerring eye for fashion and could point out exactly how a particular gown enhanced or detracted from the appearance of the wearer. She was commenting on a particularly unfortunate combination of palest pink and green, worn by a high-complexioned girl who should, she said severely, have known better, when their *tête-à-tête* was interrupted.

Alain, returning with lemonade for Gabrielle and champagne for her ladyship, brought with him a sprightly matron and her two daughters.

"Lady Harrison!" exclaimed the older lady. "Monsieur de Vignard tells us that you have a new charge." She stared with frank curiosity at Gabrielle, who rose and curtseyed as she was introduced.

The younger of the two girls was gazing at Alain with besotted eyes, and he soon took her off to dance. The others stayed in conversation, and gradually a group gathered about them. Several young men asked Gabrielle to dance, but she remained firm in her refusal, finding more and more outrageous reasons which set everyone laughing.

"Miss Darcy is a wit," explained one of the gentlemen to a newcomer attracted by the merriment.

"A dashed pretty one," he responded.

A new dance started up, and several young couples departed to take their places, but others arrived and Gabrielle soon had more new acquaintances than she could count. Lady Harrison had not been boasting when she claimed a large circle of friends.

Gabrielle was enjoying herself enormously. She waved gaily to Alain as he delivered his lovestruck partner to her mother and departed with another young lady. There was no sign of Gerard, and she hoped he was having as good a time as she was. She also hoped that Mr Everett saw how little need she had of his acknowledgment. Let him ignore her in favour of his tall blonde! She did not care.

"I see Monsieur de Vignard is popular with the ladies," she whispered to Lady Harrison, as once again he came to assure himself that they were comfortable before he went back to the dancing.

"*Oui*, he has excellent manners, besides being so very 'andsome, and the mamas like him because he makes no secret of his position and does not try to ingratiate himself, and dances with *les jeunes filles* who are ugly as well as with *les belles.*"

"He is truly good-natured!"

At that moment, a new voice addressed Lady Harrison.

"Madame, I think you know my daughter? Allow me to present my son to you."

Gabrielle looked up and gasped. The tall blond lady stood before them, a delicately beautiful young girl beside her, and next to them, Mr Everett. He bowed over Lady Harrison's hand, murmuring a polite "*Enchanté,* my lady."

" 'Ow do you do, *monsieur,*" said Lady Harrison cordially. "Lady Cecilia, *permettez* that I make known to you my young friend, Miss Darcy."

Bewildered, Gabrielle made her best curtsey. Lady Cecilia looked older close to than in the distance, but nowhere near old enough to be Mr Everett's mother. She wondered momentarily if they were for some obscure reason playing a trick on her. A single glance at the gentleman's sober face laid that notion to rest. He was regarding her with an intensity she found decidedly disturbing.

"It is hot in here, Miss Darcy," he said. "Perhaps you have not yet discovered the terrace? May I be allowed to escort you thither?"

Gabrielle cast a glance of wild appeal at her chaperone, and noticed that Lady Cecilia was looking at her with a slightly cynical smile, though not unkindly.

"Perfectly unexceptionable," she assured Lady Harrison, "It is well lit and there are a number of people outside. It *is* a warm night for the time of year, is it not?"

At that moment Alain de Vignard came up and Lady Harrison introduced him.

"I have met Monsieur de Vignard, I believe," said Mr Everett. "Are you not an associate of General Pichegru, monsieur?"

"You flatter me, sir! I am the general's secretary, no more."

Lady Cecilia looked her approval of such frankness, and made no demur when Alain asked permission to dance with Miss Everett. Dorothea smiled up at him enchantingly and they went off to join the set for the next country dance. Gabrielle watched them go and thought they must be quite the handsomest couple present.

She found herself crossing the crowded room on Mr Everett's arm. They passed through open French windows onto a wide, stone-flagged terrace colourfully decorated with Chinese paper lanterns. The cool air had enticed out a score of guests, who sat on wooden benches or strolled up and down, but there were several unoccupied corners and to one of these he led her.

"Won't you be seated, Miss Darcy?" he asked as she stood uncertainly by the bench. "You must not overtax your strength. I am surprised that your premature departure from Dover did not do you some harm."

"None at all, sir. I know my own health, I think!" She sat down and he joined her. In the faint blue light of the nearest lanterns, his face was livid. Pretty the lights might be, but not flattering. She wondered what ghastly effect they had on her own complexion. "I do not dance tonight however," she added.

"I am glad of it. I should certainly have strongly discouraged your even attending a ball so soon after your injury."

"Mr Everett, do you make a practice of issuing orders to all the females of your acquaintance?" She looked at him indignantly.

"Of course not!" He was silent for a moment, thoughtful. "I suppose I feel a sense of responsibility for you, perhaps foolishly, because of the circumstances of our meeting. I beg your pardon. I shall endeavour to avoid the appearance of commanding you."

"It would be as well. I believe I have told you before that I am unaccustomed to blind obedience."

"Gabrielle—Miss Darcy, let us not quarrel!"

70

"No. I am sorry. That was ungracious when you have already apologised. I have been hoping to see you again, for I have a thousand questions to ask you. Is it safe to talk here?"

"Little Miss Discretion! If we lower our voices and change the subject when anyone comes near, it should be safe enough. I cannot promise to answer all your questions, however. What do you wish to know?"

Gabrielle considered. "Well first of all, though it is quite irrelevant to the rest, is Lady Cecilia really your mother?"

He laughed, and she was relieved that he sounded genuinely amused and not at all offended.

"My stepmother. Did you think she had discovered the Fountain of Youth?"

"Not at all. I thought *you* prematurely aged! If she is *Lady* Cecilia, should I not call you 'my lord'?"

"No. At least, not yet. My stepmother is the daughter of an earl, I merely the son of a baron, and therefore 'the Honourable' until I succeed to the title."

"You are? You see I am woefully ignorant. I expect your sister is an Honourable too, then. She is excessively pretty."

"She is, is she not? And a most obedient child, you will be happy to hear."

Gabrielle snorted. "Crushed, I imagine. Mr Everett, who is Le Hibou, and who is de la Touche?"

"To business, then. Le Hibou is a British agent who has been passing excellent information to us for ten or fifteen years. I say British, but in fact no one knows whether he is an Englishman or a French royalist, let alone what his real name is. It is possible that my predecessor at the Foreign Office knew, but he died of apoplexy without revealing that, or a great many other facts which would have helped me immeasurably!"

"Then you *are* at the Foreign Office?"

"I am. You may consult Lord Hawkesbury if you still doubt my credentials."

"The Foreign Secretary? I should not dare! Do you still suspect me of being a French spy?"

"I cannot dismiss all my doubts," he said with devastating honesty. "If you are, you already know all that I am telling you, so I am giving nothing away. The company you keep is just such as I might expect of a French spy. Lady Harrison's house is known to be filled to the rafters with *émigrés* of all persuasions."

"Madame Aurore has an exceptionally kind heart!" retorted Gabrielle angrily.

"Lady Harrison *is* your Madame Aurore then. I have beaten Baxter to the draw."

Gabrielle forgot her anger in curiosity. "Baxter? Your servant? What has he to do with it?"

"I set him to ferret out an unknown French widow by the name of Madame Aurore. It was the only way I could think of to find you."

"You were looking for me? Because you think I am a spy?"

He did not answer at once. Then he said, "In part. For other reasons too. And Madame Aurore will be looking for you if we stay out here any longer. Come, Miss Darcy, let me return you to her." He stood up.

"As if I were a lost parcel! You have not told me yet about de la Touche."

"Tomorrow. I shall call at noon to take you driving in the park."

"Thank you, kind sir." Rising to her feet, Gabrielle was suddenly dizzy. She swayed.

His arm was instantly about her waist. He lowered her to the seat, growling, "So you know your own strength! Where the devil is that brother of yours?"

She leaned her head on her hand. "I shall be perfectly all right in a minute. Gerard is inside somewhere, but there is no need to trouble him."

"You are going home immediately. Our acquaintance is

not sufficient to allow me to take you, so you will not attempt to stir from this spot until I bring your brother to you. Understand?"

She nodded weakly. There were times, she thought, when it was much easier to obey.

— 8 —

"Davis, did you ever hear Lady Harrison referred to as 'Madame Aurore'?" Mr Everett lounged with his feet on his paper-strewn desk. It seemed to be impossible to concentrate on paperwork this morning.

"Lady Harrison, sir?" asked his lanky secretary. His spectacles caught the light from the window and gleamed blankly. "You mean Sir Cosmo's widow?"

"Yes. Did he ever call her Madame Aurore?"

"Oh no, sir! He was a very proper gentleman. But the name does sound familiar. Where did you hear it, if I might ask?"

"The person who brought Le Hibou's latest message from France is a friend of her ladyship and knows her by that name."

"Then the message is genuine. There are some documents for your signature, sir, if you wouldn't mind. Here's the order for a pension for Mrs Betsy Waterbury, for instance."

Mr Everett lowered his feet to the floor with a sigh, and took up his pen.

"I have a feeling that you know more about Madame Aurore than you are telling me," he said as he signed the first paper.

"In our business, it's best if no one knows everything, sir."

"No one but you, you mean."

"Well I've got into the habit over the years of keeping it all in my head. It's safer not to put it on paper."

"So if you die unexpectedly, I shall be left in the lurch!"

"Let's hope it won't happen, sir, least till Boney's been beat. But you could run things without me. You know the beginnings of the threads, how to get hold of the right people. I don't know much more myself. For instance, when you told me to send a message to Le Hibou asking for more information about de la Touche's connection with Fouché, I just told a certain person what you want, and it goes right down the line till the Owl gets it. We don't need to know every link in the chain, not by a long chalk. We have our people here and he has his over there, and one way or another they get together."

"Do you know who Le Hibou is?"

"Sir Cosmo never saw fit to tell me. I won't say I don't have an idea, but I've got no proof, and I'd rather not say, sir, if you don't mind."

"I sometimes think I'm nothing but a figurehead in this office," complained Mr Everett.

"Oh, no, sir, not at all!" The secretary was shocked. "It's true I know a bit more about *how* things get done, but you're the one that says *what* gets done. It's you as sets policy, decides what information we need and what to do with it when we get it. Like asking Le Hibou for that Russian stuff. We're not at war with Russia. I'd never of thought we might need that stuff. It's you that gives the orders, sir, and without that the whole network would be useless. So if you was to order me to say who I think Le Hibou is, or where I've heard of madame Aurore—well, I ask you, sir, have I ever disobeyed an order?"

"Not to my knowledge," Mr Everett admitted. "Since you have implied that Lady Harrison is above suspicion, I will leave you your secrets. I only hope that you are right."

The secretary nodded his head indulgently and presented the next document.

Mr Everett left the office shortly before noon. As he drove his tilbury towards Russell Square, a swirl of wind enveloped him in a flurry of raindrops. He looked up at the sky and frowned.

"Damn!" he said aloud. A threatening pall of grey hung overhead. If it was going to rain, that was the end of his drive with Miss Darcy.

In spite of the unfashionable address, a number of fashionable visitors had found their way to Lady Harrison's house that morning. Her ladyship's young friends had aroused the curiosity of the ton, particularly in view of Miss Darcy's Cinderella-like disappearance from the ball.

Miss Darcy was blooming, in sharp contrast to her brother's pallid, hangdog air. Mr Everett was happy to see her looking well, but a closer look at the admirers clustered about her brought a frown to his face. Among the sprigs of fashion and the dashing blades, Sir Hubert Rathwycke lounged at his ease. Devil take the man! Dorrie had followed his advice to discourage the man's rakish attentions, but he had no illusions that a word in Gabrielle's ear would have anything like the same effect!

Another dismaying fact was that, though several matrons of unquestionable gentility were conversing with Lady Harrison, no young ladies formed part of Miss Darcy's group. Her ladyship, it seemed, was an adequate chaperone but not a sufficiently elevated sponsor for a girl of unknown origins. Careful mothers would not care to risk their daughters' reputations by calling on Miss Darcy before her respectability was thoroughly established.

Cecilia, thought Mr Everett, was the one to deal with that.

Gerard noticed his presence and came to greet him. With his bloodshot eyes half closed against the light of day, he reminded Mr Everett of his condition at their first meeting.

"How do you do, sir." he mumbled. "You are come to take Gabrielle driving?"

"I had hoped to, but it is raining. If I might make so bold, did you by any chance shoot the cat last night?"

Gerard flushed. "I went out again after I brought Gaby home. Alain introduced me to a bunch of good fellows last night and we played cards until rather late. You won't tell Gaby?"

"It is none of my business. But you are young and your father is not here to guide you. Be careful what you are about until you have gathered a little town bronze! It is easy to find oneself over one's head when suddenly plunged into the amusements of London."

"I'll be careful, sir. To tell the truth, I feel devilish just now, and I didn't even enjoy the drinking above half. I shan't do it again."

Without voicing his disbelief, Mr Everett passed on to make his bow to Lady Harrison and Miss Darcy.

Gabrielle smiled at him.

"Is it noon already?" she asked. "Gentlemen, you must excuse me. I am promised to drive out with Mr Everett."

Amid laughing protests, the others took their leave. Mr Everett let them go before he pointed out that the outing would have to be postponed because of the rain.

Gabrielle looked out of the window. "It is scarcely raining at all," she said scornfully. "I walked across France in worse weather. I am not made of marchpane, you know!"

"But you are not yet fully recovered . . ."

"A little faintness now and then! That has nothing whatever to do with rain! Besides, I suppose your carriage has a hood? I have been looking forward all morning to going to the park with you, and I vow I shall be ill if I do not have a little fresh air!"

"You have been looking forward to it?" Mr Everett's face was slightly flushed. "With your admirers flocking about you, you must have been too busy to spare a thought for me."

"Those popinjays! They are amusing, I grant you, but

uninteresting. I do not suppose one of them has ever had a serious thought, far less done anything worthy of note."

"You find none of them attractive? I am glad of it, for one of them at least is a notable libertine."

"Which? Do tell me! He sounds more interesting than the rest."

"I should not dream of telling you. Indeed I have already said more than I ought."

"Next you will forbid me to speak to him."

"Which would doubtless be enough to make you seek out his company!"

Gabrielle looked at him questioningly, a little hurt. "Is that what you think?" she asked. "You misunderstand me. I have no more intention of deliberately flouting your . . . suggestions than of following them simply because you make them. I will go and fetch my cloak."

Mr Everett could only be grateful that she had not refused to go with him. He wandered over to the window and was glad to see that the rain had stopped, though clouds still obscured the sky. He was standing there, pondering Gabrielle's words, when a voice offered, "A penny for your thoughts, sir."

It was Alain de Vignard. "Pardon my intrusion," he continued. "I wish merely to ascertain whether you have any objection to my calling on your sister? And Lady Cecilia, of course! They were kind enough to invite me, but I do not wish to encroach."

"I've no objection," said Mr Everett, "if you can squeeze into their drawing room. It seems to be full whenever they are at home. Oh, de Vignard, be so good as to tell me to whom you introduced young Gerard last night."

Alain looked at him strangely, but mentioned several names. All belonged to unexceptionable scions of the nobility. Mr Everett ceased to worry about the company Gerard had fallen into. He was taken aback when Alain asked tentatively,

"You have known Gerard for some time, sir?"

"What? Oh, no. I met him last night for the first time. But you may have noticed that he looked to be in queer stirrups this morning. His sister is concerned about him, and I hoped to reassure her."

Alain seemed unconvinced, but let the matter drop. Gabrielle came back, cloaked and booted, and they set off for Hyde Park.

A light rain was falling again, but the wind had dropped and the tilbury's hood and apron kept them dry. The streets were as busy as ever, and Gabrielle looked about with interest at the carriages of the rich; hawkers selling everything from "sweet water, penny a bucket," to "fine, strong bootlaces"; liveried footmen running errands; and apprentices in leather jerkins striding jauntily along with their arms full of packages.

"How lively it is!" she exclaimed. "I quite understand why Madame Aurore did not want to live in Neuchâtel."

Mr Everett, concentrating on passing a slow-moving stage coach with twelve passengers on its roof, did not answer. Gabrielle held her breath as a high-perch phaeton drawn by four lively horses dashed towards them. The tilbury swung aside just in time.

"Neatly done! I was sure we should be overset. You handle the ribbons in prime form, Mr Everett."

"I do not claim to be a top sawyer," he said modestly, "but I think I am not a mere whipster. There was little danger, however. It generally looks worse than it is."

"I should like to learn to drive."

"I shall be happy to teach you, Miss Darcy, when you are perfectly recovered."

"If you refer once more to that . . . that *dratted* bullet hole," cried Gabrielle, "I shall never speak to you again. I daresay I should be already perfectly recovered if I were not reminded of it every time we meet!"

Mr Everett did not respond, but drove on in silence, his face forbidding.

As they turned in through the park gates, Gabrielle

asked him, "Are you angry? I am sorry if I have offended you. It is very kind of you to take such an interest in my welfare. I have not been used to such solicitude since dear Miss Wilford left us, and to tell the truth I am uncertain how to accept it."

"My poor child!" He gathered the reins in one hand and laid the other on hers. "It is for me to beg your pardon. I seem unable to speak without ruffling your feathers."

She smiled at him tremulously. "Let us talk of other things before I burst into tears and disgrace myself utterly. You were going to tell me about de la Touche."

"Ah yes, de la Touche. He came from France in February and contacted the French royalist leaders here. He claims to represent a group of republicans, led by General Moreau, who are willing to make common cause with them to overthrow Bonaparte. There are plans afoot for uprisings in various parts of the country, and the British government is being asked to subsidise them."

"And if de la Touche is Fouché's man?"

"Citizen Fouché is a sly and subtle man. Although he is no longer Minister of Police, he keeps a network of agents at his beck and call. It is possible that he might be behind a plot to overthrow his master, but it is more likely that he is attempting to lure Pichegru and Cadoudal to their doom while at the same time unmasking any hidden opposition in France. You see, the situation is complicated. It is little wonder that they do not heed my warnings."

"It is very foolish of them," said Gabrielle indignantly. "Surely they realise that you would not alarm them unnecessarily. Do they not know that you are the Man in the Green Coat?"

Well, not precisely." Mr Everett paused to exchange bows with a lady and gentleman in a smart barouche. "They think that I am in charge of British intelligence."

"You are? I had not realised your position was so exalted! I thought you a courier."

He looked a little embarrassed. "Of course it is not

necessary for me to run errands in person. To tell the truth, I do it for my own pleasure, for a change of scene. The business is fascinating, but I do not care to spend my entire life in an office."

"Naturally. It is most commendable that you choose to do useful work at all. It is not common in gentlemen of your rank."

Mr Everett accepted her praise with a feeling of guilt but without demur. It would be most improper to reveal that his father's gambling had driven him to seek gainful employment.

"By the bye," he said as they turned onto a drive beside the Serpentine, "How much have you told Gerard about my activities?"

Gabrielle was gazing out over the grey, wind-ruffled water, remembering the Lac de Neuchâtel sparkling in the sun. A proud mother mallard bobbed by, followed by six fluffy ducklings.

"Look!" cried Gabrielle. "Are they not adorable?"

"You are not listening," said her companion severely.

"Yes I am, indeed I am. You asked how much I have told Gerard. The answer is nothing. It has been difficult, but it seemed to me better that he should not know. And Madame Aurore does not even know about me being shot."

"You are quite discreet enough to be a spy yourself, Miss Darcy. Thank you. I should not like to think that the story had reached Sir Oswald Harrison."

"Madame never speaks to Sir Oswald if she can help it, so you are quite safe there. Why is it important that he, in particular, should be kept in ignorance?"

"No real reason. Only that he is constantly snooping around my office. He seems to believe that because his father worked there, he is entitled to know exactly what we are doing. As a matter of both policy and pride, the less he finds out the better."

"He will learn nothing from me, I promise."

"Have you met him?"

"No, and after hearing what you and Madame have said of him, I have no desire to do so. She dislikes him amazingly."

"His is not a prepossessing character."

They turned away from the Serpentine, heading back towards the park gates. There was quite a crush of carriages and riders now. They stopped several times to exchange greetings with acquaintances, mostly Mr Everett's, but a few whom Gabrielle had met the night before. She was beginning to feel more at home in London.

"On the whole," she said consideringly, "I am glad to discover that you are in charge of your office and not merely a courier. I daresay I should not say so, for you are sufficiently set up in your own conceit, and always ready enough to issue orders to all and sundry. But even though no one else suspected it, it was sadly lowering to my dignity to drive out with an errand boy!"

"Wretch!" said Mr Everett, grinning.

The next two weeks passed in a whirl. There were balls and routs, masquerades and musicales, riding and driving in Hyde Park, a picnic in Richmond Park, morning calls and shopping expeditions. Gabrielle and Madame Aurore were seldom home; nor was Gerard, who had found his own friends and gone his own way.

In fact, Gabrielle saw more of Alain de Vignard, who frequently escorted them, than of her brother. Among her other new friends and acquaintances, Lady Cecilia and the Honourable Dorothea Everett often attended the same parties, and they had even paid a morning visit to Russell Square. With Lady Cecilia approving her, the starchiest of matrons ceased to question her gentility, and soon there were as many young ladies calling as admiring gentlemen.

Though Gabrielle had more in common with livelier damsels, she made a special effort to get to know Dorothea. The girl was not at all shy in female company, but when addressed by a gentleman she was reduced to monosyllabic acquiescence. She was given to quoting her half brother as an authority on propriety and correct behaviour, which so annoyed Gabrielle that she tackled Mr Everett.

"Your sister takes your slightest suggestion as the word of God," she said. "I am sure such submissiveness cannot be healthy."

Eyes icy, lips thinned, he said curtly, "Thank you for your solicitude, Miss Darcy, but my relationship with Dorothea is none of your business."

After such a set-down, she was out of charity with him for several days.

It was during this period that Alain invited her to walk with him in Kensington Gardens one sunny morning. Lady Harrison sent her abigail, Marie, to act as unwilling chaperone. Muttering complaints, she followed them down paths between flowerbeds bright with purple stock and orange pot-marigolds. Early roses scented the air.

As they entered a shrubbery, they came face to face with Dorothea Everett, accompanied only by her maid. She blushed scarlet, and Alain started back with an air of surprise so patently false that Gabrielle wanted to laugh. She contented herself with saying,

"How do you do, Miss Everett. Is it not a beautiful day? Do you care to join us for a turn about the gardens?"

"Oh, yes!" exclaimed Dorothea. "I mean, thank you, that would be delightful, Miss Darcy."

In no time she was clinging to Alain's arm and the two of them were deep in conversation, quite forgetting Gabrielle's presence as they wandered on. She strolled behind them, irritated to find herself without an escort other than the two maids, but pleased to see Dorothea getting on so famously with a gentleman, any gentleman. The fact that she was fairly certain that Mr Everett would disapprove only added spice to the situation.

She was still annoyed with him, but however many elegant and witty gentlemen she met, she still liked him better than the rest. She forgave him his snub; he, it seemed, forgave her impertinence. He persuaded Lady Cecilia to invite Lady Harrison and her young guests to join them in their box at the theatre.

On this occasion, Gabrielle made the acquaintance of Lord Everett. The baron, a hearty, good-natured man, was up from Kent to transact some business in town. He was a good deal older than his wife, but she was delighted by his arrival and he obviously adored her.

Gabrielle liked him immediately, though she was somewhat disconcerted to find him, more than once, staring at her and Gerard with a puzzled look on his face. Gerard, to be sure, was not looking his best. His face was pasty and there were dark rings about his eyes she had not noticed before. She herself was dressed in a new gown of lilac *barège*, vastly becoming, and her hair had at last grown to a respectable length. Mr Everett had complimented her on her charming appearance, and she did not see why his father should stare so.

There were several empty boxes in the theatre. London was beginning to grow thin of company as the season drew to an end and the *Haut Ton* headed for the country. Lady Cecilia enquired after her children, and remarked with great satisfaction that it would be delightful to see them all again in a few weeks.

"Will it not be pleasant to be back at Wrotham, Dorrie?" she asked.

"I hope Dorrie will not find it dull after the gaiety of London," said her father fondly.

"Oh, no, Papa!" cried Dorothea, but Gabrielle thought she did not seem happy at the prospect.

Gabrielle herself was not looking forward to spending the summer in London. Already the streets were dusty, the heat oppressive at noon on a fine day. She remembered with regret the clean neatness of Neuchâtel, the cool breeze blowing off the sparkling lake, the green meadows and the chime of bells every evening as the patient cows came slowly home for milking.

"You look as if you were a thousand miles away," Gerard whispered in her ear. "What is the matter?"

"Nothing. Nothing important. Only I wish Papa would come!"

"So do I!" he agreed feelingly.

—9—

THE NEXT DAY, after breakfast, Gabrielle went to Madame Aurore's chamber to bid her good morning and discuss their plans for the day. Marie opened the door to her knock.

"*Entrez, mademoiselle*," she said, her face if possible sourer than usual. "One must hope that you can do something to aid milady."

Dismayed, Gabrielle saw that Madame Aurore was weeping, her plump face crinkled and pink as the bed hangings. She ran to the bed and hugged her, heedless of the scattered papers she brushed onto the floor.

"Dear Madame, what is it?" she demanded. "Have you had bad news? Tell me, pray tell me at once."

Lady Harrison sniffed and wiped her eyes with the dainty lace handkerchief she was clutching.

"It is these bills, *chérie*. There are so very many, and I hoped they would wait until the end of the quarter, but today comes a dun from the coal-seller, of all people, and you know the chandler was threatening me until Gerard paid him, and the bailiffs will be here by the end of the week and I shall be lucky if I am not clapped up in the Marshalsea!"

"Surely not! It is scarce two weeks until quarter day. They must be persuaded to wait. Has Gerard been over your figures, as he promised?

"I gave him all my bills, and the key to the desk in the library where Sir Cosmo kept his important papers. But he has been excessively busy, *chérie*. I daresay he has not had time to look at them."

"If he has not, he will have me to answer to," said Gabrielle grimly. "I shall go and ask him at once."

There was no answer when she knocked on the door of the chamber Gerard still shared with Alain. She peeped in. One bed was empty, rumpled. In the other her brother sprawled on his stomach, a pillow hiding his head, clasped to him by one arm.

She went to the window and flung open the curtains. Then she seized the pillow and pulled it away from him.

"Wake up, lazybones," she cried.

He groaned and tried to burrow under the blankets.

"Come on, Gerard," she said, exasperated. "Madame Aurore needs you. Wake up."

"Go 'way. My head hurts. I can't think at this hour of the morning."

"Your head hurts? You are not ill, are you?"

"No. Be a good girl, Gab, and go away."

"I believe you have been drinking! Is that it?"

"What if it is?" he said sulkily, sitting up at last with another groan. "Draw the curtains, the light is too bright. Everyone drinks. I was only a little disguised, not completely foxed. What do you want? Can't it wait?"

"No. Madame Aurore thinks she is about to be dragged off to prison. Have you been over her accounts yet?"

"Yes, and they're damned fishy. I'm not saying she doesn't spend a pretty penny, because she does. But I found a copy of Sir Cosmo's will in the desk, and her jointure should cover her expenses easily. It's my belief that what's-his-name, her stepson, is chousing her out of what's due to her."

"Oh Gerard, how dreadful! Are you sure? Whatever can we do about it?"

"Don't ask me. Now go away and let me sleep."

"But we must do something! At least let us give her enough to pay the bills until the end of the month. We are hanging on her sleeve just like all the others. How much can we spare?"

"I don't know. You can't expect me to keep a track of what you are spending as well as checking Madame's figures. I'm not a clerk."

"You must have some idea, though. We must help her even if it means you cannot join the army until Papa comes."

"I'm not going to join the army. If you want to know the truth, that money is spent already." He flopped down on the bed again with his back to her.

"Spent! We cannot have spent so much! I have made all my own dresses and I have bought very little otherwise. Where has it all gone?"

"I've lost it." Gerard's voice was muffled in the pillow. "I've lost close to a thousand pounds. On wagers. All the fellows squander the blunt as if there were no tomorrow, betting on raindrops running down the window pane, and how many minutes late the Bristol Mail will be, and stuff like that. When I'm with them, I just don't notice it going. I'm sorry, Gabrielle. I'm truly sorry. I went to see Mr Dickens at Hoare's Bank yesterday, and he says we have forty pounds left."

Her legs weak with shock, Gabrielle sat down on the edge of the bed. She laid her hand on his shoulder and felt it trembling.

"It's all right, little brother," she said, trying not to let her voice shake. "It's all right. Just give me time to think! Forty pounds, and Madame will get her allowance at the beginning of next month. Gerard, you must help me. What are Madame's biggest expenses?"

"Running the house. Coal and candles, of course, and servants' wages and such. And you wouldn't believe how much the spongers who live here eat! Alain is the only one who pays any of his own expenses. Madame hardly spends a thing on herself. You know she doesn't even keep a carriage, but takes a hackney or a chair when she goes out."

"How selfish we have been!" said Gabrielle wretchedly. "I have been so taken up with enjoying myself, I never once thought that she might really be short of money. When Marie groused, I thought she was just being bad-tempered as usual."

"What shall we do?" Gerard sat up again. "I wish Papa were here!"

"But he is not, so we must think for ourselves." Gabrielle hugged him.

He put his arms around her and held her tight, whispering into her hair, "I'm so sorry, Gab. It's all my fault."

"Well, I will let you take most of the blame for *our* problem, but not for Madame's. If Sir Oswald is really cheating her, you may be instrumental in saving her. So go back to sleep now, and by the time you awake, maybe I shall have found a solution."

"You're the best sister in the world! I'll do anything you say, I promise."

Gabrielle slowly made her way back to Lady Harrison's chamber, thinking hard. There were three important points: to persuade the most pressing creditors to wait just two more weeks; to cut expenses immediately; and to start an investigation of Sir Oswald's financial finagling.

The first could probably be dealt with by offering a few pounds on account, though it would sadly deplete their small reserve.

As far as Sir Oswald was concerned, she would consult Mr Everett, who already disliked the baronet and would know how to go about instigating an enquiry.

And to save money, they must close up the town house and find a cottage in the country that could be rented cheaply for the summer! Gabrielle smiled as the idea came to her. At one stroke that would dispose of the unwanted guests, remove Gerard from the temptations of London, and provide a pleasant retreat for the long, hot summer months.

"Madame!" she cried, bursting into the room, "How should you like to remove to the country?"

Madame thought it a delightful notion. In no time her face was wreathed in smiles. Marie was equally approving, though no hint of a smile touched her mouth. She, however, was the one to put her finger on the weak spot in the plan.

"*Comment*," she asked, "*est-ce que vous allez trouver cette chaumière, mademoiselle?*"

"How am I going to find a cottage? Oh dear, I hadn't thought of that. But never mind. I have to consult Mr Everett about Sir Oswald and I expect he will be able to advise me on that, too. There may be something suitable near his family's place," said Gabrielle hopefully. "In the meantime, Marie, I think you should be the one to tell people that they will have to move out in two weeks because the house will be shut up."

A slow smile distorted the maid's gloomy features. "*Avec plaisir, mademoiselle!*" she said. "I go at once."

"How shall I dismiss the servants?" wailed Lady Harrison. "I am sure they will have every right to be upset."

"I shall do it," Gabrielle proposed. "Marie must come with us, of course. Mrs Hodge, and any others who have been with you a long time, should be paid their wages and told that they are to take an extended holiday. It will still cost less than trying to keep the house running. So that just leaves the footman and a few maids, does it not? I expect they will soon find new positions. So do not worry about anything, Madame. Leave everything to me!"

Gabrielle found it more difficult than she had expected to compose a note summoning Mr Everett to her side. She had nearly decided to wait until she saw him in the normal course of things, but then Gerard came downstairs, bleary-eyed, and asked if she had settled on a course of action. He was enthusiastic about her ideas until it came to asking Mr Everett's assistance.

"But Gaby!" he said, shocked, "what can you be thinking of? It is not at all the thing to beg aid of a stranger in such a personal matter!"

"Mr Everett is not a stranger—and *don't* call me Gaby! The help he gave us in Dover was much more personal, and he has been most amiable ever since."

"It was a deal *too* personal. I should never have allowed him to interfere."

"You were in no shape to stop him, nor to help me yourself! Don't be a nodcock, Gerard. It is perfectly unexceptionable to approach him in this."

He shrugged sulkily. "Do as you will, then. You always do anyway. There's no need to insult me. I'm going for a walk to clear my head."

Trying to stifle her own doubts, Gabrielle dashed off a note and sent the footman to deliver it. Then she set about the unpleasant task of giving notice to the rest of the servants.

To her relief, thay all took it philosophically—except Mrs Hodge, who wept into her apron even though she was not actually being dismissed. Gabrielle had to promise that if the cottage they found was big enough, the cook should be allowed to join them in their rural exile. It would be one more mouth to feed, but at least they would not have to find someone locally to come in and cook for them.

By the time Mr Everett arrived, she was feeling hot and harassed, and very uncertain whether she was doing the right thing.

"You sent for me, Miss Darcy?" he asked in a cool voice, as Roger ushered him into the drawing room.

She looked up at him appealingly. "Was my letter so abrupt? I did not mean to presume. I wrote in a hurry, but my intention was to request a visit at your earliest convenience."

"Which is precisely what you said." The quirk of his lips reassured her. "I gather I misinterpreted haste as effrontery. You see me here, anyway. What can I do for you?"

"Thank you for coming. However, if you jumped so easily to the conclusion that I was being discourteous, perhaps Gerard was right and I should not consult you. I am sorry to have troubled you for nothing, sir."

"Oh no, you shall not get off so easily!" He sat down on a chair near her. "Gerard was certainly wrong, and it is essential that you consult me. About what?"

"I own I cannot think where else to turn."

"You are unflattering! Am I a last resort, then?"

"Not at all. An *only* resort, for I do not yet know anyone else in London so well—except Madame Aurore, of course, and it is her problem as much as ours."

"I am intrigued. Pray continue, Miss Darcy. I shall endeavour to give you good advice."

"I don't doubt it. You are expert at telling me what to do. However, it is practical assistance of which we stand in need, not mere advice."

"I am at your service."

Mr Everett was frowning now. Gabrielle hoped it was a frown of concern and not of irritation. She explained their suspicions of Sir Oswald.

"How sure are you that Lady Harrison is not simply spending more than she can account for?" asked Mr Everett. "It is all too easy to lose heavily at cards, for instance, with nothing to show for it."

She shook her head. "Not Madame. She enjoys cards, but she always avoids parties where there is deep play. I know for a fact that she has turned down two invitations this week for that very reason. No, Gerard is sure she is being cheated. There must be something we can do?"

"Has her ladyship consulted the family lawyer?"

"Sir Oswald changed lawyers on his father's death. Madame does not trust Mr Hubble any more than she trusts her stepson."

"Sir Oswald was at the Foreign Office again this morning. I caught him looking through some papers on my desk. I cannot believe that Sir Cosmo's son is spying for the

French, but I'd like to know if there is a reason for his inquisitiveness. I'll set a couple of my men onto it."

"How useful it is to know a spymaster! I doubt you'll find my other request so easily fulfilled. Can you tell me how to find a furnished cottage in the country to rent for the summer?"

"I've not the least idea. You intend to join the rest of the ton in the exodus from London?"

"We are driven to it, sir! Madame's greatest expense is running this house, and we are not in a position to aid her at present."

He looked at her sharply. She avoided his eyes.

"Gerard?" he asked. "I have seen enough of you to know that you are not drawing the bustle. Do not tell me that he is addicted to gaming already!"

"You are quick to lay all misfortunes to the evils of gambling, Mr Everett."

"I have my reasons. Gerard has been playing deep, then. How bad are matters?"

"I cannot think that that concerns you. We should be perfectly all right if my father would only come! I take it you do not care to help us."

He reached to take her hand. "Of course I care to help you, Gabrielle. You have not asked for a loan. Is that what you wish?"

"No!" She pulled her hand away. "Why do you persist in misunderstanding me? All I want is to know how to find cheap accomodations in the country!"

Her voice trembled on the edge of tears. He moved swiftly to sit beside her on the sofa, and put his arm around her shoulders in what he hoped was a brotherly fashion.

"We seem to be more than usually at odds this morning," he said ruefully. "I'm sorry! Do not cry, I beg you."

"I've no intention of crying!" Gabrielle raised her chin and straightened her shoulders, leaving him with no excuse to continue his comforting gesture. He leaned back in the corner of the seat and regarded her with mixed regret and approval.

"That's my girl! Never fear, I shall find you your cottage, if I have to send out every spy in the kingdom to search for it!"

She turned to look at him in surprise. "Surely you would not . . . Oh, now you are teasing me!" She smiled and shook her head. "I hope you have a more practical plan."

"I believe I shall consult my stepmother. In fact, I had best go immediately to catch her before she goes out. Never fear, Miss Darcy, I shan't let you be rolled up." He stood and raised her hand to his lips.

"Thank you," she said. "I never thought it would be so difficult to ask you, but I'm very glad I did."

"My pleasure." He bowed and departed.

When Mr Everett reached home, Lady Cecilia had already departed to pay some morning calls. Miss Dorothea, announced the butler, was in the drawing room, having stayed home with, he understood, a slight headache.

The scene that met his eyes when he entered the drawing room brought a look of disapproval to his face. Dorrie sat on a small sofa, a book lying neglected in her lap. As close to her as he could be while sitting in a different chair, Alain de Vignard was talking quietly with her. Her eyes shone, her cheeks were delicately tinted with rose, but they paled as the door opened and she saw her brother.

Alain jumped to his feet.

"Mr Everett! I was just about to leave. Goodbye, Miss Everett." He made a move to take her hand, quickly suppressed it, bowed hurriedly, and made his escape.

Mr Everett watched him cynically. Dorothea read his expression and said,

"He *was* just leaving, Luke. He has to be at the general's house at noon."

"I need not tell you, I suppose, that it is highly improper

for you to meet alone with a young man, especially one you are scarcely acquainted with."

She smiled, with a faraway look. "Oh, no, I know Monsieur de Vignard very well. And besides," she came back to earth, "we were not alone, for there is my maid!" She pointed at the window, and her brother saw that her maid was indeed sitting there sewing.

It dawned on him that there had been no servant present during his recent interview with Miss Darcy. Of course, the circumstances were completely different, he decided.

"If you feel you know de Vignard well, you must have been living in his pocket for the last two weeks!" he countered. "Is your mother aware of it? I'll wager she approves him no more than I do. He is a nobody, a secretary."

"He makes no secret of it. You cannot say I should not know him, for I met him through your friends, the Darcys and Lady Harrison. And Mama has twice taken me to call on them. And what is more, Alain says he asked your permission to call here, and you gave it!"

"Your mother has taken you to visit Russell Square! Strange. I did not know she was on such terms with Lady Harrison."

"She but passes the day with my lady. It is Miss Darcy she talks to. I like Miss Darcy. Are you in love with her?"

"Don't be impertinent!"

Dorothea was crushed. "I'm sorry," she said with trembling lips. "I didn't mean to pry."

"It is fortunate that you will be returning to Wrotham shortly. In the meantime, you are not to see de Vignard."

She raised her chin in a gesture that reminded him of Gabrielle.

"I cannot help but do so, for he is received everywhere. I suppose you do not wish me to cut him, or to cease to go about?"

"That would cause comment. But do not let me see you

again in his company. Indeed, Dorrie, it is bound to be talked of if he pays you such particular attentions."

To his surprise she looked rebellious, but she did not retort and he was satisfied.

"Tell your mother I should like to see her at three o'clock." he requested, "if she has no pressing engagements. I must go back to the office now." He kissed her cheek, squeezed her hand, and was gone.

As he drove towards Downing Street, his sister's question haunted him. Was he in love with Gabrielle? His feelings for her were nothing like the agony he had gone through at sixteen, when he had worshipped Cecilia and thought she could do no wrong—and then seen her marry his father. Gabrielle frequently irritated him. Her independent spirit made it impossible to know how she would act next.

On the other hand, her independence and courage had led to his receipt of important news from France. He was grateful for that, and having taken responsibility for her in Dover, he found it impossible to leave her now to sink or swim. If only her wretched father would turn up, he could hand over the responsibility and return to his former tranquil life.

Somehow the prospect was not enticing.

— 10 —

"SHALL I INVITE them to stay with us?" asked Lady Cecilia guardedly.

"Would you?" Her stepson's face lit up, then fell again. "No, best not."

"I must admit it would look most particular, and it would be bound to occasion comment, which I daresay you would not like." There was a hint of a question in her tone. When he did not respond she went on, "Perhaps the Dower House?"

"Lord no! I cannot imagine Gab—Miss Darcy in such a gloomy setting."

Lady Cecilia hid a smile. "Have you visited it since your grandmother died? I remember being taken to meet her there, and gloomy was indeed the word for it. She never had the shutters opened for fear the carpets would fade, and never had a fire lit in winter for fear the house would burn down. Not only gloomy but downright damp!"

"There you are then. It is quite unsuitable."

"Not at all. It has been thoroughly heated and aired, and due to her care the carpets are in fine condition, as are the curtains and everything else. The furnishings are very old-fashioned of course. There is a great deal of velvet and heavy brocade. In fact, I had been thinking of redecorating but I do not know where to start. If Lady Harrison would give me some ideas it would be of the greatest assistance, for she has exquisite taste."

"But it will be many years before you retire there!"

"I trust so. I was hoping that the time might come when you would like to live there, Luke."

He jumped up and strode to the window, where he stood looking out at the tiny garden behind the house.

"I cannot afford to marry," he said harshly, then turned and smiled at her apologetically. "But I will offer Miss Darcy the Dower House if you think it suitable. Thank you."

"If she likes the idea, I shall write an invitation to Lady Harrison."

Lady Cecilia thought back to the last conversation they had had, when he had denied ever having loved anyone but herself.

There were definitely signs of progress.

On his way to Russell Square, Mr Everett was suddenly assailed by doubt. Gabrielle was looking to rent a cottage, and she had indignantly refused to borrow money. Would she consider the loan of the Dower House an insult? The last thing he wanted was to offend her.

Puzzling over the best way to present the invitation, he handed Lady Harrison's butler his hat and gloves and asked Miss Darcy's whereabouts.

"In Sir Cosmo's study, sir. Miss is engaged. If you care to wait in the drawing room, sir, I'll see if Miss can see you now."

Mr Everett was suddenly aware of a loud, harsh voice, apparently raised in anger, booming from the back of the house. He raised his eyebrows at the butler, who shrugged helplessly. His face grim, he hurried towards the sound.

The study door was open. Silhouetted against a window was a giant of a man. Tall, wide of girth, he bulged with knotted muscles beneath his grimy shirt of blue homespun. The panelled room seemed to vibrate from the roar of his fury.

Mr Everett stepped in and saw Gabrielle sitting stiffly at a desk, looking tiny in comparison with her adversary, as delicate and defenseless as his sister. However, her chin was raised in that familiar gesture and her eyes sparkled.

The colossus paused for breath.

"You are perfectly unreasonable, Mr Riddlecombe," said Gabrielle quietly, her tone self-possessed. "I have offered you something on account, and the total will be paid on quarter day. I cannot do more."

"Aye, I've 'eard that tale afore, gorblimey if I hain't. Quarter day comes and quarter day goes, and be damned if I sees a penny. You just fork out right here and now, young woman, or I'll 'ave the bailiffs in the 'ouse, quick as winking."

Mr Everett moved forward and bowed to Gabrielle.

"My apologies for interrupting, Miss Darcy. Perhaps I might be of assistance?" He turned and surveyed Mr Riddlecombe with disapproval. Streaks of black dust liberally adorned the huge man's clothes and person. "You are a coal-heaver, fellow?"

"Merchant," growled the other truculently, glaring down at him. "Riddlecombe and Sons of Wapping Wharf, and all I wants is what's rightfully due!"

"Miss Darcy's proposal seems eminently appropriate." His voice was calm, but something in his gaze made the coal-merchant shift uneasily and wipe his hands on his trousers. No change was visible in either hands or trousers.

"Werl, it's like this, sir . . ."

"I suggest you accept what the lady has offered you. You have my word that the balance will be paid on quarter day."

"Werl, if you says so, sir . . ." He extended a paw like a dinnerplate and Gabrielle gave him a banknote. He studied it suspiciously, folded it with care, and stuffed it into the nether regions of his shirt. "Quarter day, mind!" he said, touched his forelock sullenly in farewell, and tramped out.

"Thank you!" said Gabrielle with fervour, standing up and giving Mr Everett both her hands. "He had me quaking in my shoes until you intervened."

"That is hard to believe. I thought you quite unperturbed."

"Oh no, it was much more frightening than being chased by French soldiers, I assure you. He was so excessively large! But it never serves to show someone that you are afraid of them, does it? Though I daresay you have never been afraid of anyone in your life."

"You are out there, Miss Darcy." He led her to one of the leather-covered armchairs with which the study was furnished and took his seat in another. "I was used to be terrified of my paternal grandmother."

"I never knew Papa's mother," she said wistfully. "And *Grand'mère* did not care for children."

"You'd not have wanted to know the Dowager Baroness. I was taken to visit her sometimes, at the Dower House. She lived there for—oh, nearly twenty years, I suppose, and she grew quite eccentric towards the end. But the Dower House has been empty for many years now. My stepmother is planning to redecorate it, and she tells me she would greatly appreciate Lady Harrison's advice. I gather her ladyship has superb taste. Should you mind giving up your cottage and spending the summer in the Dower House at Wrotham?"

"It is very kind of Lady Cecilia," said Gabrielle slowly, "and how tactful of her to say she wants advice! Though it is true that Madame has exquisite taste. Just think how beautiful her drawing room is."

"I never notice anything but you when I enter it."

She smiled at him, slightly pink-cheeked. "Because Madame designs all my dresses, no doubt!" she said. "But tell me, is not the house rather large? It is useless if we exchange one expensive household for another."

"Part of it is shut up," he hastened to reassure her. "There is a couple living there, and a woman goes in regularly to clean. You would only need a personal maid. As for coal, surely you cannot use much during the summer!"

"As long as we do not buy it from Riddlecombe and Sons, I care not how much we use! Your offer is very tempting, sir, only I have a lowering feeling I ought not to accept."

"Why?"

"It's . . . I . . ." Gabrielle looked down at her hands as if her inspiration, then raised her eyes to his. "Was it Lady Cecilia's idea to invite us?"

"Entirely. I asked her how to go about finding a cottage, nothing more."

"How very kind she is! It sounds ideal. To tell the truth, I had some difficulty picturing Madame in a cottage, though she was no whit dismayed by the suggestion. But this will suit her much better."

"Good. Lady Cecilia will write to her as soon as I tell her you accept. They go down to Kent on the fifth of July, I believe. I expect you will wish to travel with them."

"You are staying in London all summer?"

"Unless Boney suddenly surrenders! But Wrotham is less than thirty miles from town. I daresay I shall visit my family from time to time. I go to Dover at least once a month, and it is not far out of my way. In fact, I must go next week, so I shall make sure that all is being readied for you."

"Oh dear, it sounds as if we are going to cause a lot of extra work. I cannot like being under such an obligation to Lady Cecilla. Why, she barely knows us!"

"I can see that I must hurry off before you change your mind. Shall you be at Mrs Albright's party tonight?"

"Yes, I believe so." Gabrielle still looked anxious. "And you?"

"Most certainly! Till then, Miss Darcy."

She rose and went with him to the door. When they reached it he turned and put one hand on her shoulder, while with the other he gently smoothed her wrinkled brow.

"Stop worrying!" he ordered.

"Yes, sir," she said smiling, and curtsied.

As soon as he was gone, she went to find Lady Harrison. Her ladyship was in the small upstairs parlour, talking with Alain. They both fell silent as Gabrielle entered.

Then Alain said brightly, "I'm trying to persuade milady that we will survive without her hospitality, Miss Darcy. I was shocked to hear to what straits her generosity has brought her."

"I am sure Alain will do well," said Lady Harrison mournfully, "but *le pauvre* Monsieur Bellavant, and Mademoiselle de Grivis, and the others—where will they go?"

"They will get by," Gabrielle assured her. "Hundreds of other *émigrés* have managed. You have protected them as long as you could, so pray do not fall into the megrims now. I have wonderful news!"

"Monsieur Everett has found us a cottage already?"

"Better. Lady Cecilia has invited us to spend the summer in the Dower House, at Wrotham!"

"At Wrotham!" Alain was startled. "Doro—Miss Everett has spoken to me about her home. I had never hoped to see it, but perhaps I may visit you there?"

"*Mais naturellement!*" her ladyship beamed. "Gabrielle, *ce sera tout à fait merveilleux! A vrai dire*, I do not think that a cottage would suit me."

"That is what I feared, dear Madame, since our respectable house in Neuchâtel was too bourgeois for you! I was right to accept, then?"

"Of course, *chérie*." Lady Harrison had no more qualms about accepting hospitality than she had about offering it. "This Dower House, what sort of house is it?"

Gabrielle told what little she knew. Madame was delighted to hear that her advice on decorating was requested, and charmed at the prospect of travelling into Kent with the Everetts. If she was also amazed at the lengths to which Mr Everett would go for Gabrielle's sake, after knowing her so short a time, she kept that to herself.

Alain begged off accompanying the ladies to Mrs Albright's rout, but Gerard, still pale and repentant, offered his escort. Lady Harrison was struggling into her best gunmetal-grey silk evening gown when Lady Cecilia's promised formal invitation was delivered. Putting off the moment of truth, she sat down at once to write a graceful acceptance.

Dorothea begged off accompanying her mother and brother to Mrs Albright's rout. Her best friend had invited her to a small party for young people (well chaperoned of course), to play at fish and forfeits and spillikins and such nursery games, and perhaps stand up for a country dance or two. It sounded much more amusing than another grand crush, said Dorrie.

Mr Everett was struggling into his tight-fitting coat, and wishing he had had the sense to continue his self-imposed exile from the amusements of the Beau Monde, when a note was delivered. Scrawled in an uneducated hand on a tattered scrap of paper, it was addressed to Baxter, but the valet handed it to his master at once.

"From Ted?" enquired Mr Everett, unfolding the missive and attempting to decipher the writing.

"Sir," affirmed the monosyllabic manservant with a nod of his bald head.

"It seems Sir Oswald's lawyer has the reputation of a shyster. How perceptive of Lady Harrison! Ted has located Mr Hubble's offices at Lincoln's Inn. I believe I shall go and see Mr Hubble tomorrow."

"Sir."

"No, on second thoughts, if the man is a shady character himself, he might get the wind up and destroy evidence, or even warn our quarry. Baxter, tell Ted to see if he can worm his way in and find any papers relating to the Harrison family. He is not to take anything. Nothing to be put in writing, and if he's caught doing anything illegal we don't know him."

"Sir."

"I pray I never meet your friend Ted in a dark alley." Mr Everett examined himself in the mirror on his dressing table. He looked, he thought, unexceptionable. Vaguely dissatisfied, he swept his hand through his hair, leaving it in fashionable disarray. Now he looked merely unkempt. With a sigh he picked up his brush and restored it to order. "Thank you, Baxter, that is all. I may be late tonight, don't wait up."

"Sir."

Mrs Albright had described her party as a rout rather than a ball because of the unfortunate absence of a formal ballroom in her town house, about which she had been complaining for years. To make up for this deficiency, she had cleared every stick of furniture out of her large drawing room, hung it with Indian silk, and hired just two musicians so that they would not take up too much space. She had also provided a variety of attractions in other rooms in the hope that not too many of her guests would choose to dance.

Mr Everett wandered through the house searching for Gabrielle. She was not listening to the soprano in the conservatory. She was not playing silver loo in the library. She was not making polite conversation, nor exchanging gossip, in the small drawing room. She was not in the dining room sampling the lobster patties. She was not in the billiard room, but Gerard was, watching the play, and Mr Everett approached him.

"Good evening," he said. "Where is your sister?"

"I'm not betting," said Gerard defensively. "Just watching."

Mr Everett's lips twitched, but he said with perfect gravity, "I am glad to see you are not in the card room."

"Oh, I don't care for cards above half. Nor dice, either. It's the other things, like curricle races and how long it takes to down a pint of porter, that's what did it. But I do think it was downright treacherous of Gaby to have squeaked beef to you!"

"Take a damper, young man. She didn't. I guessed."

"Oh. I see."

"She said it was none of my business how you came to land in the suds."

"She's a right one, Gabrielle! She never used to tattle to Miss Wilford or Papa when I found myself in a hobble, just helped me out. I say, sir, thank you for finding us a place for the summer. Is there good shooting at Wrotham?"

"Come and see me tomorrow and I'll tell you all about Wrotham. At present I am looking for your sister!"

"She was dancing last time I saw her, with Sir Hubert Rathwycke, I think."

"Thank you," said Mr Everett, with a calmness he was far from feeling. Sir Hubert again! Was Miss Darcy attracted by the undoubtedly handsome young rake? He scowled at himself in the hallway mirror as he hurried towards the sound of music.

He was in time to see the end of the dance. Gabrielle and Sir Hubert were a good-looking couple, both with dark, vivid colouring, and they twirled about the floor as if they had been practising together. Mr Everett ground his teeth audibly, earning a surprised glance from an elderly matron standing nearby.

The cotillion came to an end. Ladies curtsied to their partners. Pink and breathless, Gabrielle approached the door on Sir Hubert's arm, saw Mr Everett, and greeted him eagerly.

"May I have the next dance, Miss Darcy?" he requested, nodding curtly to her companion.

"Of course, if you will sit it out with me. I could not stand up again immediately to save my life." She fanned herself vigorously. "Pray excuse me, Sir Hubert, Mr Everett will take me to Lady Harrison."

Dismissed, the baronet took his leave with a bow and a smile.

"He is a monstrous fine dancer," said Gabrielle as soon as he was out of earshot, "But a prodigious bore! Is it not provoking? He has no conversation beyond fulsome compliments, which are very pleasant for the first five minutes and then become insupportable."

Mr Everett's face lost its glower. "Don't, I beg of you, let him hear you say that!" he advised her with a grin. "I can think of nothing he would consider more insulting."

"No, for he fancies himself a nonpareil, and God's gift to the ladies. Madame says he has a raffish reputation and I should not be seen with him, but he is such an accomplished dancer and I cannot think it dangerous to stand up with him now and then."

"So long as you do nothing to set the tabbies' tongues wagging. I have news for you. Is there somewhere we may be private?"

"What, and set the tabbies' tongues to wagging?" she mocked. "The conservatory is the traditional place for such assignations, is it not?"

"So I believe, though I am not practised in the art. However, Mrs Albright has provided her conservatory with an operatic soprano, and I expect her audience would boo and hiss were we to talk there."

"Suppose I challenge you to a friendly game of piquet? It will have to be for farthing points, for I am bound to lose. I can never remember the rules, so talking over the cards cannot spoil my play."

They made their way to the card room. All the tables were occupied, so they reserved one and went on to the supper room. There they joined a group of friends and acquaintances who were making inroads on the magnificent buffet of cold hams and sirloins, jellies and creams, strawberry tarts and pigeon pies.

A waiter served champagne. Thirsty after her exertions on the dance floor, Gabrielle drank two glasses. She was used to wine, having been brought up on it in the French fashion, but the bubbles went to her head and made her giggle like a schoolgirl.

Mr Everett thought her enchanting, but sent for lemonade. He had no wish to take advantage of her condition to win at piquet, even at a farthing a point.

A servant came to tell them that their card table was free. When some of the gentlemen proposed to come and watch their play, Gabrielle—eyes sparkling—forbade them. How could she concentrate on her cards, she demanded, with doubtless well-meaning advice flowing from every quarter? She and Mr Everett escaped into the other room and settled down at a green baize table in a quiet corner.

As he unwrapped the fresh pack of cards, sorted and shuffled them, Mr Everett reminded Gabrielle of the rules. She listened intently, but as she then asked with considerable indignation why there were no trumps, he decided that she thought she was playing whist.

"Should there not be four players?" she said uncertainly.

"No, no, Miss Darcy, we are playing piquet." He smiled at her and patted her hand. "Should you like to deal first?"

"Certainly. You must not think I am confused because of the champagne. I simply do not understand cards very well, I fear."

"I look forward to an interesting game!" he said, laughing. "I hope you avoid playing with hardened gamesters? Wait—just twelve cards each."

"What is your news?" she asked, picking up her hand. "You said I can discard five cards?"

"Yes, or fewer if you wish. One of my men has already tracked down the lawyer Hubble. Are you sure you mean to discard that queen?"

"I think so. It is not a trump, is it? What did he have to say about Hubble?"

"It seems the man is not known for his probity."

"A knave?"

"No, that is a king. Oh, you mean Hubble. I hesitate to

go so far when I have so little information, but I decided not to confront him in case he took fright. You have a quatorze, Miss Darcy."

"I thought four knaves must be good for something. What shall you do next?"

"I shall add up my points, and then we play for tricks. I ordered Ted to search Hubble's offices for papers related to the Harrisons' affairs."

"Is that not hazardous for him?"

"I am not personally acquainted with Ted, but from Baxter's hints I gather that he is an accomplished burglar."

Gabrielle frowned as she lost the fourth trick. "I do not think you should expect your hirelings to take risks that you are unwilling to share. Bother, I meant to play my ace."

"Don't tell me what you have left in your hand! He is not likely to be caught, and he has strict instructions to take nothing."

"If he is a burglar by trade, he may not be able to resist temptation. You ought to go with him. Besides, he might be unable to recognise anything of importance."

"He has worked for me before with every success."

Mr Everett dealt for the second game of the *partie*.

"All the same, you should go with him," said Gabrielle obstinately, picking up her cards.

"If you insist, Miss Darcy! There, I have a sequence of eight. Beat that if you can."

They played in silence for a while, but it was obvious that Gabrielle's mind was not on the game. She lost dismally, shuffled and dealt with an abstracted look.

This time her cards were so good that no amount of inattention could make her lose. She took nine of the twelve tricks, and at the end was only fifty-five points behind her opponent.

"I'm sorry," she said, as he dealt the last game. "I said you should not make your man take risks you would not take, but you are doing just that for me. Or at least for Madame."

"Then I do not have to go?" He accidentally discarded a ten, which she picked up.

"Oh yes, but I will go with you."

"No, you most certainly will not!" Mr Everett lost his composure, his concentration, and trick after trick.

"Yes, I shall. I shall borrow Gerard's clothes again, as I did to cross France, so you need not fear that anyone will recognise me."

"I shan't tell you where it is nor when I am going."

"I'm sure I can find out for myself, and if you do not give me the time, I shall go on my own. And as I shall not have an expert burglar with me, I daresay I shall be taken up by the watch and sent to Botany Bay!"

"Piqued, repiqued and capotted!" groaned Mr Everett, totting up the points. "I owe you tuppence ha'penny, Miss Darcy. Will you accept my avowal?"

"When do you intend to redeem it, sir?"

"If you insist, ma'am, two days hence at midnight, at Lincoln's Inn!"

—11—

THE NIGHT MIST crept up the river, under Blackfriars
Bridge, and swirled across Thames Street. Sneaking down
narrow alleys and passageways, it lost its way in Clare
Market and wandered patchily, now hiding now revealing
the dark, silent tenements.

It deadened the furtive footsteps of the small man,
carrying a dark lantern, who hurried down Bird Lane and
peered round the corner of the gin shop. Silently approaching the two figures waiting there, he tapped the larger on
the shoulder.

Startled, the man swung around.

"Ted?"

"Right, guv." Ted put his finger to his lips and winked
significantly. "Let's 'ave a bit of 'ush now, though," he said
in a hoarse whisper. "Y'reddy?"

"Ready? Yes. We've been waiting near half an hour in
this counfounded place."

"Sorry, guv. 'Ad a bit of a set-to with the missus.
Wimmin!" He spat accurately into the fetid gutter running
down the centre of the pavement. " 'Ad to tell 'er tonight's
business is fer King and Country. Wotcher bring the lad
for, then?"

"She—he insisted on coming," said Mr Everett drily.
"Shall we go?"

"Ri'chare, guv. T'ain't far. Foller me."

He dived into the maze of alleys and lanes. The others
hurried to keep up, sure that if they lost sight of him they

would never find their way out. An occasional lamplit window or torch guttering before a tavern compensated for the blowing mist, but left sinister corners of a deeper darkness where anything might have lurked. Gabrielle reached for Mr Everett's hand.

"Sorry you came?" he whispered.

"Not in the least, only I should not like to find myself alone here! I cannot think how he finds his way."

They emerged from a particularly noisome alley into a small, paved courtyard with a horse trough in the centre. The mist had not penetrated here, and the starlight was bright enough to show an iron railing running across the opposite side of the square. A beam of light from the lantern shone upon their guide, crouching towards one end and fumbling with the lock of a narrow gate. They heard the clink of metal on metal, then a grating noise, and a creak as the gate swung open.

"Quick!" hissed Ted, and closed the lantern.

Once again he seemed to know exactly where he was going as he led them between tall brick buildings, under archways, up and down steps. At last he paused in a street somewhat wider than most, peered around, and darted across to take shelter in a doorway no different from a hundred others.

Mr Everett and Gabrielle joined him. He spilled a little light onto a crooked sign and they read, "Hubble, Blayne and Hubble, Attorneys-at-Law."

As Ted poked at the door lock, they heard a mournful cry in the distance: "One o'clock and all's well! One o'clock and all's well!"

A bobbing light rounded the corner of the street, and they pressed back into the shadows as the watchman trudged towards them.

The door swung open. Ted caught it with a not quite silent oath before it hit the wall. They squeezed past him into the pitch-darkness of a musty corridor, then the faint oblong of the doorway vanished with a click.

"That's better!" breathed Ted. " 'Arf a mo, just let 'im pass and we'll 'ave a bit o' light in 'ere."

Gabrielle, clinging to Mr Everett's arm, held her breath as the thud of the watchman's staff approached.

"One o'clock and all's well! One o'clock and all's well!"

The sound retreated. Gabrielle stifled a desire to giggle with relief.

" 'E'll be gorn a nower at least," promised Ted, and slid back the panels on the lantern.

The corridor was grimy as well as musty, and the office into which he now let them with practised ease was no better. Gabrielle looked round in dismay at the row of desks with their tall stools, the piles of dusty documents, huge volumes bound in stained black leather, boxes undoubtedly full of yet more papers.

"Wherever shall we begin?" she gasped.

"Werl, you can fergit this lot to start wiv," advised Ted, waving his arm around the room. "Won't be nuffing intristing in 'ere, fer all the world to see."

Mr Everett nodded agreement and opened the door into the inner chamber. Ted pushed past him, set the lantern on the desk and draped a filthy rag over the small window, then turned to survey Mr Hubble's private office.

"You are the expert," said Mr Everett. "Give us our instructions."

"Whyncha tike the desk, guv. Better go through all the drawers. I'll tackle the strongbox, seein' as I'm good at locks. And that cupboard might 'ave summat in it if you was to look, miss."

With a minatory glance at Mr Everett, whose slip of the tongue had betrayed her disguise, Gabrielle opened the cupboard. A cloud of dust wafted past her, smelling strongly of mildew and making her cough.

"I don't believe anyone has touched this stuff for years," she snorted. "No, wait, the top and bottom shelves have been undisturbed since the crusades, but this one in the middle is comparatively clean. I've never seen so much

115

paper in my life! I can't see much, though. Is there a lamp?"

Ted abandoned the cast iron strongbox, which seemed to be giving him some trouble, and found and lighted a lamp for her. She flipped unhopefully through pile after pile of close-written documents, peering at titles, headings, names. There was a heap of rolled papers, tied with red cotton, at one end of the shelf. She picked up an armful and dumped them on the desk to take a closer look.

"I'll try these," said Mr Everett. "There's nothing of interest in the drawers."

Gabrielle went back to her cupboard and moved some more rolls. Behind them was a smaller version of the strongbox with which Ted was still struggling. It was heavy, and she nearly dropped it as she pulled it out.

At that moment, Ted managed to open the lock. They crowded round as he opened the box, to reveal a sheaf of papers of every size and shape, from official-looking documents with seals to scrawled scraps.

Mr Everett took them and looked through them. "Promissory notes," he grunted.

Ted was far more interested in what was underneath. He plunged his hands into the box and drew them forth full of gleaming sovereigns. "Cor blimey!" he breathed reverently. "Me dreams 'ave come true!"

"No!" Mr Everett's voice was sharp and firm. "Not while I am employing you."

"Just a couple of 'andfuls, guvnor!" pleaded Ted. " 'E'll never miss 'em."

"Not one. You are being well paid for this night's work, and there will be others if you can restrain yourself now. You know well that in this kind of work it is essential not to arouse suspicions."

Ted looked downcast and somewhat sullen, but let the coins fall with a ringing noise. "Fer King and Country," he said, sighing heavily. "And wot 'as the King done fer me lately, is wot I'd like to know?"

Gabrielle patted his arm consolingly.

"There's another box in the cupboard," she told him. "It's too heavy for me. Will you get it out?"

"Ri'chare, miss." He lifted it down onto the desk. Its lock presented no problems to his pick, and a moment later they were studying yet more papers.

"Good heavens!" said Gabrielle. "The Duke of . . ."

"Lady Bonner!" exclaimed Mr Everett. "I always wondered why . . ."

"Breach of promise . . ."

"Misappropriation of funds . . ."

"These go back to the South Sea Bubble! Hubble's father must have . . ."

"I got nuffing but numbers," complained Ted. "But this one 'ere's got 'Arrison wrote on it."

"Let me see!" Gabrielle and Mr Everett spoke and reached in unison. Having longer arms, Mr Everett won. He sat down at the desk and she leaned against the chair, reading over his shoulder.

"Hubble's been taking half the difference!" said Gabrielle a few minutes later.

"That's what it looks like. He found out about Sir Oswald's thievery three years ago and has been claiming his share ever since. Her ladyship has been receiving less than two thirds of what is due to her, if I understand this aright." He heard a chink and looked up to see Ted's hand emerging from his pocket. The burglar's face, unnaturally innocent, paled before his gaze.

"I'll put 'em back," he said hastily. "I don't want no trouble, guv, honest. Somefing come over me all of a sudden, like."

"Here, put these papers back in and lock it up again," said Mr Everett resignedly. "And this little one, too. We've found what we needed. You'll note that I am *not* taking it with me, though it would doubtless be useful. The knowledge that it exists will have to serve for the moment."

"Right, guv." Ted cheered up. "Now we knows as it's 'ere, we can come and get it any time."

Mr Everett looked at him suspiciously, but decided to

ignore the implications. "We must put everything back just as it was," he said.

This took them several minutes. Gabrielle had just decided that the room looked much as it had when they entered it, except perhaps for the redistribution of dust, when she heard a faint sound.

"Listen!" She moved to the window.

"Two o'clock and all's well!"

"It's the watchman!"

Mr Everett jumped to douse the lamp, and Ted closed his lantern. In breathless, claustrophobic silence they listened to the beating of their own hearts. Suddenly the voice rang out just outside the window.

"Two o'clock and all's well!"

For an eternity they waited, until they heard the cry once more in the distance.

Ted opened the lantern. Gabrielle took down the rag from the window and presented it to him with a creditable bow. Stepping softly they crept out of Mr Hubble's chambers and hurried back through Lincoln's Inn, through the gate in the iron fence, through the stinking alleys of Clare Market, to emerge in bright moonlight on High Holborn.

Gabrielle looked round. Their tame burglar had melted away like a vision. She rubbed her eyes.

"Tired?"

"A little."

"Not far to go."

Five minutes later they reached Russell Square and stopped outside Lady Harrison's house.

"You never paid me that tuppence ha'penny," said Gabrielle.

"I forgot to bring it. Have you change for a shilling?"

"No." She giggled. "You can give it to me tomorrow." She was suddenly overcome by helpless laughter.

Mr Everett grinned, then joined in. They clung to the railings, shaking with laughter. A nightwatchman paused on his rounds to shake his head indulgently. There was no knowing what the Quality would get up to when they went on the mop, he thought. They saw him move on and their mirth redoubled.

"Two o'clock and all's well!" gasped Gabrielle. "Only it must be near three now, and how I shall explain to Madame when I can't wake up in the morning after going early to bed, I cannot imagine. Goodnight, sir, and thank you for letting me go with you."

"Much choice I had!" He gave her a quick hug and watched her go up the steps. She opened the door, turned to wave, then disappeared inside.

Mr Everett wandered home, walking on air.

—12—

Mr Everett scowled.

Coming down considerably later than was his wont, he found Alain de Vignard donning his hat in the hallway.

"Just leaving again, monsieur?" he asked unpleasantly.

"Yes, sir." Alain, no whit disconcerted, took his gloves from the footman. "I went first to the Foreign Office, but you were not yet arrived, and when I came here I found you still abovestairs. I have left a note with your butler, but since you are here, I will tell you its import: Monsieur le Général Pichegru requests a meeting with you at your earliest convenience."

"Indeed!" Mr Everett was taken aback, having imagined quite another reason for the young man's presence in his house. "I have not breakfasted as yet. If you care to join me, I shall accompany you to the general's house."

"Thank you, but I had best return at once," said Alain hastily. A *tête-à-tête* was not, it seemed, to his liking. "I shall inform the general that you will be with him shortly."

He was pulling on his gloves when Dorothea appeared, dressed for walking and followed by her maid.

"Luke!" she exclaimed, pink-faced. "I thought you had gone out long since!"

"Indeed!" said her brother grimly.

"I am going to Hatchard's," Dorrie went on quickly, gesturing at the books her maid was carrying. "Have you any volumes to be returned there?"

"I have not. But if you will wait a few minutes, I shall walk with you."

"I cannot wait. Mama is taking me to visit the Dartingtons in a little while." Her delicate features were suffused with colour, but her voice was firm.

She stepped past him. The footman opened the door and Mr Everett, helpless, watched her patter down the steps, followed by the maid and Alain de Vignard. With two servants and a stranger present, there was nothing he could do to stop her.

"Tell my lady I wish to speak to her before she goes out," he ordered the footman.

"Yes, sir. Your breakfast is ready, sir."

"Thank you. I'll serve myself."

Still furious, he strode to the breakfast room and rapidly consumed a plateful of cold beef and ham, two coddled eggs and several muffins. Burglary was good for the appetite, he thought. Remembering last night, his expression softened, until his stepmother rustled in.

"Good morning, Luke, though it is nearly afternoon, I vow. It is not like you to lie abed so late! Sit down, sit down and finish your meal. You may spread me a muffin, if you please." Lady Cecilia pulled out a chair beside him and sat down. "What did you want to see me about?"

"Dorrie! She and this de Vignard are thick as thieves. Have you not noticed it?"

Her ladyship frowned. "She likes him, certainly, but he makes no secret of his station and she knows that there can be no question of a serious connection. De Vignard has excellent address, easy manners and superior understanding, and I do not believe he has ever acted with anything other than irreproachable propriety. Dorrie has many friends and there can be no harm in adding him to their number."

"Many friends, yes, but if I am not mistaken, all the other gentlemen are little more than schoolboys. Has she shown partiality for any other old enough to think of marriage?"

"You read too much into it, Luke. I'm sure the attachment will die a natural death when we return to Wrotham and she sees no more of him."

"Precisely. I must ask you, Ma'am, to put forward your departure." His face wore a stern, inflexible look that his stepmother rarely saw.

"It is not so easy. We have a number of engagements in the next two weeks."

"Beg off!"

"You are unreasonable! Dorothea is a tractable child. If you truly think it necessary, I will drop a word in her ear and that will be the end of it."

"I doubt it. I have already spoken to her without altering her behaviour in the least. I cannot order *your* movements, ma'am, but I insist that Dorothea go into the country within the week!"

General Pichegru wanted more information about de la Touche.

"*Mon jeune collègue, Georges Cadoudal, ne croît guère qu'il soit ennemi,*" he explained to Mr Everett.

Alain de Vignard translated: "Monsieur Cadoudal does not believe your warning, sir. He is asking the British government to give him a million francs to support a royalist revolution in France. *Monsieur le général* is more cautious."

"I have no information beyond the warning I have already given. We are trying to discover more, but I am sure the general understands that communication with France is difficult."

"*Bien sûr!*" The general was all too aware of the fact. But General Moreau, their proposed contact, had fought with him against Austria. While he thought him unlikely to turn royalist, he was no lover of Napoleon and might well be willing to make common cause against him. If so, he must be supported.

Mr Everett shrugged irritably and stood up. "Doubtless it will take some time to weasel the money out of the government. With luck I shall have more news before it is necessary to make a decision. If the general will excuse me?"

"With his thanks, sir. He is going to make up a list of other Frenchmen who might help overthrow Bonaparte."

"I beg him to commit nothing to paper!"

"I will convey your concern to the general, sir," Alain assured him.

Mr Everett next called upon Lady Harrison. Though he actually did have business with her ladyship, he was disappointed to learn that Gabrielle had gone riding in the park with a group of friends.

He knotted ten farthings in his handkerchief and gave them to the footman to give to her, then went on into the drawing room. Since she was not there, he had leisure to study the colour scheme, and found it as elegant as promised. Lady Cecilia had some justification, then, for asking Lady Harrison's advice.

My lady fluttered in, a smile on her plump face.

"Good afternoon, Mr Everett. Will you take a glass of wine?"

"No thank you, ma'am. I am come to consult you on a number of matters."

"Gabrielle tells me you have evidence that *mon beau-fils* has been robbing me! Poor Sir Cosmo must be turning in his grave."

"It seems so. However, my investigations are incomplete. I hope you will wait a while yet before taking action."

"As you wish, monsieur. Since Lady Cecilia has so kindly invited us to Wrotham, there is no hurry at present.

"That is my next subject. Do not be alarmed, my lady! The invitation stands! Only the date has changed. I must go into Kent on Tuesday and Lady Cecilia has decided to accept my escort. So if you can be ready by then, I hope you will go with us."

"Tuesday? *D'accord*. Everyone but Alain will be gone by

124

then so there will be no difficulty. The dear boy is going to stay on here to look after the house."

"You trust de Vignard to do that for you? Might I ask just what you know of him?"

"Of Alain? He is the son of the Vicomte de Vignard, whose wife was a dear friend of mine. Like my husband and so many others, they lost their lives in the Terror. Alain was a mere boy when he escaped; his little sister disappeared and has not been heard of since. So I am his only family and you may be sure that I trust him."

"So he *is* the Vicomte de Vignard!"

"*Oui*, but of what use is such a title here, when the Comtesse de Guéry makes ices in her café for the Prince of Wales? It is best that he forgets such things."

"I daresay you are right, ma'am. We shall expect you to join us on Tuesday, then." He bowed and took his leave.

It was mid-afternoon by the time Mr Everett arrived in Downing Street. His secretary looked up in surprise when he walked into the office.

"I didn't expect you today, sir," he said, pulling a large silver watch out of his pocket and consulting it ostentatiously.

"I worked late last night, Davis. Very late. Sir Oswald is undoubtedly stealing Lady Harrison blind."

"Sir Cosmo's son a thief? How very shocking!"

"Do we have anything on her stepson, from our point of view?"

"Not yet, sir. It's early days for that sort of investigation. I've two men down in Kent working on it, and I've put out feelers all over town, especially right here in the Foreign Office."

"Good. Do we have a file on an *émigré* by the name of Alain de Vignard?"

"General Pitchgrew's secretary? He was cleared when he first came over, sir. I don't know as anyone's had a look at him since."

"Put someone onto it. I suppose the general's clean?"

"Well, he did fight for Boney for a while, but Sir Cosmo was sure he changed sides right enough. Monsewer Cadoudal seems to trust him, and he's a royalist for sure. Fought in the Vendee, he did."

"Royalist and warrior he may be, but I've no opinion of his common sense," snorted Mr Everett. "He's ignoring the warning I passed on. I hope there's a message from Le Hibou when I go down to Dover on Tuesday."

— 13 —

AT NINE O'CLOCK on Tuesday morning, Gerard was on the lookout at the drawing room window when a procession drove into Russell Square and pulled up before Lady Harrison's house.

"Three carriages," he reported, "and there's no luggage strapped on, so they must have sent it ahead. There will be plenty of room for our bags, madame, so you need fret no longer. I hope Mr Everett invites me to ride in his tilbury, for I do not care to be shut up with females in a coach all day."

"It will only be two or three hours at most," said Gabrielle, who rather hoped that the invitation would be extended to her.

Mr Everett had had every intention of driving Miss Darcy, but a single look at her brother's face forced him to reconsider. With a sigh he decided that both propriety and common sense dictated that Gerard should be his passenger. Gabrielle's disappointment hurt him, but he noted with admiration that she at once turned to Dorothea with a smile.

"Say you will ride with me, Miss Everett. It is past time we came to know each other better."

Dorothea, who was looking somewhat wan, assented with more politeness than enthusiasm. With the luggage safely bestowed, Lady Cecilia, Lady Harrison and their two maids settled in the first carriage, the girls and

Dorothea's maid in the second, and the gentlemen climbed up into the tilbury.

"Let us go ahead," Gabrielle heard her brother say. "Those heavy coaches will slow us down."

Mr Everett replied in a voice full of amusement, "Sorry, Gerard, but it is our duty to escort the ladies, not to race them. We will go last, so that if any mishap befalls we shall see it and be able to render prompt aid."

"You mean there might be an accident, or even highwaymen?" asked Gerard eagerly.

The coach jolted into movement and Gabrielle missed the response.

They rumbled along the busy streets of the city, over the Thames and through the southern suburbs, past the Elephant and Castle. Dorothea made polite if desultory conversation, but it was plain that her mind was elsewhere. When they reached New Cross and branched south onto the Folkestone road, now really in the country, Gabrielle decided it was time to discover why her companion was in the mopes.

"It is kind of your brother to escort us," she said, "though I daresay you are sorry to have missed the last few parties of the season."

"I do not care for parties," said Dorothea, her lips trembling, "and it is not in the least kind of Luke to go with us when it is all his doing."

"His doing?'

"He told Mama we must leave early. She had no notion of doing so, but he made her."

"How can Mr Everett make Lady Cecilia do anything she does not wish to do? He is her stepson, not her husband!"

"Everyone always does just as he orders. There's something about the way he looks at you. Even Papa gave up living in town because Luke said he must."

"Lord Everett obeys his son?" gasped Gabrielle. "How

can that be? I know just what you mean about the way he looks at you, though it has never given me the least desire to do as he says, but that he should dare command his father is beyond anything!"

"It is all because of gambling. Papa was used to be a great gamester. He lost a vast deal of money and the house was already mortgaged, so he could not pay his debts without selling land. I do not precisely understand it, but there is something called an entail, which means that the heir must approve the sale of any part of the estate."

"And Luke—Mr Everett refused?"

"I believe so. It was five years ago, and I was still in the schoolroom, so no one told me anything, but Rolf and I put things together for ourselves. Rolf is my older brother, my *real* brother. Luke would not let Papa sell any land. Papa had to sell his racehorses instead, and Mama sold some jewels. And even so, Luke has to work at that horrid Foreign Office. So Papa retired to Wrotham to make money from the farms and things, to pay off the mortgages. And I must say it is much more comfortable to have them living at home instead of in London all the time, and Papa seems to be perfectly happy. Mama too."

"So that is why Luke works at the Foreign Office!"

"Yes, to pay my dowry and the boys' schooling. But there is no need to be sorry for him, for he enjoys it amazingly."

"No doubt! It provides him with a new group of people to give orders to!"

Dorothea giggled, but sobered immediately. "I ought not to have told you all this, Miss Darcy. It is our skeleton in the cupboard. Rolf thinks Mama has not even told my grandfather—for he is quite rich, and could have helped so that Luke need not work."

"I won't tell anyone," promised Gabrielle. "But you have not yet told me why Luke insisted that you come down into Kent today."

"Mama would not say," said Dorothea evasively, flushing. "Look, there is Eltham Palace. You can see the downs from here and we shall soon cross into Kent."

Gabrielle allowed herself to be diverted into a discussion of why a range of uplands should be known as 'downs.' She learned a great deal about the topography of Kent, and Dorothea seemed to be distracted from her megrims. Nonetheless, she remained determined to find out just what had caused them.

The long, gentle ascent of the north side of the downs was pretty enough in the summer sun, especially after the city's grime. Gabrielle politely expressed her admiration of the grassy slopes dotted with oaks and sheep. Here and there mowers were at work, cutting the longer grass for hay. It reminded her of Switzerland, on a less grand, more cosy scale, and suddenly she was homesick for the lake and the green mountain meadows, the sound of cowbells and their neat little house in Neuchâtel. Until Papa joined them, England would never truly seem like home.

The carriage rocked to a halt.

"We are at the top," said Dorothea. "We always stop here for a moment."

"To let the horses take breath?"

"Partly, but mostly just to look. Do pray get out with me, Miss Darcy. It is well worth the effort."

The coachman was opening the door and letting down the step. Gabrielle followed Dorothea out, and turned to see what she was pointing at. She looked over mile after mile of rolling country: first, steep slopes of short, wiry turf, down to groves of trees in orderly rows; then fields and woods and villages stretching as far as the eye could see. She almost expected the Alps to tower out of the hazy distance.

Mr Everett came to her side.

"This is our land," he said softly. "Is it not beautiful?" The pride in his voice told her he had refused to sell this land because he loved it.

"Yes, oh yes!"

He took her elbow and turned to face the northeast. "Do you see a glint of blue? That's the Thames estuary. Chatham is down there, with the Royal Navy yards, and Rochester. I'll take you to see the castle one day, if you should care to go."

"We'll take a picnic," suggested Dorothea.

"I should like to see the Navy yards," added Gerard. "Is it possible to tour them?"

Mr Everett looked at him suddenly with narrowed eyes, then shook his head—apparently at himself, since he then said, "I'll see what I can do. Will you travel the rest of the way with me, Miss Darcy? There is scarce a mile left to go."

Gabrielle accepted his help to climb into the tilbury, but did not smile her thanks. As they set off cautiously down the hill, following the other carriages, she looked up at his face, intent on the road ahead.

"You still suspect us, don't you?" she said. "Of being French spies?"

"No!" His denial came fast and firm.

Too fast, thought Gabrielle, as if he was expecting her challenge. How was she ever to persuade him of her innocence? She scarcely noticed the surroundings as they drove on in silence. Questions flooded into her mind. Did she care that he suspected her? Yes. Why? What did it matter to her that this dictatorial gentleman should think ill of her?

It did matter. It hurt her. She had considered him a friend, the kind of friend one can turn to in times of trouble. At the back of her mind, she realised, she had counted on him to come to the rescue if her father never returned. She had even dared to hope that his regard for her was such that he might marry her, give her and Gerard a home and family, if Papa never came back.

She bowed her head and her eyes filled with tears of anguish and humiliation. Clasping her hands tight in her lap, she blinked hard, praying that he would not turn and look at her, would not say something that demanded a response.

The silence grew between them, an impassable hedge of thorns.

She ventured a quick glance at his face. It was troubled, frowning, his gaze fixed on some inner landscape. Without his guidance, the horses followed the other carriages down the hill and through a gate in a wall of faintly greenish stone.

Beyond a flower garden riotous with roses stood an L-shaped house of age-mellowed red brick. The gravel drive led to a paved court in the angle of the L, but instead of approaching it, they turned into a narrower way to the left.

The track was scarce more than a grassy ride. Mr Everett came to himself with a start as they jounced over the tussocks in the centre. He quickly straightened their course so that the wheels ran smoothly, then turned to smile at Gabrielle.

"I beg your pardon, Miss Darcy! Instead of pointing out to you the beauties of the countryside, I have been lost in a brown study." He pointed ahead with his whip. "The Dower House is just behind those trees. You will see the chimneys in a moment."

The track curved round a huge copper beech with benches about its bole. They pulled up behind the other carriages, in front of a square, friendly-looking house of the same brick as the main house. The green front door stood open and an elderly couple hurried down the steps to greet them.

"Mr and Mrs Tombaugh," said Mr Everett. "They used to look after my grandmother, and stayed on as caretakers. They are supposed to have set the place in order for you."

While Tombaugh helped the coachmen untie trunks and boxes, his wife ushered the party into the house. Though small, it was furnished with an oppressive grandeur that dismayed Gabrielle. The dining room, where a light luncheon had been set out, was wainscotted in dark oak and hung with portraits of Jacobean ancestors, all of whom seemed to be wearing black. The window curtains were of crimson velvet and on the floor, beneath an overlarge ebony table, a Turkey carpet in burgundy and navy added to the gloom.

"Rose and cream!" exclaimed Lady Harrison. "And a much smaller table in some light-coloured wood. Only think, dear Lady Cecilia, how charming this *salle à manger* could be! The carpet is magnificent. But should you mind removing *ces peintures abominables?*"

"Not in the least," said Lady Cecilia, laughing. "They are dreadful, aren't they? I hope all those stern faces staring down will not destroy your appetite."

"I fear not," replied the older lady gloomily. "Nothing has been known to do so. But here in the country I shall walk daily and see if I cannot dispose of some of my *embonpoint.*"

After luncheon, the Everetts drove back to their home, which was known locally as the Great House, to distinguish it from the Dower House. Madame retired to her chamber for a nap, and Gabrielle and Gerard decided to explore their surroundings.

—14—

THE BROTHER AND sister strolled down the hill and soon found themselves walking through orchards of apples and pears, with sheep grazing among the trees. Gerard picked a small, pink-cheeked apple and took a bite.

"Ugh!" He spat it out and tossed the remainder into the trees. "It'll be a few months before those are ready to eat!"

A large crow sitting on a high branch regarded him cynically, so he picked another fruit to hurl at it. It flapped away cawing loudly.

A pair of rabbits sat up and looked at them with twitching noses, then hopped to a new patch of grass a little farther off. Gerard raised an imaginary shotgun to his shoulder and took aim.

"Do you suppose Lord Everett would lend me a gun?" he asked hopefully.

"I daresay. You men are all horridly bloodthirsty."

"Rabbits are pests," protested Gerard. "Crows, too. Let's go up to the Great House now, and ask."

"Not today. Lady Cecilia is but now arrived home, and they will be too busy by far to receive us. Tomorrow we must pay a courtesy call, and you may ask then, but we must not presume upon their kindness. Just because they have lent us the house it does not mean that they are anxious for our company."

"Fustian! Why should they have settled us so close at

hand if they do not wish to see us? You are making a piece of work of nothing, Gab. I expect Lady Cecilia hopes that you will be a companion for Dorothea."

"Miss Everett, to you. Truly we must not appear encroaching," said Gabrielle stubbornly.

The next orchard was of cherries. Ripe, red fruit dangled in irresistible bunches, and they did not long resist. Gabrielle was satisfied with a handful, but Gerard gorged himself until his sister was moved to protest.

"You call crows pests!" she exclaimed. "I am sure their depredations are not half so great as yours!"

Walking on, they crossed a field of vines covered with odd-looking yellowish flowers. In one corner stood several small, circular buildings with curious conical roofs. Near these they passed through a gate in a hazel hedge and found themselves in a lane. It led them into a pretty village built about a crossroads, whose chief features were an ancient-looking church and a tavern called the Everett Arms.

"Let's look in the church," proposed Gabrielle, just as her brother said, "I could do with a mug of ale."

"Meet me in fifteen minutes," suggested Gabrielle, looking up at the church clock.

Quarter of an hour later, they met at the church gate.

"Those round buildings are oast-houses," said Gerard. "They dry hops in them, off those vines. They are used for flavouring beer."

"The church is full of brasses," said Gabrielle. "Most of them are in memory of Everetts. The family has been here for hundreds of years!" No wonder Mr Everett had refused to let his father sell the land, she thought, especially as it seemed to be exceptionally productive.

They walked back up the lane and through the main gates of the estate. Gabrielle wanted to wander among the roses, whose perfume was wafted to them on the breeze, but she was afraid that she might be seen from the Great House and someone might feel obliged to come out to her.

More and more she felt she had made a mistake in accepting Lady Cecilia's invitation.

Unwilling to go back into the cheerless house, they sat on a bench under the copper beech. The bronze leaves rustled above them and the shade was pleasant after their long walk. Gerard lolled back against the smooth grey bark.

"This is something like!" he said. "However did you persuade Mr Everett to ask us here? If only his lordship will lend me a gun. I wonder what sort of cattle he has in his stable?"

"You are *not* to ask Lord Everett to mount you! And I did *not* persuade Mr Everett to invite us. It was entirely Lady Cecilia's idea."

"Doing it much too brown! At all events, I am glad you did, for I had much rather live in the country. Where do you suppose we shall live when Papa comes?"

"Gerard, have you ever thought that maybe Papa will never come? He told us to come to England if he had not returned after six months, and now it has been nearly ten. Anything might have happened."

Gerard sat up straight and gazed at her in alarm. "No!" he said sharply. "Of course he will come! We cannot sponge on Madame for the rest of our lives!"

"Of course not. We shall have to find work. I could be a governess, perhaps, or companion, and you could be a clerk. Your handwriting is excellent."

"Thank you for nothing. I had rather be a gamekeeper. Are you quite sure you have no idea as to Papa's family?"

"None. I suppose we could contact all the Darcys we can find, but it must be a humiliating process, particularly if our grandfather should cast us off as he did Papa."

"He must be dead anyway, or Papa would not propose to return to England."

"True. Gerard, Madame once hinted that she knew more than we do."

"Why has she not told us then? You must have misunder-

137

stood her. You had best ask her directly, though. None of this female beating about the bush! I'm going to see if Mrs Tombaugh will give me something to eat, for I've not been so sharp-set since we left France!"

"I wonder when she serves dinner?" mused Gabrielle. "Wait, I'm coming with you."

The sound of scolding female voices led them to the kitchen.

"*Madame Tombeau!*" hissed Marie. "A fitting name for one who will drive milady to her grave."

"I baked 'em special," insisted Mrs Tombaugh, who was as plump as Marie was scrawny, "and I can't see no harm in my lady taking a raspberry tart with her cup of tea."

Gerard looked round, spotted a tray with a plate of tarts, and sat down at the kitchen table to help himself.

"What is going on?" asked Gabrielle. "No, don't both speak at once. Marie, you first."

Since Marie would not dream of criticising her mistress, except to her face, she found it difficult to explain why she had strictly forbidden the provision of pastries at four o'clock in the afternoon. Mrs Tombaugh was under no such restriction. With virtuous verbosity she pointed out that my lady need not eat the tarts if she did not want them; that she was known far and wide for a light hand with pastry but that she wouldn't take offence; and that it was not the place of a mere abigail to see to the menus.

"If her ladyship does not wish to review your menus, bring them to me," said Gabrielle. "Marie is right, however, in that you must not send up any cakes that her ladyship does not specifically ask for." She knew all to well that Madame's good resolutions vanished at the sight of food. "As for the tarts, you need not fear that they will not be appreciated, for I see that my brother has demolished every one!"

"Very light hand with the pastry," mumbled Gerard, wiping sticky crumbs off his chin.

Both antagonists seemed to think they had won the

battle. Mrs Tombaugh beamed, and Marie, casting her a glance of mingled triumph and enmity, picked up the tea-tray and stalked out.

"Pig!" said Gabrielle. "You might have left me one."

"I was being diplomatic," explained Gerard unconvincingly. "Look how I helped your argument."

"There's more in the oven, miss," said Mrs Tombaugh. "I'll have 'em out in a jiffy, and another pot of tea on the table."

When Gabrielle, full of raspberry tarts, went upstairs, she found Madame in her dressing room reclining on a gilt-and brocade chaise longue.

"You will have a cup of tea, *cherie?*" she asked. "A barbarous English custom but one to which I have grown used. Marie, fetch a cup for mademoiselle."

"No, thank you, madame. I have just had tea in the kitchen. I should like to talk to you for a minute, if you please."

Marie discreetly retired into the bedchamber, and Gabrielle sat down on a stool at the dressing table.

"*Qu'est-ce que c'est?*" asked Lady Harrison. "You have the air of worry that I do not like to see on the face of a pretty girl."

"It's Papa, madame. He has been gone for ten months, without a word! Do you think he . . . he might be dead?"

"Anything is possible, my poor child, but I do not think it likely. Maurice is *un homme très adroit.*"

"He is clever, isn't he? I expect you are right and he will turn up one day, with never an explanation as to where he went or what he's been doing. But if he does not, Gerard and I will have to seek positions where we can keep ourselves, unless you can help us to contact Papa's family."

Her ladyship jumped to her feet, swooped on Gabrielle and enveloped her in a scented embrace. "*Jamais!*" she cried. "Never while I live shall Maurice's children work for a living!"

"Even if Sir Oswald is forced to give you your full

allowance, we cannot let you keep us, madame. We are agreed on that."

"I shall tell you of your family, but not yet. It is plain that *le bon papa* does not want you to know until he is here, so we will allow him a little more time, *n'est-ce pas?* If he does not come by the end of the summer, when we must return to London, than I will tell you all I know. *Ça va, chérie?* In the meantime, you will enjoy the little vacation in the country and not worry."

"Very well, madame. But I shall hold you to it. Come September, I intend to know just who we are!"

Gabrielle kissed Lady Harrison and went to her chamber. All her clothes had been put away already. Unlike the grand chambers below, the room was simply furnished with sturdy Jacobean furniture, the walls whitewashed and a white rag rug on the well-polished floor. It might seem cold in winter, but at this time of year it was refreshing.

She sat down on the bed. Feeling suddenly weary, she leaned back against the pillows and swung her legs up. The window was directly before her, framed by flowered chintz curtains. Through a gap in the trees she could see all the way up the grassy slope to the Great House.

Did one of the windows belong to Mr Everett's room? Was he in it, changing for dinner perhaps, looking down the hill and wondering what she was doing?

With a sigh, she decided that it was unlikely. Mrs Tombaugh had said that his lordship didn't hold with country hours. They dined at eight at the Great House, and if miss didn't mind they'd do the same here, for otherwise there'd be no end of confusion. And besides, she'd enough to do without hurrying to get dinner on the table by five or six.

Gabrielle did not say that she had no expectation of being invited to dine at the Great House. Eight o'clock would be fine, she agreed.

"Oh dear!" said Lady Harrison at breakfast the next

morning. "You are perfectly correct, Gabrielle, that we must pay a courtesy call this morning, but how am I to get there? We have no carriage, and this is not London where one can simply send a servant out for a hackney or a chair!"

"You will have to walk, madame," said Gerard, grinning. "Come, did we not hear you saying that you plan to exercise regularly while in the country?"

"I intend to take a gentle stroll in the shrubbery. It must be a good *mile* to the Great House!" she wailed.

"Not much more than half a mile," soothed Gabrielle, "and we will go slowly."

"Uphill all the way!"

"Think how pleasant it will be on the way back."

"I have not the proper shoes."

"I distinctly remember that you had a pair made especially before we left London. Let us send for Marie and ask her."

"No," sighed Lady Harrison. "You are quite right. But I refuse to turn around and come home after a polite quarter hour. It will take me much longer to get my breath!"

By the time they reached the Great House, she was indeed panting and very pink in the face. While Gerard rang the bell, Gabrielle folded her parasol for her and fanned her vigorously. When the butler admitted them, she sank into a chair in the spacious entrance hall, looking as if she would never move again. Gabrielle continued to fan her.

"I will see if her ladyship is at home," pronounced the butler, and left with measured tread, no whit disconcerted at the arrival of a plump and breathless lady on foot.

"If Lady Cecilia is not at home," gasped Lady Harrison, "I shall have died for nothing!"

Fortunately, the butler returned to announce that Lady Cecilia would receive them in the morning room. It proved to be a small sunny parlour looking out over the rose garden. Gerard was dismayed to find that the three Misses Everett were also present.

"Devil take it!" he whispered to his sister. "A house full of females!"

To his relief, after an exchange of courtesies Lady Cecilia suggested that he should go and look for her eldest son.

"He will be in the gun room or the stables," she added. "Just ask one of the servants."

"The gun room or the stables!" repeated Gerard joyfully. "Thank you, ma'am, I shall certainly find him!"

"Rolf is up at Cambridge," Lady Cecillia explained to Lady Harrison, "but he is no scholar. He spends all his time at home in sporting pursuits."

"Our brothers are certain to become friends, Miss Everett," said Gabrielle to Dorothea, "if yours is indeed as mad for horses and guns as is mine!"

"Rolf thinks of nothing else, I vow." Dorothea set a careful stitch in her embroidery. "Except the army, that is. Now that we are at war with France again, I expect Papa will let him leave the university and join the cavalry."

"Gerard also wishes to become a soldier!" Gabrielle did not feel inclined to add that he himself had made this course impossible by gambling away all their money.

"Men are all the same, I vow," said one of the younger girls scornfully. Sturdy, good-natured schoolroom misses, with none of Dorothea's delicate beauty, they sat at a table looking through some fashion magazines their sister had brought them from her season in London.

"Luke is not," said the other. "I have never heard him express the least desire to join the army."

"No, but he likes to ride and shoot and hunt when he is at home."

"You like to ride yourself!"

"Do stop squabbling!" begged Dorothea. "What will Miss Darcy think of you?"

"Only that I wish I had had a sister. Though brothers are all very well in their way. I expect Mr Everett spends as much time here as he can spare?"

"He usually comes quite often in the summer. But when

he left this morning, he said he should be particularly busy for the next month or two and that we must not expect him."

"He is gone already? I had thought he meant to stay at least a day or two. And he will not be back this summer!"

The sun shone as bright as ever through the wide windows, but to Gabrielle the day seemed suddenly grey.

—15—

GERARD WAS NOT seen again until five minutes before dinner, when he burst into the Dower House's resplendent drawing room with muddy breeches and a rip in his jacket.

"Rolf Everett is a very good fellow," he announced. "I bagged five rabbits."

"Go and change at once!" ordered his sister firmly. "That is no way to appear before madame, and dinner will be ready any minute."

"Good! We had no luncheon and I am starving. All right, all right, I'm going! Don't wait for me."

"We shan't," Gabrielle assured his departing back.

Ten minutes later he appeared in the dining room, reasonably clean and tidy, though a London dandy would have stared at his neckcloth. He helped himself to a large slice of pigeon pie, surrounded it with well-buttered potatoes, permitted Gabrielle to add a few mushroom fritters, and set to.

"We are invited to dine at the Great House the day after tomorrow," said Lady Harrison.

"Mph."

"Lady Cecilia kindly sent me home in a gig."

"Mph."

"She says we may borrow any carriage we wish whenever it is not in use."

"Mph."

"You are a great conversationalist," said his sister. "It

may interest you to know that I walked home, with Dorothea, and that we are on first-name terms."

"Dashed unnecessary fuss you females make about such things." Gerard took another mouthful, disposed of it, and added, "Have you had some of this pie? Best crust I ever tasted. Rolf and I are going riding early tomorrow. He says he is certain his father can have no objection if I borrow a hack. So I shall not have to ask Lord Everett after all."

"You must still ask his permission, when we go to dine. No, do not rip up at me! I did not say you may not ride tomorrow. I am heartily glad that you and Rolf are become friends so quickly, and I do not mean to meddle, I assure you."

"Good," said Gerard, and reached for a bowl of cherries.

He was disgusted, two days later, to discover that he was expected to don knee-breeches for dinner at the Great House.

"What is the use of living in the country," he complained bitterly, "if you have to dress as though you were in town?"

Gabrielle had no patience with him.

"Don't be a clunch," she said. "If Rolf says knee breeches are customary, then you will wear them. Do you want to seem an underbred hayseed? Be thankful that at least you can get into them with ease."

A piercing groan from Lady Harrison's chamber lent meaning to her words. However, when her ladyship appeared, she announced with pride that Marie thought she had already lost an inch or two. Gerard rose to the occasion.

"If I am to escort two such beautiful ladies," he said, "then I do not mind so much that I have to wear knee breeches."

The Everetts sent a carriage to fetch them, a propitious beginning to a thoroughly enjoyable evening. Gabrielle was disconcerted to note that Lord Everett again kept glancing at her with a puzzled look, but she was soon won over by his charm and kindness.

Without the least condescension, he satisfied her curiosity about the multifarious crops growing on the Wrotham lands, and even offered to show her about the estate and the farms if she should like it. Whatever persuasion it had taken to force him to retire to the country, it was plain that he now took great pride in his once-neglected land.

By the time the ladies retired from the table, Gabrielle was perfectly able to understand why Lady Cecilia had chosen to wed a gentleman so many years her senior.

When the schoolroom party joined them in the drawing room later, she was pleased to note that his lordship extended his polite consideration to the governess. Since she might one day have to seek such a situation for herself, it was good to know that such employers could be found. Lord Everett also showed himself to be a benign, even indulgent, parent. It was Lady Cecilia who hushed the children when the game of lottery tickets grew noisy, and she who sent them up to bed before the tea tray was carried in.

All in all, thought Gabrielle sleepily, lying in bed and gazing out of the open window at the moonlit park, it had been the most delightful evening she had ever spent. Only one thing had made it less than perfect: Luke's absence.

And Papa's, she added guiltily.

At that very moment, Lord Everett was entering his wife's dressing room, clad in a dragon-embroidered dressing gown of Chinese silk. He dismissed her maid, kissed the back of her neck, and sat down in the comfortable wing chair which was set there for just that purpose.

"You don't need that," he said indulgently, watching her splash her face with Distilled Water of Green Pineapples. "You have the best complexion I've ever seen. Tell me, where did Luke come by the Darcys?"

"Do you like them?"

"Yes. They made a good first impression when I met them in London, and they improve upon acquaintance. Especially the girl. But I should like to know who they are and what they are doing in my Dower House. And do not tell me that story about consulting Lady Harrison about redecorating the place. You have never shown the least inclination in doing the place over before, and it has been in its present state these thirty years and more!"

"Lady Harrison *does* have exquisite taste."

"Cut line, my lady!"

Lady Cecilia went to sit on the arm of his chair, and ran her fingers through his silver hair.

"I have hopes that Luke may marry the young lady," she confessed.

"Ha, so that's it! What makes you think that this one is any different from the dozens of eligible maidens you have cast in his way any time these ten years? He has not so much as risen to a one of them."

"It's true he has never taken the bait, but Miss Darcy is not of my choosing. He positively insisted that I presume upon an exceeding slight acquaintance with Lady Harrison in order to obtain an introduction to the Darcys. However, I cannot get it out of my head that he had met her before. Since she is but recently come from France, it may be that she is in some way connected with his work at the Foreign Office."

"A spy! Good God! And you want me to take her into the bosom of my family?"

"Not a spy precisely. Though if she was, I am sure she would be on our side, for you know how patriotic Luke is. But she is by far too well bred to be a vulgar spy. Do you not think that she is of gentle birth?"

"On the wrong side of the blanket, most like. She does resemble someone I know, though I cannot bring to mind just who. But all this is beside the point. She has no fortune, I take it? Luke cannot afford to marry for love."

Knowing well how much he blamed himself for the situation, she kissed his furrowed brow and gently stroked his clenched fist until it relaxed in her warm clasp.

"Henry," she said, "I have always respected your decision not to inform my parents about our difficulties. But if it is a matter of Luke's future, if it would make the difference between his losing or gaining the hand of the woman he loves, then I will not let pride stand in the way. Neither mine nor yours."

Bowing his head, he gripped her hands fiercely in both his, then slowly nodded.

"As you will."

He picked her up and carried her in still-strong arms into their bedchamber.

In the morning, Lord Everett sent a groom with a note to Gabrielle, asking whether it would be convenient for him to call for her at noon to ride about the estate. She dressed with care in her only riding habit, of deep red Circassian cloth. The red-dyed feather in her hat had broken on the journey, but Marie managed to trim it so that it was at least respectable. Remembering his lordship's speculative gaze, scarcely less piercing than his son's, she was determined to appear immaculate.

On the dot of twelve, the doorbell rang. Lord Everett's courtesy extended to punctuality, it seemed. Gabrielle pulled on her gloves while Tombaugh opened the front door. Facing the bright sunshine, she made out only the silhouette of the gentleman standing on the step. It was not the baron, whose figure, though admirable for his age, had undeniably lost its youthful leanness.

"Are you ready, Miss Darcy?"

"Luke! I mean, Mr Everett!"

"Luke will do very well." She could hear the smile in his voice.

"I thought you were not coming back." Her fingers trembled as she laid them on his sleeve.

"There was no urgent news at Dover to send me hurrying back to London, so I yielded to inclination. I cannot stay longer than a day or two, though, so I trust you will not object if I join you and my father on your ride?"

She suddenly realised that Lord Everett was waiting, mounted on a black horse and holding the reins of two more.

"Good morning, sir. Is that mare for me? How pretty she is!"

"Not as pretty as her rider," said his lordship promptly. "I apologise for my son's presence. He arrived early and has been chafing at the bit this hour and more. It was more than I could do to persuade him that we do not wish for company."

Blushing, she allowed Luke to help her mount. He whispered in her ear something provocative about knowing she preferred to ride astride, which she pretended not to hear.

The mare was as easy-mannered as she was good-looking, and Gabrielle was soon comfortable enough to spare her attention for the guided tour. Why, then, did she find when she reached home that she retained only the vaguest impression of acres of plum trees and endless plantations of hazel bushes, laden with still-green nuts?

The only thing she recalled clearly was Luke's smiling eyes when he asked whether she cared to drive with him next day to Ightham, to see the moated manor house and the prehistoric hill fort.

"Prehistoric?" she murmured vaguely. "It sounds fascinating."

Lord Everett was much inclined to believe that his wife was right!

Lady Cecilia raised her eyebrows when the proposed outing was revealed to her.

"You will take your man, I suppose," she said, "or one of the grooms."

"Is that really necessary?" asked Luke, frowning. "It is an open carriage and it is no more than three miles." He remembered the midnight escapade to Lincoln's Inn, where their only chaperon had been a burglar, but that was not something he could describe to his stepmother!

"Yes," she answered flatly. "You know how people talk, and I am sure you will not wish to give them reason to talk about Miss Darcy."

"Of course not. But to have Baxter up behind! I know, I'll see if Dorrie and Rolf, oh, and Gerard will go with us. Rolf may drive the gig. Will that satisfy your notions of propriety, ma'am?"

"That will be unexceptionable," she said, lips twitching. A second carriage full of young people would allow Luke and Gabrielle far more privacy than a servant in the same carriage. "Just do not forget that it is Sunday. If you miss the early service you must be back for evensong."

Pulling a face, Luke agreed. In London his churchgoing was sporadic, to say the least, but here in the country one was expected to set a good example.

Informed of the treat in store for him, Rolf grumbled that if he was expected to squire his sister about, he had rather have stayed in Cambridge.

"I've seen that devilish moat a thousand times if I've seen it once," he said indignantly.

"Sorry," said his brother, grinning. "But we shall go up to the hill fort also, and you and Gerard may re-fight all the putative battles of the Stone Age."

Rolf's face lightened. "By Jove, you're right! I'll go and tell cook to put up a couple of hampers for lunch."

To his sister, Luke presented an invitation rather than an order. Dorothea accepted listlessly. She supposed she might as well do that as anything else.

Luke took her hand. "You are unhappy," he said. "Do you miss the gaiety of London?"

"Not in the least." She pulled her hand away. "I do not care for parties. Pray leave me alone, Luke. I have the headache."

Gerard, basking in the pleasure of having a friend of his

own age with whom he had no need be on guard, as he had in Switzerland, made no demur.

Only the weather could now upset Luke's plans.

The weather cooperated. A few high mare's-tails wisped in the western sky, but the sun shone bright and the cooling breeze was welcome.

The family at the Mote, the medieval manor in Ightham, were at home, delighted to see the Everetts and happy to show off their house to the Darcys. The two young ladies thought a picnic on Oldbury Hill the best idea in the world, could not imagine why they had not thought of it themselves. Their brother, who was preparing for the ministry, was persuaded that it was not unthinkably wicked to eat *al fresco* on the Lord's Day, and they joined the party.

With the group thus enlarged, Luke could not in common politeness monopolise Gabrielle. He was amused to see that the future churchman was greatly taken with her. How shocked he would be if he knew the half of her adventures!

A thin haze of clouds spread gradually over the sky, and the ladies, in their thin muslins, began to shiver as the breeze grew stronger. Two hours exploring the grass-grown ruins proved enough even for Gerard and Rolf, and the hampers had long since been emptied of all but crumbs and ants.

They walked down the hill to the carriages, and farewells were said. Gabrielle and Dorothea donned the wraps they had brought with them, Luke and Rolf took up the reins, and they set out for Wrotham.

A mile or two beyond Ightham they came to a crossroads. The gig, in the lead, went straight across.

"Are you warm enough?" asked Luke, turning to Gabrielle. "Then we will turn left here and go home a different way. It is a little longer but very pretty."

Since he forgot to watch where he was going, it turned out to be considerably longer.

"How on earth did we get here?" he said in surprise as they drove into a small town.

"The horses brought us," said Gabrielle. "Are we not where we are supposed to be?"

"No! This is Sevenoaks. I must have missed the turn. Lord, look at the time!" He pointed at the church clock. "I promised to be back by evensong and we shall never make it."

"*I* got up early and went to the eight o'clock service," said Gabrielle, putting on a saintly face. "We could stay here, look about the town, and then go to evensong here."

"I must not keep you out so long. Gerard will be wondering where you are."

"Fustian! Gerard knows better than to worry over me."

"Lady Harrison, then. I expect she and my stepmother will ring a peal over me for endangering your reputation."

"Have you endangered my reputation?"

"Not in the least. But you know how elderly ladies fuss."

"You cannot call Lady Cecilia elderly! I daresay she is not many years older than you are. And madame is of an age with my father, I believe, though she looks older because of what she refers to as her *embonpoint*."

He laughed. "All the same, we will go home now." Driving round the town square, he directed his team back down the lane by which they had arrived. "Have you not heard from your father yet?" he asked seriously.

"No, not a word."

Hearing the tremor in her voice, he said, "Communications with the continent are particularly difficult at present, as I have reason to know. You must not think that because you have received no news, he has sent none."

"If we were only expecting a message! But he told us he would follow us here if we decided to come without him. He should have arrived by now, I am sure."

"What is his business? What might have delayed him? Wait, here is the turn and I nearly missed it again." They entered a narrow lane so overhung by huge oaks that it

153

formed a long, dark tunnel. "You have a shocking effect on my driving, Miss Darcy."

"How fortunate that the evenings are so light at this season, in spite of the clouds, or I daresay we should be hopelessly lost. I wish you will call me Gabrielle, since you have said that I may call you Luke."

"May I?"

"You may, as long as you promise never to shorten it to Gaby, as Gerard does. He used to call me Gabby, when he was little. I don't know which is worse—to be named a simpleton or a chatterbox!"

"Since you are neither, Gabrielle, I have no difficulty in promising. Yours is a beautiful name that does not deserve abbreviation. Mine is different. I have always been called Luke, except when I was in a scrape as a child. I beg that you will never call me Lucius!"

"Unless I am excessively displeased with you," she said, laughing. "I make no promises; I shall hold it in reserve."

They drove out of the tunnel of oak trees. The sky was by now dark grey and threatening, and Luke urged the horses to a trot. They reached Wrotham village as the church clock struck seven, and a few minutes later pulled up outside the Dower House.

Tombaugh came out to hold the horses while Luke helped Gabrielle down from the tilbury.

"There's a visitor, miss," he said. "Come to stay a couple o' days, my lady says."

"Oh? Who is it, Tombaugh?"

"A Monser Derveenar, miss. A Frenchie, I reckon."

"Alain! How delightful! You know Alain de Vignard, don't you, Luke? Will you come in?"

"Thank you, no. I had better get on home, for I must leave early tomorrow. Goodbye, Miss Darcy."

As he climbed back into the carriage, a few drops of rain fell.

— 16 —

"I DON'T LIKE to bear tales, miss," said Tombaugh ominously.

Luke called me 'Miss Darcy!' thought Gabrielle. What is amiss?

"But the wife says as it's me clear, bounden dooty."

Perhaps he does not like it that Alain has come to visit?

"And I couldn't tell her la'ship, being as she's so almighty fond o' the woman."

He could not suppose that *she* was responsible!

"But I seen it wi' me own eyes. Swear to it in a court o' law, I would."

She had not invited him, after all. He was far more Madame's friend than hers.

"Right there, they was, under them elm trees: Mam'selle Marie hobnobbling wi' Master Luke's man Baxter."

No, he was just being discreet, observing strict propriety in the presence of Tombaugh.

"*What* did you say, Tombaugh?"

"Her la'ship's abigail, out there right early this morning she were, hobnobbling wi' Baxter."

"Hobnobbing with *Baxter!* You must be mistaken."

"Wi' me own eyes I seen it," he repeated obstinately. "Called the missus, didn't I, and she'll say the same. 'Tain't right, she says, and miss ought to be tol'."

"How odd!" Gabrielle remembered how Marie and Mrs Tombaugh had nearly come to cuffs over the raspberry tarts. Any tattle from that quarter must be taken with a pinch of salt! "I am sure there is a perfectly reasonable explanation," she soothed. "It may be that Baxter was bearing a message for Lady Harrison from Lady Cecilia."

Tombaugh snorted.

"Up to no good," he muttered. "That Baxter's allus been a queer nabs, if you was to ask me. Neither groom nor gentleman's gentleman, not properly."

"That's enough!" said Gabrielle sharply. "I do not care to hear you criticising either Mr Everett's or her ladyship's choice of servants. You will not refine upon this incident, if you please. I wish to hear no more about it."

Baxter, she knew, was far more than groom or valet to Luke. If spiteful minds had not invented the whole story, it was possible that he was engaged upon some investigation for the Foreign Office. Rumours floating about the countryside could only hinder him.

"You will not speak of this again," she repeated firmly, and went on into the drawing room.

Alain was alone there, looking out of the window as he had been the first time she had seen him, in Russell Square. When he turned, she thought he looked as handsome as ever but thinner, his face almost haggard.

"Are you unwell?" she asked, stepping forward with hands outstretched. "You do not look at all the thing."

He took both hands and raised one to his lips.

"Right as a trivet," he said with an effortful smile, "if I have that extraordinary English phrase correct. How do you go on, Miss Darcy?"

"Very well. Is madame gone up already?"

"Yes, and Gerard is not home yet. She vows that if he is late for dinner again, he shall not eat."

"No fear of that! If he may not eat in the dining room, he will do very well in the kitchen. I had best go change for dinner myself, or *I* shall be late."

"Wait! A moment, Miss Darcy. I had hoped to have a private word with you."

She looked at him closely. "There is something wrong,

isn't there. Dorothea?" Sitting down, she waved him to a chair.

He bit his lip. "Yes. I hoped we had not drawn attention to ourselves, but if you observed us, her mother and brother must have done so also. She suspected that was why she was forced to leave London early."

"So I guessed. You are come down to meet her?"

"I did not intend to. I wanted only to see her surroundings, find out whether she was well, perhaps catch a glimpse of her in the distance. I know there is no future for us, and I have told her so a thousand times. She is born for better than to be shackled to a penniless refugee, even if this ghastly business . . . even if her family did not stand in the way. I ought not to see her."

"Probably not." It was Gabrielle's turn to bite her lip. "But it is my belief she is pining for you. She has been in the megrims ever since we came here, though she has not confided in me."

"She is the dearest, sweetest angel! I cannot bear to think that she is unhappy. What must I do, Miss Darcy? I would not have her think I have abandoned her, yet to give her false hope were the act of a scoundrel!"

"What a coil! Oh dear, I do not know what to advise."

"No, it was infamous of me to burden you with our troubles. I must make up my own mind. But if I decide to ask her to meet me, will you be my messenger?"

"Yes, if you will promise that should she refuse, you will accept her decision gracefully and not attempt again to contact her."

"I promise." Alain's face was agonised. "If she should have the strength to reject me of her own free will, then all the love I bear her could not justify further endeavours on my part."

"Gabrielle!" Gerard burst into the room, this time comparatively clean but decidedly dishevelled. "Rolf is teaching me to drive the gig! Is it not famous? Oh, hello, Alain. You must come out with us tomorrow and I will show you.

I nearly made it through the gate on the second try, but the back wheel caught on the post."

"I hope you were not going too fast, then!" said Gabrielle. "But at present, speed is what is needed. We have fifteen minutes to change for dinner."

Up at the Great House, Luke had changed his clothes hurriedly and was tapping on the door of his father's dressing room.

"Come in!" called Lord Everett. "Oh, it's you, Luke. Did you have a pleasant day?"

"Delightful, thank you, sir, except for a discovery I made at the end of it."

"Discovery? What sort of discovery? Damme, my boy, cut the mystery if you please!"

"Has my stepmother told you of a young Frenchman who was seeing altogether too much of Dorothea in town?"

"She mentioned him in passing. De Vigny, or some such name. Seemed to think him a charming young man who knew his station in life too well to presume. No encroaching mushroom, she said. What of him?"

"Since he is the Vicomte de Vignard, he cannot precisely be described as a mushroom, but for all his title he ekes out a meagre living as a secretary. He is staying at the Dower House as guest of Lady Harrison."

"Hmm. You think he has designs on Dorrie?"

"What else *can* I think, sir? The man is devilish attractive to the ladies, and I fear Dorrie has warmer feelings for him than she ought."

"If he is a fortune-hunter, all we need do is drop a hint that her marriage portion cannot possibly be considered sufficient to set up household."

"Oh, I acquit him of more than a passing interest in her fortune. To speak bluntly, judging by appearances he is head over heels in love with her!"

"I shall speak to her mother about it. Dorrie was always the most obliging child. A word in her ear . . ."

"Both Lady Cecilia and I have dropped words in her ear, to no avail. He must be sent packing, sir, and forbidden to return to Wrotham."

"Come, come, Luke! I cannot possibly so insult Lady Harrison's guest on no more than a suspicion. You may be sure that I shall watch the situation, and take appropriate measures if necessary."

"Henry?" Lady Cecilia appeared at the door. "Are you ready, you two? The gong will ring in a few moments."

"Coming, my dear. Luke has been telling me that that young Frenchman you spoke of is staying at the Dower House."

"De Vignard? Oh dear! But it will not do to order Dorrie not to see him. Nothing encourages fancied love like oppression! I shall take her down there tomorrow morning, so that she may meet him unexceptionally in company."

"I'll give you ten to one," said his lordship hopefully, "that after a week's absence, she has already forgot him."

Alain was not in when Lady Cecilia and Dorothea arrived at the Dower House next day. Since her mother had thought best not to inform her of this presence, Dorothea chatted quite happily with Gabrielle, while the older ladies made plans to tour the house.

Nor did Gabrielle mention Alain. He had not yet told her his decision, and she did not want to distress her friend unnecessarily. So when he walked into the drawing room, Dorothea was unprepared. The incredulous joy on her face left no room for doubt in Lady Cecilia's mind that her husband had been too sanguine, and a glance at the young man only confirmed that their feelings were mutual.

There was nothing to cavil at in Alain's manners. He first bowed very properly over her ladyship's hand before addressing Dorothea.

"How do you do, Miss Everett?" he said, and if he held her hand an instant too long, it was only an instant.

"*Monsieur!*" she breathed, eyes aglow. Neither of them

seemed to feel the need of any further conversation, but their gazes never left each other, and both answered at random when spoken to.

Gabrielle could not help but wonder what it must be like to be so in love with someone who loved you too.

"Dorothea!" said Lady Cecilia firmly at last. "Lady Harrison is going to take me about the house and explain to me what she thinks ought to be done."

"Yes, Mama."

"You shall come with us. I am sure you cannot help but benefit from her advice against the day when you will furnish your own house."

"Oh no, Mama! I mean, I expect I should learn a great deal from her ladyship, but Gabrielle and I were going to walk down to the village."

"I am sure any errands you have can wait until the morrow. If not, you may send a maid or one of the footmen. Miss Darcy will hold you excused, will you not, Miss Darcy?"

"Of course, ma'am." Gabrielle could hardly say anything else.

Alain offered to accompany her to the village. But though he made an effort, he was not a lively companion. She showed him the church, and the endless memorials to Everett ancestors seemed to depress him still further.

On the way back he confessed that seeing Dorothea in her family setting had made him, if possible, the more aware of his unworthiness.

"But your family is just as good, is it not? The French nobility is in no way inferior to the British."

"True. By birth I am her equal. But this magnificent estate . . . compared to my single room! In London, in society, the difference was less noticeable. Here, I am nothing!"

Since she could not but agree, Gabrielle held her tongue.

Alain left the next morning, without meeting Dorothea again. No sooner had the hoofbeats of his hired horse died away than Tombaugh approached Gabrielle, his face fore-boding.

"Can I have a word wi' you, miss?"

"Of course. What is it?"

"I don't like to bear tales, miss."

"I've heard this before, Tombaugh! If you have seen Marie talking to Baxter again, pray keep it to yourself."

" 'Tweren't Baxter, miss. Monser Derveenar, it were. Right in this house! We ain't had such goings-on in this here house in a dunnamany years."

The thought of 'goings-on' between stringy, bad-tempered Marie and lovesick Alain was too much for Gabrielle's gravity. She laughed.

"I bain't joking, miss," said Tombaugh, offended. "Heard every word, I did, only they was talking that heathen Frog lingo, so I couldn't make it out. Abovestairs, just outside her la'ship's dressing room it were, and at an ungodly hour of the night, too."

"I care not what hour of the night it was!" Gabrielle was angry. "If you and Mrs Tombaugh will not drop this ridiculous feud with Marie, who has been with my lady for years, then I shall be forced to report it to Lady Cecilia."

The servant looked sulky, but bowed and said, "Very well, miss." As he left, she heard him mutter, "Just you wait till we're all a-murdered in our beds!"

There was no change in the quality of service provided by the Tombaughs, so if they had not gone so far as to mend their fences with Marie, at least they did not hold it against their temporary employers. Gerard, in fact, was a firm favorite in the kitchen, to which he repaired at any hour of the day when overcome by pangs of hunger.

Rolf frequently joined him, but their depredations on the larder were more than compensated for by the baskets of produce carried down from the Great House every day. Nothing that the gardens and orchards of Wrotham produced was lacking, from raspberries, cherries and blackcurrants to all kinds of vegetables—and even chickens, pigeons and a ham. To this Gerard added the odd rabbit, and when he was persuaded to add up the household accounts, he said he could not believe how cheap it was to live in the country.

A month passed. There were picnics, morning visits to neighbours, dinners at the Great House, a subscription ball at the Assembly Rooms in Maidstone. They were invited to attend Open Day at Knole, near Sevenoaks, the vast and magnificent mansion of the Earl of Dorset. Sponsored by Baron Everett, the Darcys merged into County society without the least effort on their part, and enjoyed it prodigiously.

Now and then they met Sir Oswald Harrison, with his pallid, subdued wife and sharp-faced daughter who, two or three years older than Gabrielle, might fairly be considered to have ended on the shelf. Their small estate was situated not far off, near Tunbridge Wells. Warned by Lady Harrison that, as far as she knew, Mr Everett's investigation was continuing, they spoke to them politely but as rarely as possible, and avoided them when they could.

Sir Oswald was jovial in his cold way, and curious beyond the bounds of politeness about their sojourn at Wrotham. They received his promise of a visit as a threat, but the weeks passed and he did not come.

Nor did Luke come, nor Alain, nor Gabrielle and Gerard's father. July passed into August, and Gabrielle knew Luke must have gone to Dover and back on his monthly visit without stopping to see them.

Had the news from France been so urgent it brooked no delay? Or was he deliberately staying away from Wrotham? And if so, why?

— 17 —

Mr Everett posted north to Harwich. The French invasion force gathering in Boulogne was so thoroughly blockaded by the British fleet that the details of its doings had to travel all the way to Holland and across the North Sea to reach England. The Man in the Green Coat paced impatiently from end to end of the coffee room of the Anchor Inn; five days he'd waited while squalls delayed the crossing.

When the news came, borne by a friendly American, it was nothing new. The Corsican Monster continued to gather his *Grande Armée;* troop transports and landing craft were abuilding by the thousand; the construction of artificial harbours proceeded apace. To the ignorant it looked thoroughly alarming.

Mr Everett wondered whether it would be worth the effort to try to persuade the government that spending millions on raising a volunteer defense force was unnecessary. Even if good weather coincided with a momentary lapse on the part of the blockading fleet, it would take the French so long to sail out of their basins that the situation would have changed before they were all at sea. And besides, the transports would be sitting ducks before the guns of the Royal Navy.

Wearily he hastened back to London. As expected, his arguments went for nothing.

Mr Everett posted south to Brighton. The Duke of York,

favourite brother of the Prince of Wales, wanted to lead an expedition to free the Dutch from the French yoke.

He spent a frustrating week of luxurious living at the magnificent Pavilion, attending balls and musicales, card parties, breakfasts and endless dinners. At last he obtained a private interview and succeeded in convincing His Royal Highness that the time was not yet ripe for an invasion of the continent.

Hurrying back to London, he found that Georges Cadoudal had talked the government into subsidising his Royalist uprising to the tune of a million francs.

Mr Everett posted east to Dover. Le Hibou did not fail him. Méhée de la Touche was indubitably an agent of Fouché. The supposed conspiracy against Bonaparte was nothing but a plot to draw *émigrés* back to France and implicate General Moreau and anyone else foolish enough to oppose the First Consul.

Back in London, red-eyed from lack of sleep, he explained the intrigue to Hawkesbury, Cadoudal and Pichegru. Pichegru agreed to put off his return to France pending further investigation. Cadoudal, with his million francs in his pocket, was making preparations to depart at the end of August and no argument could sway his determination.

Lord Hawkesbury shrugged. The money had been handed over, there was nothing he could do.

As far as Mr Everett was concerned, there was only one good point to the whole business. General Pichegru's secretary, Alain de Vignard, had been present at the meeting. Therefore he was not in Kent, dangling after Dorothea.

"What have you dug up on de Vignard?" he asked Davis the next morning, striding into the office well past noon. "And Harrison, too. Any results?"

"Good afternoon, sir. There is nothing to implicate Sir Oswald in any sort of espionage, other than his excessive curiosity when he calls in here. Nothing to suggest that he tries to pass on anything he learns."

"Then it looks as if I shall have to tackle him myself,

about the other matter. Devil take it! Strictly speaking it is none of my business. He'll have every right to take umbrage."

"If I may make so bold, sir, you might claim an interest on the grounds of being Sir Cosmo's successor here at the Foreign Office. Keeping an eye on a colleague's widow, if you see what I mean, sir."

Mr Everett frowned. "Too officious by half. Let's hope he doesn't question my interest. I shan't have a leg to stand on."

"Might *I* ask what your interest is, sir?"

"A friend requested my help," he said hurriedly, somewhat flushed. "What of the Frenchman?"

"Ah now, that's another kettle of fish, sir. The young man has been keeping unsavoury company, that's not to be denied. But there's nothing to justify arresting him. No evidence that he's passed any information, or even that he knows his contacts are on the other side."

"And if we pick up the contacts, we'll scare him off and never learn any more. There's genuine cause for suspicion though, right?"

"I'm afraid so, sir. We're keeping a close eye on him."

"I suppose there's no harm in him learning what Pichegru and Cadoudal are up to. De la Touche knows every move before they make it. Le Hibou has provided all the evidence I could ask for, and they won't listen to a word."

"There's another message from Le Hibou, sir. Came in while you were in Dover, by another route."

"What does he say?"

"He's coming to England in September, sir, and that'll be the end of it. After twenty years, Le Hibou is resigning!"

Gabrielle set a final stitch in the hem of her riding dress and shook it out.

"There," she said, "just in time. Rolf and Dorrie are fetching us at half past twelve for a picnic."

"I shall buy you a new habit," insisted Lady Harrison.

"That one grows positively shabby. I have saved a great deal of money living here, and I shall not buy any new dresses myself until I am sure I shall lose no more weight."

"You must not fade away entirely, madame! You are looking simply marvelous already."

"Marie had to take in another two inches yesterday," beamed her ladyship, preening. "I feel twenty years younger."

"And look it! Are you sure you will not come picnicking with us?"

"You go on horseback, *n'est-ce pas?* For this I am not yet ready. Where are you going?"

"To a chalk quarry up on the downs. It sounds odd, but Rolf swears it is an excellent place for a picnic, sheltered from the wind, and Dorrie says it is full of wildflowers because it is never mowed. Oh, here they are and I am not changed yet! Pray tell them I will not keep them a moment."

The quarry turned out to be as delightful as promised. Long disused, it was comfortably carpeted with the short, crisp grass of the downs. They tied their horses to a sapling near the entrance, spread rugs, and opened the hamper provided by the Everetts' cook. Being by now well acquainted with that genius, Gabrielle had eaten no breakfast and was able to fully appreciate the ham and egg pie, cold roast chicken, greengages and crumbly yellow cheese.

Satiated, they lay back and watched the snow-white cloud puffs race across the sky, talking desultorily. Dorothea named for Gabrielle the multitude of flowers surrounding them: deep blue rampion and pale blue chicory, tall foxgloves and tiny lady's-slipper, yarrow, tansy and blood-red pheasant's eye.

"What's that?" asked Gabrielle lazily, pointed at a stand of dark green plants with purple heads like thistles.

"Burdock."

"Burdock? Where?" Rolf sat up and looked around. "Oh, famous! Come on, Gerard. Let's have a battle!"

Mystified but willing, Gerard stretched and rose to his

feet. Rolf picked a handful of burrs, handling them with care, and showed him how the tiny hooks clung to the fabric of their clothes. Moments later they were pelting each other, while the girls shrieked and ran to a ledge a few feet above the floor of the quarry, well out of their way.

Sitting there, they contemplated the prodigious idiocy of brothers, and then moved on to other subjects.

Eventually the boys ran out of ammunition, or possibly enthusiasm, and paused to disentangle the burrs from each other's wildly dishevelled hair.

"Have you ever climbed out of here?" asked Gerard, seeing their sisters on the platform at the side.

"No. The chalk is not very stable."

Gerard scanned the high, uneven walls. "It's a steep slope, but it's not quite vertical. I'll wager it could be done. Look, suppose you started over there, where the girls are. Then up to that ledge on the left, about half way up. See it?"

"Yes. Then there's that sort of crack, leading up nearly to the top. Come on, let's try it."

Naturally they took no notice of Gabrielle and Dorothea's protests. They crept upwards, Gerard in the lead, moving carefully from handhold to handhold until they reached the ledge they had spotted from below.

"That's far enough!" called Gabrielle. "Come down now!"

"Not likely! We're going all the way. We'll meet you by the horses. Don't worry, it's easy!"

Rolf started up the crack, Gerard close behind him. They moved more swiftly now, sure of themselves, until suddenly Rolf stopped. The crack had looked continuous from below, but he had reached a blank patch, with no visible holds. Clinging to the soft rock, he leaned back a little and peered upwards.

"I'll have to go that way," he said, pointing above Gerard's head, "back the way we came, only higher up. You'd best wait here till I see if there's a way."

He pulled himself up until he was spreadeagled against

the face, just above Gerard, then began to inch sideways. The girls watched, holding their breath.

His foothold gave way. With a cry of dismay he scrabbled at the wall, then tumbled backwards down the cliff. A flying foot caught Gerard on the shoulder, dislodged him, and sent him sliding and slithering downwards, feet first, scoring a path in the soft chalk.

"Gerard!" Gabrielle picked up her skirts and ran to him.

Face white with chalk and shock, he stood up and turned to her, then crumpled to the ground.

"It's my ankle," he groaned, "but I'm all right. I think. What about Rolf?"

Dorothea was staring upwards, her hand to her mouth.

"He's up there," she whispered, "caught on the ledge. And he's not moving!"

"Very sensible," said Gabrielle hopefully. "At least he will not fall any farther. Rolf!" she called.

No answer. The sprawled figure lay very still.

"He's badly hurt!" Dorothea's eyes were huge with horror.

"Probably just knocked himself out," said Gerard, trying to reassure both her and himself. He grasped his sister's arm and hauled himself shakily to his feet. "Devil of it is, I don't believe I can climb up to see."

"Certainly not!" said Gabrielle. "I must ride for help."

"Oh no!" cried Dorothea in dismay. "Pray don't leave me here alone! I should not know what to do."

"Well, one of us must go and one stay. Can you ride home on your own?"

"If you will help me mount," said Dorothea. "I'll go to the hop fields, it's closer than the house and all the harvesters are there."

"Come on then, quickly. Gerard, sit right here and don't move. If your ankle is broken, you might damage it permanently. Keep an eye on Rolf, and if you see him move, shout at him to keep still."

The girls hurried towards the horses. As they left the shelter of the quarry, a rider coming up the hill reined in, then spurred forward, calling, "Miss Darcy, Miss Everett! Lady Harrison said I should find you here."

"Alain! I have never been so glad to see anyone in my life! Gerard and Rolf are hurt and Dorothea is going for help."

Dorothea looked up at him, her eyes swimming with tears. He swung down from his mount and took her hand comfortingly, but spoke to Gabrielle.

"What can I do? Shall I go with her, or do you need me?"

"Please stay. Help her mount, then come with me. If we can plan the rescue before anyone arrives, it will go much faster."

Dorothea cantered down the hill, and they hurried back into the quarry.

"Quick!" cried Gerard, as soon as he saw them. "He's moving, but I don't think he hears me."

Alain took in the situation at a glance.

"I must go up to him," he said quietly. "If I cannot bring him down, at least I can keep him still."

"No!" Gabrielle foresaw all too clearly another accident, and *three* injured men on her hands. "It is much too dangerous. We must be able to make him hear!"

Alain shook his head, took off his coat, and started up the cliff.

Gabrielle sat down and hid her face in her hands. She heard Rolf moaning, the small sounds of Alain's boots on the chalk, then Gerard's directions.

"There's a small knob just above you to the right. That's it. Now there's a bad bit, where I fell and scraped it smooth. Oh, well done! Now put your left foot a little lower. Nearly there. By Jove, I couldn't have done it better myself. How is he?"

"Very restless, not more than half conscious. His head is bleeding badly and I don't think I can reach it."

Gabrielle stood up, shaded her eyes and stared upwards.

"How badly? Will he bleed to death?"

"I don't know. Wait a bit, maybe if I crawl round here . . ."

"Oh be careful! Don't let him knock you off!"

Alain, on hands and knees, straddled Rolf's body. With one hand he wrenched off his neckcloth and pressed it to the boy's head. She could hear him talking soothingly, but could not make out the words. Gingerly, he raised his other hand from the ledge, took a handkerchief from his pocket, and used the red-stained neckcloth to bind it about the wound.

"I've bandaged it," he called down. "Now there's nothing to do but wait."

There was a sound of drumming hooves, and Lord Everett rode into the quarry.

"I met Dorothea," he explained curtly, surveying the situation. He raised his voice. "How do you do, Monsieur de Vignard? I am Dorothea's father. How is my son?"

"Not well, my lord. His head looks bad and I think he may have broken his leg. But I am no doctor."

"No, thank God, or doubtless you'd not be up there taking care of him. Dorrie will send for the sawbones as soon as she has told my harvesters to come up here. Can you manage?"

"I shall have to, my lord," said Alain drily. "Even if you could reach us, there is no room on this ledge. I cannot say that it is precisely adequate for two!"

"It's all my fault, sir," said Gerard. "It was my idea to climb the cliff."

The baron turned to regard his white-powdered, scratched, bruised face. "I daresay you did not force Rolf to go up with you," he said gently. "Nor push him down. You look as if you have suffered for your foolhardiness, and you cannot be blamed if Rolf has suffered worse for his. You've hurt your leg?"

"Yes, or I should have stood up when you came, of course. But I think my ankle is only sprained."

"Let us hope so. Miss Darcy, be so good as to go and see if the men are coming yet."

Only his unwillingness to leave the spot indicated his distress at his son's accident. Gabrielle hurried to the entrance and looked down the hill. A dozen men trudged up the slope, carrying ropes and ladders and hurdles. Seeing her waving, they quickened their steps, and a few minutes later she led them into the quarry.

They were not a moment too soon. Rolf was groaning, twisting and turning in pain, and it was all Alain could do to keep the two of them on the ledge. Standing at the bottom, Lord Everett directed the rescue, his voice calm but his fists clenched, face pale and set.

At last Rolf, roped to a hurdle and his leg splinted, reached the ground. His father knelt beside him. The makeshift bandage was soaked through with blood and there was no recognition in the boy's glazed eyes.

Gabrielle stood beside him, one hand on his shoulder. "Concussion," she said. "It is not necessarily as bad as it seems. But he needs attention quickly."

"Take him home," ordered Lord Everett harshly, and rose to clasp Alain's hand with a gratitude beyond words.

After taking care of Rolf at the Great House, the doctor drove down to the Dower House to examine Gerard's ankle.

"How is Rolf?" asked Gabrielle eagerly, as Tombaugh ushered him into her brother's chamber.

He shook his head gravely. "Not like to die, ma'am, but there's no telling yet whether the blow will affect the mind. The leg's a simple fracture, no problem there, but I can't deny I'm not happy about his head. Only time will tell. Now what's the matter with you, young man?"

Gerard endured his probing fingers with clenched teeth. To their relief the doctor decided the ankle was indeed merely sprained, though badly. Cold compresses and a few days rest were prescribed, along with a sleeping draught in case the pain should keep him awake at night.

"I shan't take it," said Gerard firmly as the door closed behind him.

"As you wish," agreed his sister. "However, you *will* stay abed. And if I find you on your feet before he permits it, there will be dire consequences!"

"You say!" he jeered, then sobered. "I *wish* I had never suggested climbing! Suppose Rolf should never properly recover!"

"You must not blame yourself. Lord Everett does not. If you feel the need of penance beyond the pain in your foot, you may look forward to entertaining your bedridden friend for the rest of the summer!"

"Yes I suppose that, whatever happens, our riding and shooting are at an end. How lucky that he taught me to drive! I shall be able to take him out in the gig when he is better."

"Just so long as you do not overturn it!" said Gabrielle. "Rest now and I shall bring up your dinner in a little while."

She went downstairs and found Lady Harrison anxiously awaiting word. She was relieved that Gerard was not badly hurt, distressed to hear that Rolf was in a bad way.

"I must write a note to Lady Cecilia," she said. "Tombaugh shall carry it up this evening."

"Where is Alain?" asked Gabrielle. "I thought he was with you."

"He went up to the Great House to comfort Dorothea. The poor boy feels sadly his own unworthiness, and does not know what to do for the best, expecially now that her parents are so deeply indebted to him." She brightened. "Gabrielle, while you were out I received great news: a message from your father!"

"Madame! Then he is still alive! Oh, what did he say?"

"He sends us all his love, and he will be with us before the end of next month!"

—18—

LUKE WOKE EARLY and contemplated the day before him with loathing. After all his travels he had spent a week catching up on paperwork, and there was at least another week's worth left before he would be able to spare the time to go down to Wrotham.

It was over a month since he had seen Gabrielle. Did she remember that day at Ightham with the same pleasure that he did? Was she enjoying herself at his home, or was she bored with country pleasures and longing for adventure? Surely it could not be as dull as her life in Neuchâtel, he reassured himself.

Baxter stuck his bald head round the door, saw that his master was awake, and came in.

"Letter, sir."

"The post cannot have come yet. Where is it from?"

"Wrotham, sir."

"Give it here." He sat up and rubbed his eyes. "Who brought it?"

"Groom, sir."

Luke scanned the brief note from his father.

"My brother has had an accident. We leave for Kent at once."

"Mr Davis, sir?"

"Yes, notify him. No, wait. Devil take it, I shall have to take some work down with me or we'll never get straight. We'll leave at noon, Baxter, on the dot."

"Sir."

Luke bounded out of bed. Mingled with his concern for Rolf was gladness at the prospect of seeing Gabrielle so soon.

They arrived at Wrotham in mid-afternoon. While Baxter, eagle-eyed, supervised the removal of several locked boxes of papers from carriage to study, Luke hurried to the drawing room.

Lady Cecilia had heard his arrival and came out, closing the door behind her.

"Luke, I am glad you are come!"

"How is he, ma'am? What happened?"

"The doctor and your father are with him now. He has broke his leg, but the chiefest worry is his head. He has what the doctor describes as a 'nasty concussion.' He has not been properly conscious since the accident."

Luke put his arm round her shoulders. "How did it come about? What was the rapscallion up to? Come and sit down, Cecilia, you are alarmingly pale."

"No, wait." She resisted the pressure of his arm towards the drawing room. "Rolf and Gerard were climbing in the old quarry. Rolf fell and knocked Gerard down, but Gerard has only a sprained ankle, you need not fear for him. Rolf was stuck on a ledge half way up, and being half conscious was in the utmost danger of rolling off. Luke, I know how you dislike and distrust Monsieur de Vignard, but you must admire him now! He climbed up there, in peril of life and limb, and stayed with Rolf until help came. We can only be thankful that he was present. Your father and I will never be able to pay our debt to him!"

Luke was at a loss for words.

"So do, pray, try to bring yourself to express your gratitude," she continued, "and at the very least, I beg you will not scowl at him in your fearful way."

"But, Cecilia, there is a very good chance that he may be a French spy!"

She gasped. "No! It cannot be!"

"We have no proof as yet, but the evidence points that

174

way. To insinuate himself into my family may be a very clever move on his part."

"You will not accuse him of causing the accident!"

"No, I cannot see how he could have done that. But . . ."

"Luke, I will not listen to you. He risked his life for Rolf, and nothing you say can change that. Perhaps one day you will arrest him and carry him off, but in the meantime he has my prayers. Now come in, and I hope you will be polite, if only so that he does not guess your suspicions!"

Besides Alain, Dorothea, Gabrielle and Lady Harrison were in the drawing room. There was a flurry of greetings, and before Luke found himself obliged to speak specifically to Alain, the doctor came in.

Silently all eyes turned to him.

"Master Rolf is much improved, my lady," he announced. "He recognised his lordship and asked after Mr Darcy. I have every expectation that his mind is undamaged. However, he is not yet out of danger. At all costs he must be kept quiet or I will not answer for the consequences."

The verdict was so uncertain that no one had anything to say. Lady Cecilia broke the silence.

"Thank you," she said to the doctor. "We will do our best to keep him calm. Lady Harrison, you will excuse me if I go up to him now."

"*Mais certainement, madame.* Gabrielle, come, it is time we went home. Gerard will be wondering where we are."

"May I go with you, ma'am?" asked Luke. "I have a lowering feeling that my presence may be considered too exciting for my brother, so I shall inflict myself on Gerard instead."

Gabrielle smiled at him, stars in her eyes. "Yes, do come," she said, "and stay for dinner. You can help Alain carry Gerard down, and then perhaps he will stop complaining about being cooped up in his chamber. He is fretted to death about Rolf, you know."

She turned to Dorothea, who was looking rather lost,

and added, "Dorrie, surely your mama will not object to you joining us?"

They strolled down through the gardens to the Dower House. At first Luke kept a strict watch on Alain en route, though he had much rather have been looking at Gabrielle, but his gaze kept sliding in a puzzled way to Lady Harrison. At last he tugged on Gabrielle's arm and held her back while the others went on.

"What has happened to your Madame Aurore?" he asked. "She is vastly changed since I last saw her, but I cannot put my finger on the difference."

She giggled. "That is because the difference is an absence. She has lost I know not how many pounds of her *embonpoint*. She begins to look almost beautiful, does she not?"

"Unquestionably. She has that superb Parisian carriage and *chic*, now that it can be seen. Would it be improper of me to congratulate her?"

"Not at all. She is prodigious proud of herself and will be delighted that you noticed. Come and tell her." She started after them.

Wait, he wanted to say, did you miss me? But suppose she laughed and said no, she had been too busy by far. Or suppose she said yes . . . He was in no position to follow that opening to its logical conclusion.

He went after her.

Lady Harrison was charmed by his awkward compliment. She was anything *but* charmed when she reached the Dower House and Tombaugh informed her that Sir Oswald Harrison had called and was awaiting her return in the drawing room.

"*Mon dieu!*" she exclaimed. "*Qu'est-ce qu'il veut, ce canaille?* What does this . . . this . . ."

"Scoundrel?" suggested Luke.

"*Ah, bon, merci!* What does this scoundrel want with me?"

"I don't know, my lady," said Tombaugh stolidly, "But

being as he said he's a fair bit from home, and your la'ship's a relative, Mrs Tombaugh made up the back bedchamber."

"*Quelle effronterie!* Mr Everett, what must I do?"

"I will confront him at once if you wish, ma'am. However, I had intended to speak to the lawyer, Hubble, first. And I still think that the best plan."

"Then I must endeavour to treat the *scélérat* with politeness." Lady Harrison swept into the drawing room, and they all followed.

Sir Oswald seemed disconcerted that Luke was present.

"Ah, Everett, you here?" he said inanely.

"As you see. Wrotham is my home, after all."

"Yes, yes, of course, but thought you was fixed in town. Didn't know you was particularly acquainted with my stepmother."

"Exceptionally well acquainted," Luke assured him smoothly. Remembering Davis, he added, "Having succeeded your late lamented father at the Foreign Office, I feel a certain obligation to look out for the interests of his widow, you see."

He was pleased to see that the baronet looked decidedly out of countenance.

Gerard came down for dinner. Between Sir Oswald's forced joviality and the thought of Rolf's uncertain condition, it was not a merry meal. He protested when Gabrielle insisted that he return to bed immediately afterwards, but in a perfunctory way. He was still aching and shaky from his fall.

He begged Luke and Alain to keep him company in a game of cards.

"Otherwise Gabrielle will hover over me," he said. "Sisters can be a dratted nuisance at times."

"They can indeed!" agreed Luke, carefully not looking at Alain, the cause of the only trouble he had ever had with Dorothea.

"You do not know how lucky you are!" the young Frenchman burst out. "If my sister were only . . . But enough! I will go and ask Lady Harrison if she feels in need of my support, and if not I shall be happy to join you in a game." He went out, leaving Luke frowning in thought.

"I've never heard him mention his sister before," said Gerard. "He's not seen her since he escaped from France. I thought she was dead."

"Maybe," said Luke noncommittally.

Alain returned to report that Sir Oswald had already retired, claiming to feel the onset of a cold. They played cards for a while, until Gerard felt sleepy and Luke remembered that he had work to do.

He and Dorothea walked up to the Great House across the moonlit park. They both cautiously avoided Alain's name. Luke ascertained that his brother was sleeping peacefully, and then settled in his father's study with his boxes of papers.

He worked steadily for three hours, until he heard the clock in the entrance hall strike one. With a sigh he put away the documents, locked the boxes, lit a candle and turned out the lamp. He walked to the French doors and looked down the hill towards the Dower House.

The moon was sinking in the western sky, casting mysterious shadows beneath the trees. The leaves, moving restlessly in the breeze, let pass the faint light from a single window. Was Gabrielle still awake? Was she looking up at his light, his single candle, and wondering what he was doing?

The window went dark. He took the candle and went to bed.

Rolf was much improved the next day. On the other hand, Sir Oswald declared himself to be far too ill to depart as intended. Grumbling mightily, Tombaugh carried up his breakfast, and later brought down an empty tray. The cold did not seem to have affected the baronet's appetite.

Lord Everett asked Luke to see after the hop harvesters for him. His determination to stay at Rolf's bedside bewildered Luke, who remembered not seeing his father for months on end during his own childhood. He spoke to Gabrielle about it as they rode between the aromatic vines, watching the men carrying baskets of hops to the oast houses to be dried.

"Dorothea has told me a little about it," she said hesitantly. "I mean, about how he used to be a sad rattle, and a member of the Prince's set, until he retired here. Perhaps you do not realise how much he has changed. I have never met anyone more devoted to his family and his land. And it is a joy to see how much he and Lady Cecilia love each other."

"They do? But he is so much older!"

"It does not seem to matter in the least. I think—you will tell me if I speak too boldly—I think perhaps you are a little jealous of her, for your mother's sake."

"My mother died when I was very small," he said, frowning. "I do not remember her at all. And my father was always in town. I am no part of the family to which he is suddenly so devoted!"

She reached towards him. "Do not say so! His first thought, when it was discovered how badly Rolf was injured, was to send for you. And if you had seen the difference in Lady Cecilia before and after you came! It was as if her burden had been lightened. Dorothea kept saying that it would never have happened had you been here. Oh, you *are* part of that family, never doubt it!"

He took her hand above the row of vines between them, and looked at her searchingly. He had never seen her so earnest, her voice so serious and full of compassion.

"Thank you," he said simply. He pressed her fingers and let go.

She smiled, though teardrops sparkled in her eyes. "I envy you your family," she said.

"You were old enough to remember losing your mother. Do you still grieve for her?"

"That was long ago and far away. One cannot weep

forever. But I have not yet told you *our* great news. My father is on his way home!"

He congratulated her with perfect sincerity, then fell thoughtfully silent. Her father's arrival could not but change his relationship with her, whether for better or worse there was no way of knowing. Who and what was Mr Darcy?

That evening he sat again in the study. On the desk before him lay a half finished report for Lord Hawkesbury, detailing his meeting with the Prince of Wales. His mind was far away.

The house was silent. Though Lord Everett insisted on dining late, he generally retired at eleven and the rest of the household followed suit. An owl hooted in the distance; Luke got up restlessly, walked to the open French door and looked out. Across the park, once again bathed in moonlight, Gabrielle's window was dark.

He returned to the desk and tried to concentrate on Prinny's exact words.

A sound on the terrace outside made him raise his head to listen. He was just beginning to turn when a shot cracked the night, and his lamp went out in a shower of glass. A second shot rang out.

There was a burning pain in his shoulder. He put his hand to it and felt a wetness already beginning to seep through his coat. Standing up, he took two paces towards the figure he dimly saw outlined against the moonlight, then crumpled to the floor.

He came to a moment later, forced himself to his feet and staggered to the mantel. Fumblingly he took the tinderbox, struck a spark and lit a candle. He turned, holding it high with his good arm.

Gabrielle leaned against the doorpost, one hand to her head, the other grasping a pistol.

"You!" he cried, aghast, and sank down on the nearest chair.

She stared at him blankly.

"Go ahead," he said, filled with a vast despair. "Finish it off. I won't try to stop you."

"Luke?" She took a wavering step toward him. Her cloak fell open to reveal the nightdress beneath. "Are you all right?"

She seemed suddenly to notice the gun in her hand, and put it down on a table. Then the enormity of his words seeped in. "Oh, Luke! You don't think *I* shot you? It was a man! I saw him from my window, sneaking up here, and I came as fast as I could. He hit me on the head as he left, and he must have dropped the gun. I don't know why I picked it up. I was a little dizzy."

Flooded with remorse, he saw the red mark on her forehead, already beginning to swell. He jumped to his feet and strode towards her.

"Come and sit down! You are pale as a ghost!"

"So are you," she responded with an attempt at a smile. Then she caught sight of the blossoming red on his shoulder. "Oh, you are hurt! I thought he had missed you. Luke, it is you that must sit down!"

She got him to a chair just as he swooned again.

Baxter was first on the scene. He found Gabrielle trying to staunch the bleeding with a strip torn off her nightdress.

"Cut his coat off," he said with his usual taciturnity. He produced a wicked-looking knife from his pocket and sliced away Luke's ruined jacket and shirt.

The wound, surrounded by a purpling bruise, was small and neat but still bleeding. Gabrielle pressed the cloth against it, recalling the agony of having the bullet dug out of her in the inn at Dover.

"Go fetch the doctor," she ordered Baxter.

"Miss."

The little man stepped aside at the door as Lord Everett appeared, followed by a footman and the butler. Magnificent in his Chinese silk robe, he took one glance at his bloody son and seemed to age ten years.

"Miss Darcy?"

"Someone has shot Luke. I do not think the bullet has touched any vital part, but there is no exit wound and it will have to be extracted. Baxter is going for the doctor."

He did not ask what she was doing in his house, in his study, at midnight. He seemed stunned. "First Rolf and now Luke!" he murmured unbelieving.

Luke opened his eyes and saw his father.

"Sorry, sir," he said with a faint smile. "Hazard of the business. Beg you will go and reassure Lady Cecilia."

The baron crossed to him and squeezed his uninjured shoulder briefly. "My dear boy!" he said helplessly. "My dear boy!"

Lady Cecilia entered the room and, after asking Gabrielle a few quiet questions, took charge. She sent the butler to tell Cook to heat water and the housekeeper to bring linen; the footman, who was busily lighting candles, was to stay, to keep out the other servants and help in any way he could; her husband she persuaded to leave by telling him Rolf was agitated and asking for him.

"Let me take your place, Miss Darcy," she offered.

Gabrielle shook her head. "Thank you, ma'am, I can manage quite well now. There is nothing to be done until the doctor comes."

"Then I shall go and see to the children. You will send for me at once if you need me."

"Thank you, ma'am." No more than Lord Everett had questioned her presence did she wonder why Lady Cecilia was willing to give over Luke's care into her hands. Everything seemed to be taking place in a dream, and one does not ask a dream for motives.

Baxter came back in, after a brief altercation with the footman, who took his duties seriously.

"Sent a groom," he explained.

"Baxter!" Luke's voice was weak but urgent. "Look on the desk."

His bald head gleaming in the candlelight, he obeyed.

"Nothing, sir."

Luke tried to sit up straight, but Gabrielle firmly held him down. "The report!" he exclaimed.

"Pen. Ink. Penknife." Baxter was forced into near loquacity. "Broken lamp. Box on floor, full of papers, lamp oil, glass."

"He's taken my report!"

"Keep still! You will start bleeding again."

"Baxter!"

The many-talented servant nodded as if he had received full instructions, slipped out of the French windows, and disappeared into the dark.

The doctor came before Baxter returned. Luke had swallowed a bumper of brandy and was lying on a sofa swathed with old sheets. He turned his blurry gaze on his manservant, who shook his head.

"Both safe abed," said Luke thickly, then he noticed Gabrielle. "No place for a woman. Messy business."

"You helped *me* in like circumstances."

"Not same 't all. Go 'way."

Her lips tightened. "Don't you tell me what to do, Luke Everett, even if you are drunk as a wheelbarrow. I'm staying."

"Jus' li'l bosky," he protested, and passed out.

—19—

AFTER TWO DAYS in bed, Luke was allowed to descend to the morning room. Gabrielle, who had refrained from visiting him, now found him there, flipping impatiently through the *Gazette*.

"At least they do not seem to have discovered Sir Oswald's stay here," he said, throwing it aside. "Good morning, Gabrielle. How did you enjoy the operation from the other side?"

"It was almost as bad," she admitted, wrinkling her nose. "They told you Sir Oswald decamped before breakfast the next day?"

"Yes. It certainly looks suspicious, but I still think it much more likely that it was de Vignard. I take it you could not identify my assailant?"

"And mine! I still have the bruise to prove it. No, you know how moonlight distorts things, and I was at a distance. In the study, though, I received the impression that it was a large man, and though Alain is tall he is not heavily built."

"Sir Oswald certainly is! Devil take the man, he has muddied the waters! I must see him, and soon."

"Not until you are perfectly recovered. I have had such a time keeping Gerard off his feet. He insisted on coming up today to see Rolf. I think he would have walked, but Lady Cecilia sent the gig. What an exceptionally kind person she is!"

"Don't change the subject. I *must* see Sir Oswald. I seem

to remember a certain someone who went about with a bullet in her side for four and twenty hours, had it extracted, and was off to London by the stage within five days. I shall take a leaf from her book, and go confront Hubble on Thursday."

Gabrielle's protests were seconded by Lady Cecilia. Beyond promising that he would take every care of his health, Luke paid them no heed.

He was closeted with his father in the study for over an hour, and when they came out Lord Everett's arm was about his shoulders, as Dorothea reported to Gabrielle. They had shaken hands heartily but wordlessly. She had no idea what they had been discussing.

On Thursday morning Luke departed for London, taking one of the Wrotham grooms to drive him and leaving Baxter behind. He went first to his office, where Davis was much shocked to see his arm in a sling and hear the story of the assault.

"How can you be sure it was not the young lady as did it, sir?" he asked. "She could have made up the whole story, couldn't she?"

"She had every opportunity to finish the job," pointed out Mr Everett curtly, "or to disappear into the night. Besides, she was hit on the head."

"Could have done that herself. Say she hit her head on the doorpost going out, and then you lit the candle so she knew she'd been seen, and she didn't have time to reload the pistol . . ."

"Gammon! Besides, the report disappeared, and she certainly had no time to hide it."

"Ah, but you were unconscious, weren't you, sir, for quite long enough for her to hide it about her person. I don't suppose you searched her after! You'd be surprised the places a female finds to hide what she wants to hide."

"I will not believe it, Davis! It was Harrison or de Vignard. Since I must in any case see Sir Oswald about

Lady Harrison's jointure, I shall investigate that possibility first. I am going to Lincoln's Inn to see the lawyer. If he knows his dishonesty is discovered, he will cease to aid the baronet."

"You'll take one of the men with you, sir."

"Surely you do not think I shall come to harm at Lincoln's Inn!"

"Better safe than sorry, sir." Davis went to the door and called down the corridor, "Billy!"

Elephantine footsteps announced the approach of a huge man dressed in sober fustian. His face bore a bovine expression, but his deepset, currant-black eyes were shrewd. Though cleaner and altogether more respectable in appearance, in size he reminded Mr Everett of the coal merchant from whom he had rescued Gabrielle.

"Yes, guv?" he enquired.

"This is the chief," said Davis. "Take care of him."

"Right, guv. How do, sir?" He touched his forehead in salute and fixed a critical stare on Mr Everett's sling. " 'Ad a bit o' trouble, 'as you? We won't 'ave no more o' that. Got me pops 'andy." He patted his pockets with a significant nod.

"Hold your tongue, Billy," ordered Davis. "He's a bit of a chatterer, sir, but never been known to let slip anything as ought to be kept quiet."

"Mum's the word, guv," said the giant amiably.

As they drove through the sultry streets towards the Law Courts, Luke wiped his forehead and wished he was back at Wrotham. His shoulder both itched and ached miserably. There had been no rain for over a week; the hot, humid air was full of dust stirred up by carriage wheels, and noisome odours floated from every alley.

Lincoln's Inn was pleasant in comparison. The narrow streets and quiet courtyards were clean, if no cooler, and an occasional tree or plot of close-mown grass provided a contrast to the tall brick buildings.

The groom enquired the way of a hurrying errand-boy, and they pulled up before a door announcing "Hubble, Blayne and Hubble, Attorneys-at-Law."

Last seen by lamplight, thought Luke. What a night that had been!

Billy helped him down solicitously, and followed no more than eighteen inches behind as he stepped up to the door.

"You need not come in with me," he said. "Wait here."

"Not bloody likely, sir! The guv'd 'ave me guts for garters if I was to let you go in there alone."

The obstinate look in his eye suggested that it would be useless to argue. Mr Everett pushed open the door, crossed the lobby, strode past gaping clerks without a word, and entered the inner office with his watchdog at his heels.

"Good afternoon, Mr Hubble," he said, tossing his hat on the desk and taking a seat.

The lawyer was a small man with thin lips and shifty eyes. Although visibly startled by Mr Everett's entrance, he made a swift recover. He picked up a pair of dusty, gold-rimmed pince-nez from the desk and settled them on his nose, effectively hiding his thoughts.

"To what do I owe the honour, Mr . . .?" he asked smoothly.

"To Sir Cosmo Harrison's will. Mr Everett fixed his piercing gaze on the man's face.

If Mr Hubble paled, it was invisible in the murky office. "Harrison . . . ah yes, Sir Cosmo. I recall it distinctly. A simple will, uncontested, passed probate in no time."

"How odd then that you remember it so distinctly. Perhaps some subsequent happening drew it to your attention? Such as the discovery that the terms were not being strictly observed by the chief beneficiary?"

"Impossible, Mr . . . er," snapped the lawyer coldly. He glanced up at the impassive Billy, the first sign he had given of having noticed his presence. "Might I enquire as to your interest in the matter?"

"You may not. I shall inform you, however, that I have seen evidence to that effect, implicating you in a scheme to defraud the dowager Lady Harrison of a considerable part of her income."

"You do not, I assume, have such evidence in your possession."

"No, but I can get it." said Mr Everett, his voice grim. "Immediately and, I believe, without much difficulty." He looked meaningfully at the cupboard door behind Hubble, then up at Billy.

The lawyer was betrayed in a quick peek behind him. "It is possible," he admitted grudgingly, "that Sir Oswald Harrison has been so ill-advised as to embezzle certain funds to which he is not entitled. Entirely without my knowledge, you understand."

"You are fortunate, Mr Hobble, that my principal does not wish for a scandal. If this peculation ceases forthwith and restitution is made, there will be no prosecution."

"I am a poor man, sir! And I cannot answer for Sir Oswald!"

"You may leave Sir Oswald to me. As for your poverty, I believe you exaggerate." Again Mr Everett looked significantly at the cupboard, though hard put to avoid smiling at the recollection of his tame burglar's efforts to pocket a share of the gold within.

Billy took it into his head to step forward at this point.

"A bank draft!" gabbled the lawyer. "At once! Let me call one of my clerks to prepare it."

"Very well." The clerks had all looked half starved, certainly no match for his bodyguard. "But I also require a letter in your own hand, against future need. I will dictate."

An hour later, tired but satisfied, Luke walked up the steps of his London house. In his pocket were a bank draft for a considerable sum, payable to Lady Harrison, and a full confession from Hubble, which he had promised not to use as long as her ladyship received regularly the entire amount of her quarterly allowance.

The next day, accompanied by Billy, he drove beneath lowering thunderclouds down to Sir Oswald Harrison's estate. They stopped at an inn in Goudhurst, the nearest village, and he took off his sling. If it had indeed been the baronet who had attacked him, he did not want to give the man the satisfaction of seeing that he was still suffering.

While the groom asked directions, Billy went into the tap for a mug of ale. When Luke called for him, he was deep in conversation with a man as tall as he was but lean as a rake. He introduced this beanpole as Albert.

"'E's bin keeping 'is eye on this 'Arrison," he explained. "There's another couple o' the boys around, but Albert'll do. 'E don't look much, but 'e's 'andy wiv a shiv."

Albert silently produced a gleaming knife and as silently hid it away again. If Billy looked like a respectable trades-man, then his colleague had more the air of a peddler. Mr Everett wondered what on earth the Harrison household would think of his companions, but by now he knew better than to try to persuade them to stay behind. Billy had slept on a pallet at his feet all night, snoring horrendously, and Albert was doubtless equally dedicated to his duty.

The butler regretted that Sir Oswald was not at home.

Billy and Albert exchanged glances.

"Ho, ain't 'e!" said Billy. "I 'ave hinformation to the contrary, my good man. Just foller Albert, sir. Knows 'is every move, 'e do." Brushing aside the butler along with his objections, Billy ushered Mr Everett in Albert's wake into a room hung with hunting trophies, barely visible in the gloom.

Warned by Billy's heavy tread, Sir Oswald was half way to the door.

"Everett!" he exclaimed. "What a surprise! That stupid man of mine did not tell me it was you, or of course I should not have denied you. What brings you to this neck of the woods? Sit down, man, sit down. And these are . . . ?"

"Friends," said Mr Everett briefly.

Billy and Albert took up posts on either side of the door. Under their concerted stare, the baronet shifted uncomfortably and ran a finger around his collar. His plump face was so pale that the dark, bushy eyebrows to which his step-mother so objected stood out like a smear of ink on a blank sheet of paper.

The uneasy silence was broken by a rumbling of thunder.

"Ah, you were passing by and came in to take shelter from the storm!" said Sir Oswald, grasping at a straw. "Delighted to be of service. Let me call for refreshments." He reached for the bell-pull.

"No!" Mr Everett's shoulder was pounding, making it hard to think. He tried to support the weight of his arm with the other hand.

Sir Oswald swallowed nervously and pulled at his collar again. "Come from Wrotham?" he asked. "How's your brother?"

"I come from London. I went up especially to visit a lawyer, Hubble by name. We had a most interesting interview."

"Oh . . . oh yes? Legal problems, eh?"

"Not mine," Mr Everett assured him. "Yours."

"I don't know what you mean."

Unnoticed, Albert had slipped around the room to a desk on the far side and ransacked it, swiftly and silently. He took a pistol from the bottom drawer, ejected the charge, and tossed it to Billy.

"Take a gander at this 'ere, sir," said Billy, presenting it to Mr Everett.

"It looks remarkably like one that was found in my father's study," he said. "Have you by any chance lost its twin, Sir Oswald? It is, I should say, a duelling pistol, one of a pair?"

A flash of lightning illuminated the baronet's face, eyes

popping, forehead bedewed with sweat. Thunder crashed as if the very heavens were accusing the malefactor. And he seemed to think so, as his bravado evaporated wholly.

"You don't know what it was like," he said in a rapid monotone. "The stupid old woman squandering all that blunt on her precious refugees, while I have a position to keep up, a family to feed, my wife always complaining, my daughter wanting a season in London. I left her plenty, more than most people spend in a decade, I daresay. She just needed to hold household a bit. God knows I've had to." He looked up at the ceiling as a new outburst of rattling grew to a roar that shook the room.

"Taking the Lord's name in vain?" asked Mr Everett.

"I didn't mean to hurt you. But I knew you were investigating, had to stop you. It seemed like a perfect opportunity. I was sure those papers must have something to do with it. I just meant to shoot out the light, then grab them while you couldn't see me."

"Haw!" snorted Billy.

"It's true, God help me!" He cast an anxious glance at the ceiling but the skies ignored him. He jumped up and started towards the desk.

Billy and Albert flanked him immediately.

"I'm just going to get the papers. Tell them, Everett. You want them back, don't you?"

"If you have no further use for them."

"Use? What use are they to me? I've no interest in Prinny's conversation. My God, you don't take me for a spy, do you?"

"The possibility had crossed my mind. You are apt to ask too many questions."

"No, really, just curious, I assure you! You can search the room, search the house, whatever you want!"

"Oh we've a'ready done that," Billy assured him jovially. "In the clear, you was, till this little business come up. 'Ave to send in a report, won't we. This it then? Confidential

Foreign Office papers found in baronet's desk. Don't look good, I 'as to say."

As Sir Oswald sank into his chair, thunder sounded again, more distantly, and a few heavy drops of rain hit the windows.

"Everett, what shall I do? I swear I'm no spy. You're in charge of that department, you can clear me."

"I ought to report our find to the Foreign Secretary . . . "

"To Lord Hawkesbury? No!"

". . . But I am devilish tired of writing reports. Of course, there is the other matter to be considered also."

"I'll pay her back! I swear it! She'll get every penny from now on."

"For your sake, I hope so." Mr Everett rose wearily from his chair. "Billy, Albert, you'll hold your tongues unless I give you the word. Oh, you can tell Mr Davis, of course, but not a hint to anyone else."

"Mum's the word," promised Billy.

Rain was falling in sheets, but Mr Everett refused the baronet's eager offers of shelter and refreshment. Leaving Albert at the inn, they set off for Wrotham. The country lanes quickly turned into a muddy morass, and it took them over three hours to cover the twenty miles.

At last they turned in at the gates. Luke ordered the groom to drive to the Dower House. He wanted to tell Lady Harrison of his success, and to bask in Gabrielle's admiration. They pulled up at the front door.

Billy lumbered up the steps to ring the bell, then returned to help him down. Suddenly weak, he leaned heavily on the big man's arm, and found himself swept off his feet.

"Overdone it. 'asn't you," said Billy severely, and carried him past Tombaugh into the house.

— 20 —

"I'M PERFECTLY ALL right," protested Luke.

Arms akimbo, Gabrielle looked down at his pale face. "I want to see that shoulder," she repeated obstinately.

"C'mon, chief, best do like the lady says," urged Billy.

Luke swung his legs off the sofa on which his bodyguard had deposited him, and stood up. He swayed.

"Sit down!" said Gabrielle and Billy in chorus.

Ruthlessly, but with amazing gentleness, Billy untied the sling, eased off coat and shirt, exposing a bandage stained with red.

"You have started it bleeding again!" Gabrielle frowned. "I knew I should not have let you out of my sight. Men simply have no idea how to take care of themselves."

She sat down beside him and began to unwind the bandage. Acutely conscious of her closeness, Luke watched her intent face. Her cropped hair had grown out into dark, glossy ringlets; long lashes veiled her eyes; her mouth was soft, serious, the tip of her tongue visible as she concentrated. He was shaken by a fierce desire to hold her in his arms, yet he hardly dared breathe for fear of drawing her attention to his emotion.

Her hand brushed his skin. As if the shock that ran through him touched her also, she raised her eyes to his momentarily and a deeper rose tinged her cheeks.

"There!" she said quickly, handing the soiled linen to Billy, who passed it on to the hovering Tombaugh. "It is bleeding only a little now, and I can see no sign of infection. If you promise to follow instructions faithfully, I will not send for the doctor. Tombaugh, bring fresh linen and the basilicum powder, if you please. And tell Mrs Tombaugh that Mr Luke will be staying here tonight."

Luke grinned. "She will have to make up a pallet for Billy beside my bed," he said. "A large pallet. I cannot persuade him to leave my side until we return to London and Davis relieves him of his duties."

"Very well," said Gabrielle, looking up at Billy, who nodded. "I hope Baxter will not take it as a reflection upon his abilities. Now put your feet up, Luke, and while we wait for Tombaugh you shall tell me what you have been doing since you left."

Luke complied. He had just reached the village of Goudhurst and removed his sling, to Gabrielle's exasperation, when Lady Harrison rustled in, looking not a day older than thirty-five in a gown of blue and grey striped silk.

"Mr Everett, you have seen Oswald? Who is *ce gros garçon* and what does he here? Gabrielle, it is not at all *convenable* for a young lady to consort with a gentleman *à demi-nu!*"

Gabrielle draped Luke's shirt across his chest.

"He has been telling me about his interview with Mr Hubble, madame, and had nearly come to Sir Oswald."

"*Recommencez!*" requested her ladyship. "I cannot follow a story begun in the middle."

Luke stopped gaping at the transformation of elderly dowager into handsome matron, pulled himself together, and obligingly returned to Lincoln's Inn.

The story had to be repeated again when Gerard returned from visiting Rolf at the Great House. He was inclined to be disappointed that no duels had been fought, but Lady Harrison and Gabrielle were as grateful and admiring as Luke could have hoped. That Alain de Vignard had returned to London only added to his expectation of an enjoyable recuperation, and he retired to bed at an early hour, somewhat greyer in the face than Gabrielle liked but in high spirits.

Gabrielle kept him at the Dower House for three days. He was not difficult to persuade. All his family came to see him there, except Rolf who was, however, suffering more now from boredom than anything else.

No trace of boredom marred Luke's convalescence. When there were no visitors, he sat with Gabrielle in the parlour or in the sunny garden, talking quietly or simply enjoying each other's company.

Billy was their constant chaperon, but he managed to make himself remarkably unobtrusive in spite of his bulk. He would sit just out of earshot, watching them with a benevolent expression. After a voluble explanation on his side and no more than a pair of words on the other, he had come to terms with Baxter. Luke had never been better looked after in his life.

Nor had he ever been happier. It was his nature to anticipate problems—to consider alternatives, ponder possibilities, lay out a course of action. But with Gabrielle beside him, he found it easy to live in the present. He was no nearer being able to support a wife, let alone her brother and her possibly indigent father, if and when that gentleman appeared, so he deliberately avoided thinking of the future.

Gabrielle, once she was satisfied that Luke's wound was healing properly, was happy too. Not until he removed to the Great House did she ask herself why.

The answer shocked her.

She was in love.

How comfortable, in retrospect, it had been to have Luke for a friend! Ever since her arrival in England she had had someone to turn to for advice and assistance. She had considered the possibility of marrying him, but only if Papa failed to turn up. Now the thought appalled her: to be married to a man who was merely fond of her, when she adored him! Not that he had ever given her the slightest hint of wishing to marry her. She was sure that he was fond of her, that he liked to be with her. It was not enough.

She sat up in bed, hugging her knees. Papa, come quick! she cried silently, desolately. I need you!

Lady Harrison was already making plans to return to London. With her finances at last in order, she had decided the time was ripe to refurbish her house in preparation for the Little Season in the autumn. Rolf and Dorothea were both dismayed at the prospect of losing their new friends, the one still confined to his bed, the other in the megrims after bidding Alain farewell. The Everetts invited the Darcys to move up to the Great House for a few more weeks. That satisfied Rolf and Gerard, but Dorothea was all too conscious that, with Lady Harrison gone, Alain would have no more excuse for visiting Wrotham.

Gabrielle was torn. Luke was well enough now to go back to his work. If she went with Madame, she might see him in town; but how painful it would be if he was too busy, or not inclined to visit. She opted to stay with his family and hope that he would come down often.

As for Luke, forced at last to consider the future, he came to the conclusion that there was no hope for his courtship. There was simply no way he could support a wife. In desperation he cast about for reasons to stop loving Gabrielle, and could find none.

He and Billy escorted Lady Harrison back to London, borrowing the Everett travelling carriage for the purpose. Lady Cecilia waved goodbye, then turned to her husband.

"A word with you, my lord," she requested.

His arm about her waist, he led her to the study. She sat down on a sofa, pulled him down beside her and kissed his cheek. For several minutes he was too busy to ask what was on her mind. At last she moved away a little and took his hands.

"My dear," she said, "I am sure you no longer doubt Luke's feelings for Gabrielle."

He stood up, crossed to the window, and gazed out. "No more than I doubt my own feelings for you, Cecy. But of what is to be done I am less sure. I have no more idea who Miss Darcy is than I had when she first came here. What is her father? An adventurer, a black sheep, the skeleton in some noble family's closet? Or a mere nobody who thought to make good abroad? I told you I found her face familiar, which leads to concerns—as to legitimacy."

"You still have not recalled whom she reminds you of?"

"No. It cannot be anyone I know well. And even if it is her real name, there are a hundred families called Darcy. I daresay I never met more than two or three of them in my life."

"Well, no matter. You remember that I told you I should not let pride stand in the way of Luke's happiness. I was not thinking of pride of birth at the time, but in the end it is as unimportant as any other kind. If Luke loves her and wants to marry her, neither her lineage nor his straitened means shall prevent it, if I have any say in the matter.

"Henry, I had a letter this morning saying that my parents will travel to Tunbridge Wells next week, to take the waters. Wrotham is not far out of their way and I should in any case have invited them to break their journey here." She went to him, put her arms around him and laid her cheek against his back. He was rigid, breathing shallowly. "When they come, I am going to ask them for money."

He turned in her arms and held her tight.

The Earl and Countess of Ipswich arrived in due course, with three carriages, eight servants and a mountain of baggage. They brought with them another guest, whose train consisted only of two carriages and five servants.

"I made sure you could have no objection, Cecilia," said Lady Ipswich, a majestic figure in purple *gros de Naples*, topped with a huge frothy hat adorned with no less than five dyed ostrich plumes. "Lord Charing is practically a neighbor of yours, after all. He happened to mention to Ipswich that he intended to stay the night in Wrotham. His health is not good, unlike your father's, and he does not care to travel above thirty miles in a day. He and Ipswich were friends many years ago. We did not like to think of him languishing at an inn when our daughter resides not a mile distant."

"Of course, Mama. We are happy to welcome Lord Charing, are we not, Henry?" She nudged her husband, who sighed and said everything proper.

The Marquis of Charing, suffering severely from gout, was carried into the house by his servants. Some seventy years of age, he looked much older than the Ipswiches, his contemporaries. He wore his hair unfashionably long, tied behind, and it was as white as if it had been powdered in the mode of his youth. His lean face was deeply lined, giving an impression of constant weariness and regret.

Lord Everett took one look at him and reached for his wife's hand. Squeezing it meaningfully, he whispered, "Family name: Darcy!"

She turned to him, startled, and when she resumed the duties of a hostess, greeting the unexpected guest and directing the servants to see to his comfort, she scrutinised his face intently.

Lord Charing retired to a hastily prepared bedchamber. The countess went straight to the schoolroom to see her younger grandchildren, while the earl visited Rolf on his sickbed.

"I see no resemblance," said Lady Cecilia to her husband.

"It is not obvious," Lord Everett responded. "I caught a hint of young Gerard about the eyes. But he is the one the Darcys reminded me of, I'd wager on it. The resemblance must have been closer when he was younger."

"He is something of a hermit, is he not? I know nothing of his family."

"I was never well acquainted with him. He is older, and

200

his heir, Lord Darcy, younger than I. I have a vague recollection of seeing in the *Gazette*, oh, perhaps fifteen months past, that Darcy was killed in some sort of accident."

"Where does that leave Gerard and Gabrielle?"

"Precisely where they were, except that we can guess at a connection. Just what it is, is still a matter for conjecture. There must be cadet branches of the house, and the connection might be distant, the resemblance pure chance."

"My parents probably know more."

Lord Everett frowned. "Don't ask them, Cecilia. We have no right to delve into the matter."

"As you wish. But I shall invite the marquis to stay for a few days, until his leg pains him less. We shall soon find out if you are right."

"We shall?"

"To be sure. Either he knows about the relationship, in which case he may repudiate it and leave at once, or he may wish to further it, so he will stay. Or else he does not know of it, in which case he will stay to investigate, if he has only an ounce of curiosity in him! But if you are mistaken in the resemblance, he will hum and haw and make a to-do about putting us out, and consider a thousand pros and cons . . ."

"All right, all right!" The baron laughed. "I daresay you have the right of it, unless Charing happens to be a man of quick decisions, or fails to note a resemblance which is there. In which case we shall learn precisely nothing!"

Lord Ipswich made Gerard's acquaintance in Rolf's room, and his wife met Gabrielle when she returned with Dorothea from a walk to the village. They were pronounced respectively "a promising youth" and "a pretty-behaved young woman." Neither the earl nor the countess remarked upon the coincidence of surnames, nor appeared to notice any likeness.

Of the rest of the household, children and staff alike, only Lord Charing's servants were aware of their master's family name. They were a taciturn lot, not given to gossiping in the servants' hall or stables; if they felt any unusual interest in the young Darcys, they kept it to themselves.

When the marquis limped into the long gallery before dinner, on the arm of his footman, Lady Cecilia's gaze never left his face. She presented Dorothea to him, but was pleased to note that his eyes kept straying to Gabrielle and Gerard, who were waiting to be introduced. When he heard their name, his look of puzzlement changed to a wary interest.

Gabrielle, having but recently nursed her brother and Luke, was quite ready to practise her new skills on another invalid. She took charge of Lord Charing, brought a stool for his bad leg, a screen to shield him from the draught, a cushion to set behind him. All was done with such an utter lack of self-consciousness that he could not possibly suppose that he was being toad-eaten. She sat down beside him and conversed politely on subjects of general interest, the very picture of a demure, well-bred young lady in her evening gown of apricot mull.

"Do you make a long stay at Wrotham, Miss Darcy?" he asked abruptly.

"Until next month, sir. Lady Cecilia has been kind enough to ask us to stay several more weeks."

"And then?"

"Then we return to town, sir."

"To your parents, no doubt."

Gabrielle chose to disregard this query. His sudden curiosity seemed odd compared to his previous courtly, somewhat old-fashioned manner.

"We have very much enjoyed spending the summer here," she said. "The countryside is magnificent, is it not? If it were only the view across the Weald from the top of the hill, it would be worth a visit."

The marquis looked a little put out at her evasion but did not press his question. Instead he described his home to her, the village of timbered houses and the remains of a palace once belonging to the Archbishop of Canterbury.

"You can still see the Great Hall," he said, "where both Henry VII and Henry VIII were entertained. It is within my grounds, so I have never had to construct an artificial Gothic ruin to please romantic ladies."

She laughed. "It sounds delightful! Are you close to Canterbury?"

"Some twelve miles."

"You must often have visited the Cathedral then. Describe it to me, pray. Is it not the oldest in England?"

"It was founded in 597, burned down in 1067, and subsequently rebuilt. It is something of a hodgepodge of styles, but well worth a visit. As is the city, which has still a great many medieval buildings."

"I should like to see it," said Gabrielle, "but Mr Everett said it is much too far for a day's outing."

Lord Charing fell silent, looking thoughtful. They soon went in to dinner, where he ate so sparingly that Lady Cecilia felt every justification, later in the evening, when she invited him to stay until he felt more the thing.

He agreed with alacrity.

Lady Cecilia was not in the least surprised, the next day, when the marquis asked to meet Rolf. After all, Gerard spent most of his time with his friend. With a touching wistfulness, his lordship angled to be included in their limited pastimes; and since they both had excellent manners, he frequently succeeded.

"Imagine having a bad leg all the time!" said Rolf to Gerard, aghast at the thought.

Lady Cecilia was mystified, however, by the marquis's determined cultivation of her daughter. Dorothea had grown worrisomely pale and wan since Alain's departure. Never talkative, she had lately become silent, and if it had not been for Gabrielle's animating presence she would have retired to her chamber to mope the days away.

Heartsick herself, Gabrielle was not one to go into a decline. She conceived it her duty to her kind hosts to encourage Dorothea to exert herself, and when Lord Charing arrived she did her utmost to see that the charge of entertaining him did not fall on Lady Cecilia.

The Everetts were grateful. When Lady Cecilia at last found an opportunity to approach her father on the subject of money, she did it as much for Gabrielle as for Luke.

Lord Ipswich was entirely unsurprised when she laid the situation before him.

"Had a notion it was low tide with you, Cecy," he said. "Well, I mean, your old father knows the time of day, what? Stands to reason you can't play deep for as many years as Everett did without getting a trifle scorched. You *would* marry him though."

"And I have never regretted it, Papa."

"Was going to offer a helping hand when he came down here. Reformed character, what? Your mother thought he'd be insulted."

"She was right. But things have changed now."

"Not run off your legs, are you? I've been looking about the place, and it looks as if Everett's brought the land into good heart, doing well."

"It is. He has a touch for estate management, now that he has put his mind to it. It's the old debts: mortgages and liens and other things I don't understand. If it was just the two of us we could get by, but the children are growing up. So far, Luke has provided for them, but . . ."

"Not another word, my love! Your stepson is an admirable young man, but there's no call for him to take care of my grandchildren when your mother and I don't spend the half of our income—in spite of her wretched hats! I shan't live forever, and when I go there will be a fair bit coming your way, without embarrassing your brother in the least. You shall have it at once, no strings attached, except I'll thank you not to let Everett gamble it away again!"

"Papa! If I didn't think you were roasting me . . . But I

knew I could count on you." Lady Cecilia hugged her father, feeling like a little girl given a shilling to spend at the fair. With the debts paid off, the estate could easily support Luke with a wife and family.

Now all she had to do was to make sure he married Gabrielle!

— 21 —

GABRIELLE HAD COME to like Lord Charing. She felt she was genuinely useful to him, and though she had heard him cursing his servants when his leg was particularly painful, he was unfailingly polite, even charming, to her.

She was walking in the garden one morning when she overheard a snippet of conversation. Unaware of her presence, Lady Cecilia's parents were sitting on a bench on the other side of a bed of gloriously scented red roses.

"I've known Charing any time these sixty years," Lord Ipswich told his wife, "and I've never seen him behave so obliging."

"Irascible is the word," agreed my lady, nodding her vast hat with its own rose garden about the brim. "But I noticed last time we met him in town that he had mellowed prodigiously. And his son has died since. That's enough to make a man ponder his life."

"That's as may be, my lady, but I'll wager that young woman has something to do with it, with her pleasing ways and the little attentions an old man likes. I'm half in love with her myself, I vow."

Gabrielle blushed and hurried away.

That same day when the marquis descended at noon, as was his custom, to join the rest of the company, he announced that he felt himself sufficiently recovered to depart on the morrow.

"My daughter-in-law will be wondering what has become of me," he explained to his hostess. "The tone of her mind has been much affected by her widowhood. In fact, I do not believe I have seen Lady Sarah smile since my son's death. It is unfortunate that she has no children to distract her thoughts."

Lady Cecilia murmured her sympathy.

With an effort the old gentleman continued. "I have found my own sorrow much eased in your house by the presence of young people. I hardly dare to ask it, ma'am, but could you see your way to allowing your daughter to come with me to Charing, in the hope of cheering her? Accompanied, of course, by Miss Darcy! Miss Darcy has expressed a wish to see Canterbury, an expedition easily accomplished from Charing."

Lady Cecilia was hard put to it not to reveal her triumph. The marquis had most certainly recognised a family resemblance, and at the very least did not intend to repudiate the connection outright. Having gone so far, he might be expected to do something for Gabrielle and Gerard even if it turned out to be a left-handed relationship.

"What a delightful idea!" she said quickly. "I am sure a change of scene cannot but benefit Dorothea, and I trust the scheme will serve to raise Lady Sarah's spirits too. Naturally I cannot answer for dear Gabrielle, but she is the most obliging girl. I doubt she will be hard to persuade if there is some expectation of doing good. I shall speak to them both, at once!"

Gabrielle's only concern was for her brother. Being assured by the Everetts that he was welcome to stay at Wrotham, she went to find him in Rolf's room. She told him of her invitation.

"I cannot leave now," he said in alarm. "Rolf will be able to leave his bed in a few days and I mean to take him out in the gig."

"That is what I am afraid of! You are bound to fall into some sort of scrape if I leave you here on your own."

"Don't fuss so, Gaby! How can you say I shall be on my

208

own when I am surrounded by Everetts? If anything comes up, Lord Everett will tell me how to go on."

"Don't call me Gaby. You promise you will send to Charing if you are in a hobble?"

"I promise," he said with a sigh of exasperation. "Now do go away, there's a good girl. We are in the middle of a game."

Gabrielle went back to the marquis and curtsied.

"Thank you, my lord," she said, "I shall be happy to go with you to Charing."

The seat of the Marquis of Charing was situated, like Wrotham, on the southern slopes of the North Downs. The house, a vast Elizabethan mansion, was largely shut up. Only the marquis and his daughter-in-law resided there now, and even before his son's fatal accident they had rarely entertained.

It was raining when Gabrielle and Dorothea arrived. The great hall was gloomy, its huge fireplace a black cave, the suits of armour guarding the stair sinister in the half-light. His lordship was suffering severely after the journey, though they had travelled less than thirty miles. Preoccupied with his pain, he left the girls to his housekeeper, a depressed-looking woman who took them to adjoining, connected bedchambers and sent a maid for hot water.

The rooms were decorated in a style outdated twenty years before. Dorothea's abigail snorted as she unpacked their clothes.

"I been in houses like this afore," she said. "Time the water comes from the kitchen it'll be lukewarm, you mark my words, miss."

Dorothea looked ready to weep, and Gabrielle could not help feeling dismal. At least Lady Sarah could have made an effort to greet them, she thought.

At that moment there was a knock on the door of her chamber and a tall, pale lady drifted in. With grey hair and a grey gown unadorned by so much as a strip of lace, she might have been a ghost.

"Miss Everett, Miss Darcy?" she said in a low, lifeless voice. "I am Lady Sarah. It is kind of you to visit this unhappy house."

The girls curtsied. Dorothea seemed too quashed to speak, so Gabrielle said, "How do you do, ma'am. I am Gabrielle Darcy and this is Dorothea. We are looking forward to staying here. Lord Charing has told me how pretty the village is, and about the ruins of the archbishop's palace, and I quite long to see them."

Lady Sarah shrugged helplessly. "Yes, of course," she murmured. "We must hope the weather improves. I expect you will want to rest after your journey. Mrs Hunney shall bring you down to the drawing room when you are ready." She drifted out again.

It was an inauspicious start to their visit, but things improved thereafter. The water was hot, the drawing room warm and comfortable, and Lady Sarah pulled herself together enough to make polite, if insipid, conversation.

Lord Charing appeared at dinner, a plain but lavish and well-cooked meal. He drew their attention to the pastries and jellies and creams, saying that they must thank his daughter-in-law, for they did not usually eat such kickshaws and he had not thought to provide for the tastes of young ladies. Dorothea, who was partial to sweets, took a second plum turnover and thanked Lady Sarah so prettily that she brought a smile to the melancholy face.

"Ha!" said his lordship triumphantly.

By the next morning the rain had ceased. Gabrielle succeeded in persuading Lady Sarah to accompany them in exploring the surroundings. She turned out to have a fund of anecdotes about the history of the area which greatly enlivened their tour of the village and their scramble through the archbishop's palace. By the time they returned to the house, her pale cheeks held a hint of pink and her eyes, though still mournful, had lost the look of being constantly about to spill over.

A few days later, Lady Sarah took them on a tour of Canterbury. Again her historical knowledge much increased their enjoyment of the ancient town, and she was plainly gratified when they told her so.

A signpost pointing to Dover caught Gabrielle's eye. They were only sixteen miles from the place where she had made her dramatic entrance into England. It was about the time of the month when Luke generally went there to take up his rôle as the Man in the Green Coat, and she wondered if he was there now, waiting at the King's Head for news from France.

Did he know she was no longer at Wrotham? Had he perhaps called in at his home on the way to Dover and found her gone? Suddenly she wished she had stayed, though she was sure by now that her visit was doing Lady Sarah a world of good. It would be beyond bearing if Luke thought she had cheerfully abandoned his family, but after all, she reminded herself, she had only come as a companion to Dorothea. Lady Cecilia would be certain to tell him so.

When they got back to Charing, Luke was there.

Luke had had a frustrating week. First Georges Cadoudal announced that he would be leaving for France by the end of the month. No argument succeeded in convincing the fiery young warrior that such a course would endanger not only himself but his anticipated allies. Lord Hawkesbury ordered Mr Everett to give him every assistance.

Mr Everett spent several days in Dover arranging to have Cadoudal smuggled across the Channel. The courier who arrived in search of the Man in the Green Coat brought new confirmation that de la Touche was an *agent provocateur*, but no evidence different enough to change minds.

Stopping in Wrotham on his way back to London, hoping for twenty-four hours respite from the exigencies of his work, Luke discovered Gabrielle and his sister both gone.

Before he mentioned that he was returning from Dover, not on his way there, his stepmother had asked him to call in at Charing.

"Dorothea writes cheerfully," she said, "but I should like to be sure that she and Gabrielle are quite comfortable. It is such an odd household, just Lord Charing and Lady Sarah Darcy."

"The family name *is* Darcy, then! I thought so. How does this come about, ma'am?"

Lady Cecilia explained the marquis's stay at Wrotham and his invitation to the girls to cheer up his daughter-in-law. "He asked Dorothea to go, and Gabrielle as her companion, but it is my opinion that it was Gabrielle he really wanted. Your father noticed a distinct resemblance, and it is unlikely that it could have escaped his lordship's eye."

"Then Gabrielle has found her family!" The thought made Luke distinctly uneasy. It was an excellent family to be related to, to be sure, but she would no longer need to turn to him in times of trouble. In spite of all his efforts at self-persuasion, he still loved her.

"Not necessarily. Henry thinks the connection is likely on the wrong side of the blanket. Since Lord Charing has gone so far, I daresay he will be willing to help them even so. But we have no reason to suppose that Gabrielle is aware of the relationship. The resemblance is more a matter of the way the marquis looked many years ago, and as for the name, it is quite possible that she has not heard it. *He* is always referred to as Lord Charing, and *she* as Lady Sarah."

"Then she has left you and gone off to Charing without even the excuse of knowing that she is related to the marquis!" exclaimed Luke, seizing eagerly on this evidence of imperfection to support his fight against his own feelings. "I had thought her more capable of gratitude than that!"

"Fustian! She has gone to accompany Dorothea and to try to comfort Lady Sarah."

Luke was not listening. Already resentful at Hawkesbury and Cadoudal's refusal to accept his warnings, his smothered anger flared at Gabrielle's apparent slight to his family.

"I must leave at once if I am to call at Charing, ma'am," he announced. "I will let you know how Dorothea fares."

Calling for Baxter, he strode out.

Gabrielle and Dorothea were delighted to see Luke, until they saw his expression. The drive, thirty miles in the wrong direction when he had hoped to be relaxing at home, had not improved his temper. Nor had the realisation that his actions were totally illogical, that he should simply have told his stepmother that he was headed the other way and put Gabrielle's misdeeds out of his mind.

Lady Sarah welcomed him with quiet courtesy, and invited him to stay to dinner and for the night.

"Thank you," he responded, "but I must refuse. I but called in passing and must be on my way presently."

"Then I shall leave you to talk to your sister in peace," she said with a sweet smile. Drawn out of her sorrow, she had proved a gentle, kindly hostess, somewhat lacking in humour but very ready to please and be pleased. "No one will interrupt you here in the drawing room," she went on. "I will tell Mrs Hunney to bring refreshments, for I am sure the girls need something if you do not." She went out, a little wearily after the unwonted exertions of the day.

Dorothea, easily alarmed, had retired to the shelter of a windowseat at the far end of the room. Luke turned to Gabrielle.

"I had thought better of you," he said bitterly. "I may once have suspected you of spying, but I never considered that you might be a mere adventuress. First you insinuate yourself into *my* family, and then, as soon as a better chance offers, you abandon them and cozen Charing into taking you in. Oh yes, he is much richer than we are—childless, doting! Do you hope to marry him, I wonder? It would suit you, I daresay, to be a wealthy widow. To think that I once considered marrying you myself, penniless as I am!"

"How prodigious kind of you! I am sure you need not have troubled, since I should not marry you if you were rich as Croesus! Of all the arrogant, overbearing, self-satisfied coxcombs is has ever been my misfortune to meet . . ."

"Enough, Miss Darcy!"

". . . So set up in your own conceit you cannot see beyond the end of your nose . . ."

"You are distressing my sister!"

Gabrielle ran to Dorothea, who was weeping in silent misery.

"I'm sorry, Dorrie darling. Don't heed him. Your brother is the most provoking wretch on the face of the earth!"

"Dorothea, you will pack your bags and return to Wrotham with me at once."

"No, I shan't. I am to stay here another week and I will not be dragged home as if I were in disgrace."

He turned on Gabrielle again. "Until she knew you, my sister was a docile creature who always did as she was bid. What a disastrous influence you have had upon her! How you must be laughing up your sleeve at the misery you have brought upon my family!"

"Go away, Luke," pleaded Dorothea, hiccupping. "You are being quite ridiculous. I'm sure I hope you do not know what you are saying!"

With a look of baffled fury, Luke stalked out.

Equally furious, Gabrielle paced up and down the room, fists clenched, cheeks pink with indignation.

"You were magnificent, Dorrie!" she exclaimed. "I never thought you had it in you to stand up to a bully like that."

"He was right about one thing," Dorothea admitted regretfully. "I should never have dared until I met you, and saw how you make your own decisions."

"Oh, dear!" Gabrielle bit her lip and went to join her friend on the window seat. "Am I really your pattern-card? I am no paragon, you know, and my decisions are sometimes wrong. Besides, our upbringings were quite different. I have had to think for myself for years, because much of the time there was no one to turn to. Believe me, I have learned from my mistakes."

"I have led a very sheltered life, I know. But if I am never allowed to make mistakes, how am I to learn? At all events, I *will* not give up Alain only because Luke says I must! He is not my father, after all, only my half-brother."

"He has an unfortunate habit of laying down the law. His reasons may be excellent, but as he does not give them, one cannot judge. Dorrie, I do not care to be the cause of a breach with your brother. I appreciate your defence, but perhaps you ought to go with him, and I will go to Madame in London."

"No." Dorothea was adamant, her delicate features suffused with determination. "If he wishes me to do as he says, he must explain himself, tell me why I should, and let me decide. You do not want me to go, do you? Pray do not hold *his* dreadful words against *me!*"

Gabrielle hugged her. "Of course not, goose. Now dry your eyes and let us go and change, or we shall be late for dinner."

The evening seemed endless. All Gabrielle wanted was to be alone so that she could consider Luke's outburst without distraction. At last she retired to her chamber, only to fall asleep as soon as she blew out her candle, tired from walking about Canterbury, and emotionally exhausted.

Though both Gabrielle and Dorothea were subdued the next day, their friendship had deepened. Dorothea's nature was not confiding, but her brother's behaviour had inadvertently broken down the barriers to intimacy, in part because his intention was so manifestly the reverse.

If Luke had thought, he might have supposed that after ten days at Charing it was impossible that Gabrielle should not know her hosts's surname. He would have been wrong. There were no visitors to reveal it. The late Lord Darcy was rarely referred to, and then as "my husband," or "my son." All the servants were as well trained and as little given to gossip about their betters as had been those who travelled with his lordship. Naturally Lady Sarah was aware of the coincidence, but her father-in-law had most strictly forbidden any reference to it.

And the family crest sported an ornate C for Charing, so that Gabrielle was even unaware of sharing an initial.

She had, indeed, received an unusually incoherent letter from Lady Harrison, upon first informing her of her destination. It was so full of heavily underlined phrases in French as to be practically unreadable. All she learned from it was that Madame was distraught about something indecipherable but that the redecoration of the house was proceeding according to plan.

September came. The pears ripened in the marquis's orchards and swallows gathered in huge flocks, ready to fly south. A date was set for Dorothea to return to Wrotham. Gabrielle was to go with her, to pick up Gerard and go on to London to await her father's arrival.

She felt oddly nervous at the thought. It was so long since she had seen him! She had changed, and their relationship must change likewise, but how she could not tell. At last she would find out who she really was, and she was not at all sure she wanted to know. She recognised that she had been floating in a vague and comforting belief that all her problems would vanish with his appearance. Closely examined, that belief faded beyond resuscitation.

On their last day at Charing, restless and dissatisfied with herself, Gabrielle went for a long ride on the mare his lordship had provided for her use, followed at a discreet distance by the groom insisted upon by Lady Sarah. When she returned at dusk, Mrs Hunney was hovering in the entrance hall, waiting for her.

"Oh miss, I'm *that* glad you're back!" the housekeeper exclaimed, her usual calmness in tatters at the edges. "My lady'd like to see you in the drawing room, if you please, right away."

Gabrielle looked down at her soiled riding habit. "I'd best change first," she said.

"Please don't, miss. Her ladyship said soon as you come in."

Alarmed, Gabrielle hurried to the drawing room. Lady Sarah was sitting in the twilight, twisting a handkerchief in her agitated hands. She started up as Gabrielle entered.

"My dear, I don't know what to do! Thank heaven you are come."

"What is it, ma'am? Have you had bad news? Where is Dorothea?"

"A gentleman came to see her. An excessively good-looking young man, with the very faintest hint of a foreign accent. I ought not to have left them alone, I know, particularly as he would not give his name, but I did not think any harm could come of it, just for a few moments."

"Alain! What happened? Oh, do not tell me she has run off with him!"

"No, no. I should have known what to do in such a case. No, he said he was come to make a final farewell, so I left them. He was here for perhaps fifteen minutes, and when he departed Dorothea ran up to her room in a fit of weeping. She will not open her door, or answer when I speak to her. But I can hear that she is still crying, and it has been over an hour now. Surely she will talk to you?"

"I hope so," said Gabrielle grimly. "I shall go and do my best to discover what is toward!"

She hastened to Dorothea's chamber and knocked. There was no response. Suddenly remembering the connecting door, she went through her own room and found her friend curled in a miserable huddle on her bed, her face red-eyed and tearstained.

"I can't cry any more," said Dorothea hopelessly. "There are no tears left."

"Good. Then you will be able to tell me just what this is all about. What did Alain say?"

"You guessed it was him?"

"Of course. But how did he find out . . . Oh, of course: Madame."

"Gabrielle, it is so dreadful I do not know how to tell you."

"Begin at the beginning. In the end it is usually easiest."

"You know Alain has a sister?"

"I know he had one. I thought she died in the Terror."

"So did he. But about eight months ago he was approached by another *émigré*, who told him she was alive. Sophie, her name is. Bonaparte had found her, or not exactly him but one of his ministers, beginning with an F, I think."

"Fouché?"

"That sounds like it. Anyway, he said that if Alain ever wanted to see her again, he must provide information about the plans of the man he works for. I can't remember his name either, it's a peculiar one."

"I know. Never mind that. Did Alain do it?"

"He kept stalling. There was someone else there, a French spy, who knew everything anyway, so he didn't have to give away any secrets at first. But two weeks ago the man came to him again. He said there was a list of names he wanted, that the spy had not been able to see. If Alain would not provide it, Sophie was to be sent to a house of ill repute for soldiers. Alain would not tell me what that is, but I think it means they would turn her into a—a *bit of muslin!*"

218

"I'm afraid you are right. So Alain has given them the list?"

"Not yet. He is on his way to Dover now, and they are supposed to have Sophie there, to hand over in exchange. He says he has betrayed the country that gave him refuge, and he will not sully my purity by his presence, ever again. But what else could he do when they have his sister?"

"He has not seen her for ten years or more. She was a mere child! The girl they have might not even be his sister. But we cannot let him go through this alone. Dorrie, we must follow him. I know where Lord Charing keeps his pistols, and he told me thay are always loaded because it was the fashion in his day to have duels without the least ceremony. Are not men odd? We'll take them, and perhaps, as they will not expect us, we shall be able to take Alain's sister away from them without giving them the list of names!"

"But I have never fired a pistol in my life," protested Dorothea, aghast.

"It is very easy. My Papa taught me years ago. You just point it and pull the trigger. But I do not expect to shoot anyone, only we must have them to point. Now do not turn all faint-hearted on me, Dorrie. I am doing this for you and Alain."

And partly for Luke, she admitted to herself. He worked so hard to keep England safe, and whoever was on the list of names, if the French wanted it he would certainly not want them to have it.

"What shall we tell Lady Sarah?"

"Leave that to me. You put on your riding habit, quickly, and a warm cloak, and come down. There is no time to lose; Alain is an hour ahead of us!

"But how shall we find him in Dover?"

"You can leave that to me, too. I just happen to know where all the spies in Dover congregate."

She could only hope that was true.

— 22 —

THE STORY GABRIELLE told Lady Sarah had little to do with the truth. Only a lady of thoroughly unsuspecting nature could have swallowed it, and then only because she was not allowed time to think it over. She did manage to persuade Gabrielle to take a groom with her, to show her the shortest way.

Within half an hour the girls were on their way, leaving Lady Sarah with the vague impression that Dorothea's brother was on his deathbed at an unnamed inn in Dover. She had enough to do, dealing with the tearful abigail they left behind, not to fret over what explanation she would give her father-in-law when he came down to dinner.

Gabrielle and Dorothea cantered across the Downs after the groom, who thought the whole business a grand lark. Gabrielle had already been in the saddle for several hours and suspected she would end up as sore as on that memorable ride out of Switzerland. At least she was riding sidesaddle so her thighs would not be rubbed raw.

They followed an ancient road along the crest of the Downs, dating from the days when the Weald was a dense and sinister forest and all travellers preferred the high ground. It soon grew dark, but a three-quarter moon shone, and high scudding clouds obscured it only briefly. When at last the groom led them down from the hills to a post-road, they had already bypassed Folkestone and Dover was no more than three miles ahead.

Guiding her mount took less concentration now, and

Gabrielle had leisure to consider her actions and wonder just what she was going to do next. It had seemed so obvious and easy. They would just walk in and force the French spies at gunpoint to hand over Alain's sister. Now it dawned on her that the enemy would undoubtedly also be armed, and that Dorothea was not likely to be of much assistance.

Suppose the wrong people were shot?

The moonlit castle loomed before them as they trotted down the main street. The flickering light of a pair of flambeaux illuminated the sign of the King's Head. Gabrielle rode under the arch into the courtyard and dismounted wearily. An ostler came out to help their groom with the horses, and they went on into the inn.

Mr Colby stepped out of the taproom to greet them. He showed no recognition of Gabrielle. Though tousled from the ride, she was a far cry from the urchin Mr Everett had carried into his establishment four months ago.

The innkeeper was inclined to be suspicious of two young ladies arriving after dark with no luggage and no more escort than a groom. However, business had been shocking since the resumption of the blockade of France. He asked them civilly what he could do for them.

Gabrielle was stymied. It seemed highly unlikely that Alain was using his own name when engaged upon such an errand. The only thing she could think of was to ask for a private parlour and use that as a base for exploration.

Dorothea took the matter out of her hands.

"We are looking for my brother," she said, somewhat breathlessly. Her fingers were crossed behind her back, Gabrielle noticed. "He is tall and dark and he's wearing a green coat. Is he here?"

A green coat! Had Alain worn it in a deliberate attempt to confuse, or was it pure chance? Gabrielle caught a look of confusion crossing the landlord's face, and a sudden desire to giggle nearly overcame her.

"There's a gentleman of that description in the house," he

222

admitted cautiously. "He's took a pair of bedchambers. He did say as how he's expecting a young lady to join him, but not two! Howsumdever, I'll have the maid show you up, miss."

The maid's eyes widened in recognition when she saw Gabrielle, who quickly put her finger to her lips. The girl nodded and hurried them up the stairs. They entered a chamber with a connecting door to the next room. Gabrielle went to it, pulled it open a crack, and peered round. No sign of Alain.

"Do you know where the gentleman who took these rooms is at present?" she asked the maid.

"Yes, miss. There's two gentlemen and a young lady as took a private parlour, and the young gentleman's with them now. Furriners they are, at least some of 'em."

"Dorrie, have you a sixpence?"

Dorothea found a coin and gave it to the girl.

"Ta, miss. Shall I tell the gentleman as you've arrived?"

"No!" said Gabrielle quickly. "We'll go down shortly."

"Right, miss." The maid curtsied and left them.

Dorothea sank into a chair.

"What shall we do now?" she wailed. "He has already met them!"

"Wait a minute, I'm thinking." Gabrielle opened the connecting door and went alone into the other room, looking vaguely for something to suggest a course of action.

On her left was a washstand, then a wardrobe with mirror door. There was a chair in the corner. In the opposite wall was a window, with a large four-poster bed in front of it, its head to the corridor wall. The door into the corridor came next. Between Gabrielle and the door was a chest of drawers, against the shared wall.

On the chest were a pair of hairbrushes, a flask, a folded road map, and several other odds and ends. Among them, a piece of paper caught her attention. She picked it up.

It was a list of names. French names.

So Alain had not yet betrayed his adopted country! He

must be bargaining with the French spies, checking that they had indeed brought his sister to him. Soon, any minute, he would come to fetch the list, or perhaps bring them up to get it. That would be the moment when she and Dorothea must act. She felt in the pocket of her cloak for the comforting weight of the pistol.

A movement caught her eye. She swung round as the door to the corridor opened.

Luke stood on the threshold.

"Gabrielle!" In two strides he was beside her, snatching the paper from her grasp and scanning it. "My God, it was you all the time! And alone in de Vignard's room in the middle of the night! Is he your lover? Did you lure him into this treason? He will go the gallows for it, but I can save you. I have fought against my cursed passion but I cannot help myself. You must marry me, as soon as I can get a special license!"

"You are determined to think the worst of me, Mr Everett. I care not what you believe, but I cannot imagine why you should wish to marry me. It is fortunate indeed that I am not obliged to obey your commands, for I desire nothing less than to be your wife!"

Gabrielle was shaking with anger and shock. Since she had come to the realisation that she loved him, she had seen Luke only twice, and both times he had poured insults and accusations upon her head. This was not the man she had fallen in love with, the cool, determined gentleman who had adopted her problems as his own and promptly solved them.

"Then run!" he exclaimed. "I will not pursue you, nor give you away, if you will only go back to France and cease tormenting me!"

"Run! This is no time for running! Alain will be here at any moment and we must be ready. Whether you will help or no, I must go and tell Dorothea what to do."

"Dorothea! You have embroiled her in this deadly business? Is there no end to your depravity?"

"She is in the next room, and it is for her sake that *I* am here." Exasperation warred with hurt. "However wicked I may be, you will surely consider her position! I take it you are come here as a spycatcher, not merely to abuse me. Have you a gun?"

"Yes," he answered, startled into attention.

"I am sure Alain will be coming up here shortly to fetch that list, and it seems to me quite likely the men you are after will come with him." She drew her own pistol. "We must hide and . . . Hush! I hear someone coming! Behind the bed!"

Looking bemused, he obeyed her, diving for cover. She ran to the connecting door, pushed it nearly closed behind her, and discovered too late that her field of vision was severely limited. She could see little but the wardrobe.

In the mirror was a view of the other door, split in two by a bedpost. As she watched, a man in a green coat appeared in the doorway, his face hidden by the post.

"What is happening?" whispered Dorothea, creeping up behind her with the other pistol drooping in her hand. "I thought I heard Luke's voice."

Gabrielle turned. "Don't hold it like that!" she hissed. "You will shoot your own foot, goose. Or me. Dorrie, your brother is here!"

Dorothea fainted.

Gabrielle managed to catch her firearm before it crashed to the floor. She set both the pistols on a chair, lifted her friend in her arms and staggered with her to the bed. Laying her down, she gazed at her in vexation.

The sound of voices came from the next room and she hurried back to the door.

"I left it here," protested Alain, in French. She saw his elbow, clad in green, moving as he searched through the clutter on the chest. "Perhaps it has fallen on the floor."

In the reflection, a hard-faced man stood near the door, his hands in the pockets of his overcoat.

"I cease to believe in this list, *mon ami*," he said sharply.

"It exists, perhaps, only in your imagination. So much the worse for *la petite!*"

"Oh no," said Luke's voice, "the list is real. I have it. Don't move!"

Alain had taken a step away from the chest of drawers and was standing with his back to Gabrielle, his hands slightly raised. She guessed that Luke must have a gun aimed at him. The Frenchman was in full view in the mirror, his features twisted with malice.

"So!" he hissed. "You have brought your English friends with you! They may save you, but as soon as my colleague below has the least suspicion that all is not going according to plan, he will shoot your sister immediately. He is Fouché's trusted aide, and those who serve Fouché do not hesitate."

Alain turned to face him, so that Gabrielle could see his profile. To her astonishment, his face wore a curious smile. She supposed that a clean death was better than the alternative fate proposed for poor Sophie.

He was about to speak when Dorothea moaned.

"Gabrielle?" she called weakly.

"Dorothea?" Alain turned towards the connecting door, his voice joined by Luke's.

Gabrielle pushed the door shut and ran to the bed. "Hush!" she whispered. "You must be perfectly quiet. I fear you distracted Luke's attention. I don't know what has happened now."

"Has Luke killed Alain?" asked Dorothea in a fearful whisper, her blue eyes swimming.

"Of course not. Dorrie, you lie here, keep still and do not make a sound. I will see if I can hear any more."

She pressed her ear to the door. Carved of solid oak, it cut off all sound from the next room. Heart in mouth, Gabrielle lifted the latch slowly and carefully, and even more slowly pulled the door towards her until it was no more than two inches open.

The reflected bedpost obliterated the French spy's face

and bisected his body, but all too clearly she could see that he held a pistol in each hand.

She raised her own gun uselessly. There was nothing to shoot at but a reflection. She could not aim at the man without stepping out into the room, and he would have plenty of time to fire before she could. She was not even sure whether she would be able to fire at a human being. She had once killed a rabbit when her father was teaching her to shoot, and the memory had haunted her for weeks.

Luke's life was at stake! He was a provoking, overweening wretch and he despised her, but she could not let him be shot down in cold blood. The Frenchman was no harmless, inoffensive creature, and if she had to kill him she would not regret it, she assured herself.

"Gabrielle!" Dorothea's tiny whisper just reached her.

She turned, finger to her lips, and the other door to the chamber caught her eye. Of course, how stupid of her! She could go out into the corridor and come round behind the spy. She looked again, to ascertain his position.

He had moved into the room three or four feet; otherwise the scene was frozen. She felt as if eons had passed; but no one in the other room had spoken, so it must have been seconds.

A pistol landed on the bed. Luke was helpless now. Everything depended on her.

"You are sensible, monsieur," said the spy. "I will attempt to persuade my colleague that the lady in the next chamber is not to be disturbed." Behind him, the door opened. "Ah, here he is now."

A man in a light brown coat stepped into the mirror, a gun in his hand. For a moment his face was obscured by the bedpost, then he moved into view. Gabrielle recognised him at once.

"Hold still!" ordered that beloved voice.

With a half-swallowed sob, Gabrielle ran back to the bed, fell to her knees and buried her face in her arms.

Her father was a French spy!

She felt a hand on her shoulder. "What is it?" whispered Dorothea. "What is the matter? Has Alain killed Luke? Has Luke killed Alain? Tell me!"

Gabrielle raised her head. "No," she said dully. No, she thought, my father is about to kill both of them. "No, nothing like that."

"Then what? Oh, pray go and see! What can they be doing?"

She forced herself to her feet and went slowly back to the connecting door. The day's exertions had suddenly caught up with her and she ached in every bone.

Dorothea followed her, pulling on her arm.

"Gabrielle, are you all right? Gabrielle! What shall we do?" The pistol wavered dangerously in her delicate hand.

"Hush! First put that down." She took the gun and laid it on the floor. "Wait a minute. Let me see what is happening."

Alain was slumped in the chair in the corner of the room, looking tired and strained.

"How is my sister?" he asked.

"As well as can be expected." Gabrielle's father sounded his usual cheerful self. She could see his face clearly in the mirror, an ordinary face, topped with crisply curling grey hair, smiling gently. He looked no more like a malevolent traitor than he ever had, yet he was capable of threatening an innocent girl to force her brother to do his will.

Mademoiselle de Vignard was waiting below stairs, ignorant of her fate, alone and afraid.

"Dorothea!" hissed Gabrielle. "Listen! You must take Alain's sister away from here. Hire a carriage, go back to Charing. She will be safe there, whatever happens."

Dorothea's frightened face gazed at her in horror. "Oh, I couldn't," she stammered. "On my own? I have no money."

"Of course you can. You must! For Alain's sake. Take the groom with you, and tell Mr Colby to put the charge on your brother's reckoning."

"On Luke's?"

"Or Alain's, if he thinks Alain is your brother. For heaven's sake, what does it matter? Go now, quickly."

With relief she saw that she had convinced Dorothea. The girl scurried towards the door into the corridor. Gabrielle turned back in time to hear her father say,

"Roussel, you appear surprised."

"*Sacre bleu!*" The Frenchman addressed as Roussel was beyond Gabrielle's view, but he sounded stunned, not merely surprised. "For eight years you have worked for Fouché, and I for you. How should I not be surprised? What are you going to do now?"

" 'E's not gonna do nowt!" declared a familiar voice. Suddenly Mr Darcy's reflection was framed on one side by a small, bald man in black, on the other by a portion of a huge, round-faced man in fustian. "Drop that pop smart now," Billy continued, "or I'm gonnarafta shoot, and I don't like killing coves, see?"

"Don't shoot!" cried Alain, springing up. "He's on our side. That is Le Hibou!"

Gabrielle's knees went weak and she sat down abruptly on the floor, head spinning. What *was* her father? Was Alain lying to gain time? Or was he really Le Hibou, the mysterious English spy who had bedevilled Boney for years, and his predecessors before him? With all her heart she hoped that it was true, that he was not after all a renegade and a turncoat.

Yet, just as Luke had believed the worst of her, so she had been ready to condemn her own father.

She wanted to run to him and ask his forgiveness. She wanted to sit still and think quietly, sort out her feelings. But Luke was speaking, his voice tired, and she must concentrate on his words.

"All right, I don't know who is who here. But until I find out, you are all under arrest. Baxter, Billy, let us escort these gentlemen belowstairs, if you please. There is a parlour reserved there, I believe, which cannot but be more convenient than this wretched bedchamber, which I begin to abhor!"

Luke was in control. For the moment she was content to have it so.

There was no need now for Dorothea and Sophie to escape to Charing. She must call them back and tell them the outcome of the confrontation. Hurrying down the stair she met Mr Colby, lumbering up, looking as worried as a man with a plump face made for jollity can look. He greeted her with relief.

"What's agoing on up there, miss?" he asked anxiously. "The young lady come down all of a fluster and ordered a chaise to be made ready, quick as winking. I don't have no objection to my house being used for certain activities what you wot well of, if you catch my drift, but I don't care for the looks of some of them as is here tonight."

"It's quite all right," Gabrielle assured him. "A certain gentleman the colour of whose coat we both wot well has everything under control. The chaise will not be needed, at least not immediately. Where is the young lady who ordered it?"

"This way, miss, if you please. She's in the parlour with the foreign miss as arrived a while back. The missus went in a few minutes agone, and she said as neither young lady don't look too well, miss."

"I shall take care of them. Pray bring us some tea, for it will do them good, and I vow it is the only thing I want in the whole world!"

She found Sophie de Vignard huddled in a wing chair by the fire. She was a thin, sickly-looking girl of fifteen or sixteen, with her brother's dark hair hanging now in lank strands about her wan face. Dorothea was sitting beside her, holding her hands. They both looked up.

"You need not go," said Gabrielle. "Luke had a pair of aces up his sleeve, and you will be quite safe here."

"He has not shot Alain?"

"No, merely arrested him until he sorts out the mess."

"Arrested! That is near as bad!" Dorothea turned to Sophie and the two chattered to each other in mixed French and English.

Gabrielle realised that for the present she was not needed. The girls were united in adoration of Alain and worry over his safety. A wave of intense loneliness unexpectedly engulfed her, and she sank onto a sofa on the other side of the room.

At any moment Luke would come in with his prisoners. She did not want to face him. Two thoughts chased each other through her mind, refusing to stand still for rational examination.

Papa was found and Luke was lost.

The maid brought in a tray of tea and set it on the table. Gabrielle was pouring from the heavy earthenware pot when voices were heard in the hall. The French spy, Roussel, came into the parlour, guarded by Baxter. Next came Alain, with Billy towering over him, then Mr Darcy, and lastly Luke, pistol in hand.

Mr Darcy looked back at him. "I can see that I shall have to produce reams of evidence to satisfy you as to my credentials," he said. "Perhaps you will at least explain to me just where *you* come into the picture?"

"He is the man in the green coat, Papa," said Gabrielle.

Mr Darcy stopped dead. She had never seen him taken by surprise before. His face was momentarily completely blank, but when he spoke it was in his usual calm voice.

"Gabrielle, my love, what the devil are you doing here?"

"I came to rescue Alain, Papa." Her own voice was unnaturally calm.

Luke gazed at her in astonishment. Apparently he had not yet learned his prisoner's name, and thus his connection with Gabrielle. She tried to avoid looking at his face.

"To rescue Alain!" Her father was undoubtedly taken

aback. He looked from her to Alain and back, and frowned. "You are in love with Alain, *mon petit chou?* I cannot like a marriage between first cousins."

Gabrielle scarce heard his last comment.

"No," she cried, "I am in love with the Man in the Green Coat!" Her control broke and she ran to hide her face in her father's waistcoat. "Tell him to go away, Papa," she sobbed. "I never want to see him again!"

— 23 —

"I CANNOT UNDERSTAND him!" exclaimed Lord Everett. "I told him that the debts are paid and that henceforth he will receive an allowance suitable to his position, and it sent him into a flat despair!"

Lady Cecilia nodded wisely. "I thought there was something amiss. Let me talk to him."

"I wish you will, and that before he wears out the carpet in my study."

Luke was pacing up and down from desk to window and back. Now and then he paused at the window and gazed down to the Dower House, then shook his head fiercely and turned away. His stepmother watched him for a few moments before announcing her presence.

"Luke?"

Startled, he swung round.

"What is wrong?" she asked bluntly, advancing into the room and taking a seat.

He flung himself into a chair, then got up again and went back to the window.

"I don't know what to do!" he said, not looking at her.

"About Gabrielle? She is at Charing, is she not, and you are on your way there?"

"She told her father that she loves me, and that she never wants to see me again."

Lady Cecilia laughed gently. "Is that all? You must have made her very, very angry."

"I insulted her in every conceivable way. Not only the last time we met, but the time before also."

"Then you can hardly wonder that the poor girl does not want to see you! I daresay she expects more of the same."

"I cannot think what came over me! I have never before fallen into such a rage that I lost control of my tongue!"

"No, it is not like you. But there is nothing in the world so painful as to think ill of the one you love. I take it your suspicions were unfounded?"

"Of course! I cannot tell you all because it is secret government business, connected with my position at the Foreign Office. But you know that Gabrielle's father is come. He and I decided to gather together everyone involved to explain the situation, and since Lord Charing must be present and his ill health makes travel inadvisable, I am on my way to Charing now. If it were not for that, I should probably never see her again."

"It is up to you to make use of the opportunity. Luke, I cannot tell you what to say, only to make very sure that she knows you love her."

"I do, Cecilia. Very much."

She went to him, squeezed his hand and kissed his cheek.

"Then you will know what to do." Struggling with an unexpected and unwanted pang of jealousy, she left him. For too many years she had had his silent devotion. She had always hoped that he would find a woman he could love and wed; yet now that the moment had come, it hurt a little. She went to look for her husband.

The huge fireplace in the great hall at Charing was filled with dancing flames. Newly burnished, the suits of armour guarding the stair gleamed. A vase of magnificent Chinese chrysanthemums, bronze, white and yellow, added their spicy scent to the fragrance of woodsmoke.

Lady Harrison looked around with an air of satisfaction. Barbaric splendour it might be, but it was a vast improvement over the gloomy den she had walked into when

Maurice brought her here three days earlier. Outside was a raw September morning; inside was as near cosy as such a large room could be.

She looked up as Gabrielle came down the wide oak staircase. *Ah, bon!* The girl was dressed in her new lilac morning gown and Marie had done wonders with her hair, not that those dark ringlets needed a great deal of arranging. A touch of rouge would not have come amiss, thought my lady. Gabrielle had been alarmingly listless since Maurice's return.

There could be only one reason for melancholy in a young lady recently reunited with her long-lost father. Lady Harrison swept forward and gently pinched Gabrielle's cheeks to bring a little colour into them.

"You must not let him believe you pine away, *ma chérie!*"

Lord Charing's halting step was heard approaching. Busy settling him in a comfortable chair by the fire, Gabrielle scarcely noticed the arrival of the rest of the company. She glanced up to find that her father, Gerard, Alain, Sophie de Vignard, Lady Sarah and Luke Everett had joined them. Marie and Baxter were also present, sitting a little apart from the rest.

She sat down quickly on a footstool, leaning against the arm of his lordship's chair and half hidden by a sofa occupied by Gerard and Alain. She could see clearly only Sophie, seated opposite, with Lady Sarah and Lady Harrison on either side of her, a strange contrast of quiet simplicity with fashionable elegance.

Her father came to Lord Charing and kissed his hand. "With your permission, sir?" he said.

"I will speak first," said the marquis firmly. He raised his voice. "Welcome to Charing. My son has brought you all together to clear up any doubts and misapprehensions as to his identity and history. Yes, Maurice Darcy is my younger son, now my heir.

"You will forgive an old man who feels a need to divulge the reasons for our estrangement. Maurice married against

235

my wishes. I held, and still do hold, that the majority of the French nobility were mere lapdogs, fit for nothing but to scurry about the throne." He held up his hand. "My apologies, Lady Harrison, Monsieur de Vignard—I did say, the majority! However reasonable my beliefs, I acted on them unreasonably.

"I disinherited my son, forbidding his return to his native land and giving his patrimony to his brother, my heir. In the years since, I came to regret my decision but did not choose to expose my error by setting afoot a search. How foolish I was, I leave you to judge. How I might have watched my grandchildren grow up, perhaps saved their mother . . ." He was unable to continue. Gabrielle took his shaking hand and held it tight.

There was a moment of silence, and then the new Lord Darcy, standing with his back to the fire, took up the tale.

"My brother, with his good lady's support . . ."

Lady Sarah blushed.

". . . secretly found me out and insisted on sending me that portion of his income which he considered rightfully mine. I settled in Paris. And now I come to the part of my tale which must never leave this room. You, sir," he turned to the marquis, "Lady Sarah, Mademoiselle de Vignard, and my son are the only ones present who know nothing of what I am about to reveal. I must ask your word that you will never speak of it."

The four pledged silence—Lord Charing with curiosity, the ladies uneasily, Gerard casting a glance of resentment at Gabrielle. It was most unfair that his sister should know more than he did.

Their father continued.

"While living in France, I occasionally came across odd facts that I thought might be of interest to the British government. At first I did nothing, but eventually I reported an item of particular significance to our ambassador. He put me in contact with Mr Cosmo Harrison, as he then was, at the Foreign Office. Gradually I found myself spending more and more of my time not merely reporting, but actually searching out information.

"The political situation in France deteriorated, and my position grew more dangerous. We developed between us a network of couriers and code names, so that in the event of hostilities my part should not be obvious. Sir Cosmo, by now created baronet for services to the Crown, was known as 'the Man in the Green Coat.' "

"Poor Sir Cosmo always was partial to green," mourned Lady Harrison.

"I became Le Hibou, the Owl, the silent, invisible predator of the night. A romantic image, I confess, but I was still young enough to consider my rôle romantic."

Gabrielle looked up at her father. Of course it was romantic! she thought. Not that Papa looked romantic. He looked rather ordinary. Even now, holding the floor, he had a quietly unassuming appearance, until you noticed the commanding eyes. Just like Luke's.

Had she fallen in love with Luke because he reminded her of her father?

Lord Darcy was talking now about the Revolution. His wife's sister, who had married the Vicomte de Vignard and lived near Avignon, fled to Paris with her two children when her home was burned, her husband murdered by the peasants. There was no safety in the chaos of the capital. He had told her to join the exodus to England, given her Sir Cosmo's name and direction, and seen no more of her.

Three months later the *ci-devant vicomtesse de Vignard* was listed among the *aristos* sent to the guillotine. The children had vanished.

"I lost Sophie," said Alain, his head bowed. *"Maman* told me to take care of her, to take her to Sir Cosmo in England, but I lost her."

With a little wordless cry, Sophie jumped up and ran to him. She hugged him tightly, then squeezed in between him and Gerard on the sofa, holding his hand.

"I found my way to England," he went on, smiling

tenderly down at his sister. "I had forgotten Sir Cosmo's last name, but after a long search I found him, and he gave me work to do—nothing secret, just translations and such. Then Madame Aurore arrived."

"*J'arrive!*" crowed Lady Harrison. "I leave *mon cher Maurice* in Neuchâtel, *une ville bien bourgeoise*, and I come to *Londres*. Me, I know who is Monsieur D'Arcy and who is Le Hibou! I come to Sir Cosmo and I tell him all. He receives many messages from Le Hibou, but how to send to him he does not know. I arrange! Such long letters I write, full of the gossip. No censor will read all the babblings, *n'est-ce pas?* And with great secrecy I tell *le feu* Lord Darcy where is his brother. Through me, he sends the money.

"Marie is of the greatest assistance. *Une femme de chambre*, a lady's maid, she can speak with many people without the least suspicion. Also a boy—Alain was not yet twenty!— may go anywhere and no one will notice. He is the nephew of Le Hibou, so Sir Cosmo employs him in the secret work.

"Then my poor Sir Cosmo dies. The Foreign Secretary, who does not take *assez sérieusement* the spying, appoints a young man of no experience. Patience, Monsieur Everett! I mean no insult. *Le bon* Davis, Sir Cosmo's secretary, he must teach the young man. He learns very fast, but Davis knows only a part of the whole. He knows of Marie, but of me and of Alain he knows nothing! Still, the messages go to Le Hibou, and the messages come back to Monsieur Everett, who is now the Man in the Green Coat."

Luke stood up. Gabrielle fixed her eyes on her hands, but she heard him pacing as he talked.

"I had no idea of Le Hibou's identity, but he was the source of our best information from France—not surprisingly, as I now gather he had been posing for years as an aide to the Minister of Police. A year ago, I asked him to go to Russia, to investigate various matters there. We heard nothing from him for several months. Then came a message from France in his name, borne by an unknown courier and disclosing a conspiracy."

Gabrielle prayed that he was not about to reveal her part in the delivery of that message. She had told her father, but the fewer people who knew of her arrival in England, dressed as a boy and with a bullet in her, the better.

"I will not go into details," he continued, to her relief. "It is government business, and the less said the better. We heard from Le Hibou two or three times more, and then we received word that he was resigning. Lord Darcy?"

"Thank you. Just before I left for St Petersburg, I heard that my brother was dead. My father discovered from his papers that he had been supporting me, and through the same channels wrote to say that I was now his heir. I chose to believe that he had forgiven me."

He smiled at the marquis, who nodded his white head and whispered to Gabrielle that in actual fact he had begged his son's forgiveness.

"However, I had to complete my mission to Russia before I could go home. It was, to say the least, a hazardous mission and uncertain of outcome. I had no idea how long I should be away. My dear children were used to long absences, but I told them that if I was gone for more than a certain peiod without sending news, or if it seemed likely that war would break out, they were to go to Aurore in London. As indeed they did.

"I must apologise to them, and to you, my lord, for asking Aurore to keep silent about my family. It seemed best that they should await my arrival, or certain knowledge of my death, before approaching you. I gather this has led to some confusion, and for that I must apologise also to Mr Everett."

Gabrielle felt her face crimson and turned her eyes again firmly on her lap. What would he say next? She should never have told him that Luke had thought her a base-born adventurer, a harlot and a French spy!

"In the meantime, I returned from St Petersburg and found my children gone. I reported to Fouché such intelligence of Russia as I thought fit, and laid my plans to come

239

to England. That was when I discovered the plot to which Mr Everett referred, and learned that my nephew was being drawn into it.

"Fouché knew that Alain worked for a key figure in the conspiracy. He somehow found his sister and used her to induce him to betray his employer."

"What would you have done?" asked Alain, his arm round Sophie's shoulders, his gaze passing from one to another of his listeners. "They threatened her with a life far worse than death. I had failed her before, when I left her behind in France. I prepared to cooperate, praying that my uncle, Le Hibou, would find some way to intervene, but ready to give up a thousand bloody-handed Frenchmen to save her!"

There was a moment of heavy silence.

"Of course you were," said Lady Harrison firmly. "And of course Maurice *did* intervene!"

Lord Darcy patted her shoulder. "I did indeed, *chérie*, but Mr Everett was a step ahead of me—and his henchman nearly put an end to me!" He waved a salute to Baxter. "However, they now have Monsieur Roussel in secure custody, Sophie is restored to us, and I am happy to inform you all that Aurore has consented to become my wife!"

Lady Harrison, her sea-green silk rustling, swept forward, and knelt before the marquis.

"I ask you for *la bénédiction*, milord," she said, smiling up at him coquettishly.

"With pleasure, my dear," he responded, and kissed her forehead. "And now, if the explanations are over, Maurice, we shall repair to the morning room to drink your lady's health in the best French champagne."

She helped him out of his chair and she and Gerard supported his steps from the room.

In a daze, Gabrielle went to the nearest window and leaned her forehead against the cool glass. Papa to marry Madame! And now that Alain, too, had found his family, doubtless he would marry Dorothea, and Gerard might as well take Sophie, who was turning out to be almost as pretty as her brother was handsome.

And she herself would just turn into an old maid and spend the rest of her life on the shelf.

"Miss Darcy?"

She froze.

"Gabrielle?" Luke's voice was having trouble emerging. He cleared his throat. "I know you said you never want to see me again, but I must talk to you!"

Her own voice was misbehaving now. She wanted to ask what there was to talk about, but all that came out was a grunt.

Apparently this was sufficient encouragement.

"Forgive me! I had no right to say all those terrible things to you, and I knew in my heart that they weren't true, however bad it looked. It was pure anguish! I wanted to marry you, and I knew I couldn't. I was trying to persuade myself that you were unworthy. But even when I half believed it, I still wanted you for my wife. You cannot imagine how it felt."

"I was in anguish."

He was silent. Somehow he had not thought of that. He had known she was angry, had every right to be angry, but he had not considered that she might hurt as much as he did.

"Can you ever forgive me?" he whispered wretchedly.

She was fighting tears. If she spoke they would escape, and she despised weeping females. She closed her eyes tight, bit her lips, pressed harder against the windowpane.

"Gabrielle!"

His cry was filled with despair. She turned and flung her arms about him, hid her face in his chest, and let the tears come.

Fortunately Luke had a large, clean handkerchief. He carried her to a sofa and held her while she wept. He was somewhat puzzled, having seen her go through the most painful experiences without the slightest sign of tears; but

241

as long as she let him keep his arms around her, he had no objection.

At last the sobbing turned to sniffling. She looked up at him, her eyes red, and he kissed them.

"I adore you," he said.

She snuggled closer.

"Do you really?" she asked. "It seemed odd to me that you wanted to marry me when you despised me."

"I didn't think it possible that I could ever want to marry you more than I did then, but I do now. If you follow me. I truly do adore you. Will you be my wife?"

"Kiss me again while I think about it."

He obliged.

Gerard rushed into the room.

"Gaby," he shouted, "Papa says I can join a cavalry regiment!"

"Do go away, there's a good fellow," urged Luke.

"And Gerard," said Gabrielle with a sigh, "*don't* call me Gaby!"

HISTORICAL NOTE

General Pichegru followed Georges Cadoudal to France in January 1804. They were both arrested, along with General Moreau and other conspirators.

Pichegru committed suicide in his cell; Cadoudal was shot. Fouché failed to implicate Moreau in the plot, but Bonaparte exiled him anyway. He went to America, returning in 1813 to fight with the allies again his ex-master.